Contents

ISBN: 979-8218183233 (pbk.)

Dear reader,

Ever since I was a kid, I would go to sleep at night, and have the most vivid dreams. It almost seems like when I'm asleep, I either visit my past lives, or I journey through alternate universes/other dimensions. Years ago, I started a dream journal and after reading through my entries, I realized that my dreams were good plots and story lines. So, I decided to turn them into books. "April's Fool" is the first book of my *Dream Catchers* collection. I hope you enjoy and learn from the journeys as you read.

Sincerely yours,

Anetta Tiquila

TRIGGER WARNINGS: Death/murder, suicide, AIDS, mental illness (Schizophrenia), hallucinations and profanity.

This book is a cautionary tale about the extremes a mentally unstable person might be willing take to get revenge. The story is intended to change thoughts and toxic behavior patterns by exploring the worse that can happen in situations where people are struggling with mental illness.

Anetta Tiquila does not encourage nor condone any of the actions related to the issues regarding the trigger warnings announced. As you read this book, come to grips with what *NOT* to do, and learn from the characters, their mistakes and the ultimate consequences that they have to face. This story is also not meant to mock anyone's lifestyle or judge their life choices, so please be mindful of that as you flip to the last page!

Please do not attempt to engage in any of the stunts, behaviors/ thoughts or actions contained in this book

MATURE AUDIENCES ONLY!!

Chapter 1

Allen

I'll be dead by dawn if everything goes as planned. Life is overrated, and I anticipate the moment I can close my eyes for good. *This* type of darkness, I wouldn't wish on my worse enemy. Well, That's not *entirely* true.

There's still some lights I want to put out before I leave this earth. Some people, I want to save. but then there are some people I want to cover in dirt, a few heads I want to spin and some hearts I want to make bleed.

I have no regrets for releasing this wave of heat, and as I sit here in darkness contemplating the last day of *my* life, I realize two things: for one, when my mother brought me into this world she pushed me out through the wrong hole.

She didn't birth me like your mother may have done with you - she shitted me out. At least that's how I've come to feel, being that she treated me like crap from the moment I peeked into existence, and all the way up until the day her clock stopped ticking. Had she been a woman of her word and aborted me like she promised my father, She would've saved a lot of lives.

The other thing I realize is that a lot of people fake being happy, and they're happy being fake. If you look closely you'll see the words *'fuck you'* ease through the slit of their lips with every grin.

Happy people, an old-folk's tale.

Every other person I come across is living that lie. Some of them are so caught up in a fantasy, they overlook the fact that their seconds left on earth are numbered.

Smiling faces seem to be marked with the same total, *ZERO*. Like halos hovering above their heads, standing upright. I always know what to do When I see that number pop up. My hands turn red, and people turn up dead - After walking around like they were *safe*.

They should've asked the last person who showed me their teeth thinking I was just going to let that fake shit slide; the self-proclaimed *angel* had said to me with a straight face, yet the corners of her mouth spreading wide, '*if it's my time to go, it's my time to go.*'

Her halo took on a vertical stance as she spewed those words toward my ears, not even realizing her number had just been called. That's just how much I hate a smile. The sight of it makes my blood boil. Like, stop trying to '*fake it 'til you make it*' - just be yourself.

Instead of looking like ventriloquist dummies dangling from strings because if there's one thing I can't stand, it's a dummy. Like this married couple who's been renting out space in my head for twenty Summers; Mr. and Mrs. Wright - Two dummies that like to tap dance on my last nerves.

The sound of their voices makes my brain vibrate and my skin shrivels up. Like most people, the Wrights seem to be oblivious to impending doom and dangling numbers. *Fate*. Resonated in a continuous rhythym of ticks; A noise that calms me when I find myself trapped in the "*Wright storm.*"

That's what I call it now, because It feels like a natural disaster when Mr. Wright disagrees with his wife. He always does this little thing to make her get quiet; he reaches into his bag of tricks and pulls out a bottle of bubbles. Every time Mrs. Wright says something he doesn't like he starts blowing those bubbles and as they pop, they seem to drown out his wife's voice.

This shit unbelievable. Sometimes Mrs. Wright would part her lips and before she could push a word out, Mr. Wright would have already started blowing. The sight and sound of those bubbles make her cringe, and now every time she sees her husband reach into his bag, she just walks away.

Her disconnection from their war is the only thing that has kept them both alive up to this point, but the more I absorb the zing of their artificial happiness the harder it is for me to manage the rage brewing in my soul.

It's like I can't catch a break. One minute my body is hot to the touch, and in the very next second my skin is crawling with chills. I'm always being pulled in so many directions, I don't even know where I stand anymore unless I'm stuck in the middle of a war with the Wrights, and they fight about everything under the moon.

Not once has there been a time where they agreed on *anything.* Mrs. Wright would say it's cold outside and Mr. Wright would hiss, '*uh-no, it's lukewarm, YING.*'

The storm never ends. On the way to our meeting yesterday Mr. Wright told me I should make a right turn at the upcoming stop sign, but Mrs. Wright retorted, '*no, turn left. YANG is going to make us late!*'

I sided with Mrs. Wright and got caught at a red light. '*last time we stopped here we waited three minutes for this light to change. You always listen to her, and look where it gets you.*'

As quiet as I had kept it, I actually needed those extra three minutes to think; I couldn't decide whether to dispose of the waste in my trunk *before*, or *after* the meeting. I ended up waiting until the Wrights engaged on another honeymoon phase, and I decluttered in a wooded area along Crystal Springs Drive with my mind on lock and key. I didn't need them overcrowding my thoughts yet *again*. I've had it up to the top of my head with their dirty energy. They truly are some of the worst people I've ever met.

The worse part about it is, no matter how many times I wish them away, I can't evict them from their corners. Believe me, I have tried. I've come to the conclusion that the only way to get rid of these two idiots is to *blow*'em away. But first, I need to get *this other* issue off my chest.

Staring at the shoes on the billboard ahead, the world becomes a shade brighter as the sun makes it's morning debut. With My middle finger dancing along my steering wheel, I listen to the Wrights go from arguing, to laughing at random crap, then they go right back to war. In the midst of trying to figure out what the hell could be so funny, I could hear their timers slow from a rhythmic tick, to a stuttering pause.

TiCK,TiCK,TiCK... TiCK

not just yet

That melodious sound of the timer counting down the seconds of their existence is just enough to keep me calm, for now. So I let their muffling voices travel in and out of my ears whilst my eyes remain stuck on the call-to-action ahead of me.

The colors orange and red never looked good together to me - they always seem to cancel each other out. But on these shoes, the colors are a perfect match. Reminds me of a flickering flame of fire. The athletic ankles protruding from the sneakers reminds me of a friend turned foe, and encoded in a single bend of the foot there is a message: *'just do it.'*

I really hate that it's come to this, but I can't take another day living on the same planet with, *"happy people."* **The Wrights** are constant reminders that it's time to put it all to an end. Hours pass and they're still at each other's throat. Forcing me toward my breaking point, they turn to face each other head on and amid their tug-of-war with my thoughts, they brain-bop *me* blow for blow.

'you've caused enough trouble already hun – please, don't do it.' Mrs. Wright's voice feels like dirty water clogging my ear. I can't even agree to disagree before her husband chimes in, *'people smiling in your direction is like saying fuck what you're going through,'* he nods toward the billboard, *'don't listen to Ying, she*

laughs at you behind your back.'

'You mean the way you laugh every time he listens to YOU, and winds up with his hands covered in red?!'

'ah, passion. Come on Al, do it!'

'No!'

Doesn't matter how hard I beg these two flip-flops for silence, they never shut up. Mr. Wright throws his hands in the air, *'It's NOW, or NEVER! – Do it Al - now!'*

He obviously doesn't understand that if I *'do it,'* I'd have to get rid of him and his wife sooner than later. I don't know why, but today of all days, their voices are super loud, and I don't like people to scream at me. Like, lower your tone.

Over time the Wrights have mastered the skill of accessing parts of my mind that I have closed off to others, so to stop them from reading my darkest thoughts I often whisper to myself. I could feel my muscles tighten then my jawbone flex when Mrs. Wright repeats, *'don't do it Al'*

"*Cuz*," I chant through clenched teeth, "*I'm tired of this shit. Tired of everybody thinkin' I'm a pussy ass nigga.*"

I twist in my seat, temporarily disconnecting my attention from the command up ahead and I glance toward the building just as the door swings open and a laughing crowd of people pour out and down the steps - looking *too* happy.

What could be so funny?

Don't they know what's about to happen?

I had given them a warning many sessions ago, but the story of my life is, people refuse to take me seriously.

Just looking at these *"happy"* people -- Men, women, and *others*, covered in dark colors. Walking and talking in circles around each other... it makes me squirm so hard that moisture oozes from my pores. This type of fake shit, I can't be a part of. People walking around smiling, acting like they won't **get pierced by an anonymous slug.**

'Just think for a minute Allen.'

Ying's advisory causes a burst of rage to force my fist into the steering wheel as words rise from my throat and blast through my lips, "Shut the fuck up!"

HONK!

Temporarily snatched out of my angry state, I turn my attention back to the sign. *'Think for a minute Al,'* Ying repeats despite my demand for silence. Seconds later Yang's voice comes out of left field, Zooming toward my ears like a struck baseball, *'Shoot!'*

Eyelids tightly squeezed, palms slapped against ears and jaws full of hot air. My brain is now rattled beyond repair.

'Do it, now!.'

'No Al!'

'Now!'

'... Wait!'

I'm already on the edge of the edge, and it's hard as hell trying to mind to the business I'm tending to with these two micro-midget clowns filling my head space. Two taps on the window rescue me from the warfare.

"sup big Al, you alright?"

"Yes," I lie, giving this bull-faced idiot the green light to back up. But of course, he keeps flapping his dick suckers, "you're just in time for the noon session, we're heading over to –"

"Nah I'm good." I crash my forehead into the steering wheel, sounding the horn off again. A peppery-hot flow of blood zips through my veins. Other than Ying and Yang, there's no voice I hate more than this dummy's standing at my car. He pushes his face toward the opening of my window, and before I could push the button to close the space he says, "you're not coming in?"

Peeking inside my ride, his breath smells like hot ass and

firecrackers. All the while, I'm still being bullied by the billboard. Between that and the Wrights, I'm starting to lose my sense of reason. My glove compartment is seconds away from being popped open but for some reason, my hand won't budge. The contents of my skull, bouncing around like the hot whirling globs of a lava lamp

'Do it, now!'

'No! don't do it!'

The smell coming through my window pushes the simmering vomit from my stomach and onto my steering wheel. With each rise and fall of this idiots chest his throat releases fumes that punch me in the nose, and every time I take in a breath, I feel like I could vomit again. It gets so hard to breathe that I decide not to but holding my breath only makes my face goes numb, and my heart feels like it's about to explode inside my chest.

"You need me to go get Daniel?" The irritant asks me. Before I could respond, I hear his feet leading him away from my car at about three steps per second and when I open my eyes, I turn to look just as the door to the building closes behind him.

If nothing else, I'm glad to have his stank breath out of my face. I can't *stand* that cum wad, and every time he looks at me, I come up with different ways to see him dead. Seconds later the door swings open again, and out comes Daniel with stank breath right behind him, both rushing towards my car.

"Open up Al, let's get you inside," Daniel insists. When he pulls the door open, an ice-cold breeze rushes inside, causing my skin to rattle and shrink. While twisting the ignition off, Daniel positions his hip at the threshold so that I won't fall to the ground.

Staring at the dark blue Khakis he's wearing, my vision fades to black, and the world starts spinning. Now I'm stuck somewhere between time and space. I could feel my feet separate from the ground in the same moment Daniel's distant voice increases in volume, "You need a wheelchair, Al?"

'No,' Yang demands, 'he's not handicap. stand up Al,   WALK.'

'*Are you nuts?*' Ying snaps, '*He's gonna fall on his ass, you need a wheelchair, Al - NOW!*'

'*He doesn't need a wheelchair, he needs a set of balls.*'

'*He doesn't need another set of balls, he needs a wheelchair!*'

I'm so gone I can't even hear myself yell, "Would you two motherfuckers shut up?!"

"Al," Daniel whispers, "come, let's get you inside. It's me - Danny. You gonna be alright, just lean against my shoulder, I got'chu." Daniel strong arms me to my feet and he steadies himself.

"Sam!" Daniel yells to stank breath, "grab his keys and lock the door!" I stagger up the steps, poor Daniel using his scrawny arms and legs to help me to the waiting room. Once inside, he guides me to a seat and supports the weight of my body as I flop down in the chair.

He then walks over to the water **fountain and** fills up a paper cup, returns and sits down in the seat next to me, "take a sip", he says, handing me the water, "remember, mindful breathing – slow, deep breath in," he commits the breath and I imitate his actions, "slow, deep breath out."

As I exhale, tears start diving down my cheeks. I'm more pissed than anything that stank breath can't seem to find his way to his business. When I look up there he is, giving me that look

'*Nosey bastard - Curse'em out*!'

'*Be nice Al, say hello. He's just trying to help.*'

Turning my head to look at stank breath, I yell in his direction, "Hi!"

"*Tuh,*" he twists his neck and flips his locks over his shoulders, "I just wanted to make sure you was good, but let me get outta here before I say some shit to make you dance." Sam stands up, and switches out of the door, slamming it behind him as he tosses my keys to Daniel.

"what's going on?" Daniel finally asks. Sucking in shallow breaths I rest my forehead on my fists, "I wish motherfuckers would shut up, I can barely hear myself think."

I try to stand, but when Daniel sees me flinch toward the door he places his hand on my shoulder, "relax Mr. Vaugh, here - have a seat." Once I crash back down into the chair I ponder my next move. Kill, steal, destroy - in *that* order. Daniel slides his chair closer to mine, "I can't help you if I don't know what's going on."

"You couldn't help me if you *did* know."

"Let me try, talk to me."

"Talk, talk, talk. Talking ain't fixing nothing. I'm so sick and over this shit - I just want to make it all go away."

"Is it Ying this time, or is it Yang again?" He looks at me from under his glasses and raises a brow. Shingles of anger crawl down my spine and my arms stiffen in turn. Shifting in my seat, I try to dodge the static crackling along my skin. Feels like I'm seconds away from being struck by lightening.

CLACK!

"... get a little fresh air flowing through here," Daniel says after walking over to the window and pulling the lever. Smelling cow manuer seep through, I'm pulled back into the moment, "It's Ying, *and* it's Yang,"

Rage

Hatred

Jealousy

I shiver and look away as I inform my Therapist of my worsening mental dysfunction, "and come to find out, these motherfuckers done had kids."

Chapter 2

Allen

Two weeks later, Yang swipes the toothpick from his clenched teeth and flings it into the air, *'Why won't you just do it?'* he asks with a roar. After rubbing my tongue across the inside of my cheek, I shake my head, "I, I'm trying to be the bigger man." In lieu of fresh tulips and lavendar, an illusional smell of iron and gun powder makes my water; complimentary of Yang's amplifying voice

'Is that what he did for you?'

"No"

'Didn't he betray you?'

"yes"

'So, you're just going to let that shit slide?'

"Hell naw."

I feel my eyes lower as I stare at Omar, my head nearly falling off the side of my neck. As I study him, I chant between clenched teeth, trying to talk myself out of doing the unthinkable. But even in the midst of my reluctancy, I just can't figure out why his clothes keep changing colors.

His button-up seems to turn from beige, to red in certain spots. Like, right where his heart and his stomach is. All of this as he stands ahead of me smiling and blushing – looking all *happy*. Time and time again, his life plays out like a horror movie in my head. With each blink of my eyes, I see him die. When I turn my head, there I am at his funeral where he lies in his coffin – stiff, cold... useless.

The images are haunting; They fold me while bringing tears to my eyes in a wave of side-splitting laughter. It's crazy - I know. But his demise is a thought I entertain often. It's something I can't let go of. My animosity towards him has become a part of my DNA, almost like a cancerous tumor that spreads from one part of your body to another, killing you from inside out.

In a dog-eat-dog world, I'm always the dog that gets bitten first. Well, not always, but most of the time. I mean, I've gotten hungry a time or two and enjoyed a few meals, but never once have I hungered for the blood of a best friend. Someone I have called my brother since childhood. My *"brothers"* and I, we've shared everything from lunches to video games - even a female or two.

My circle has always been small enough to wrap around my pinky finger. Like many other crews Michael, Omar, and I have always had this brother hood code: *bros before hoes.* That code was one of the things that kept us tight and right. Blood couldn't make us any closer. But everything is different now and this snake they call *Omar*, he's managed to bump himself to the top of my *'to-kill'* list.

What's the root of my hatred? Well, Just imagine your best friend smiling in your face while slithering their way into your lover's heart. And then having the nerve to say, *'we didn't mean for this to happen.'* I don't care nothing about those damage control apologies - that snake knew what he was doing. How is he *NOT* gonna know? I was a serial cheater, true enough. But who is *he* to step in and be a better man to *MY* woman?! I treated Olivia bad, and I know it.

But how was I supposed to know she was really getting tired of me? I mean, she had loved on me for so long, I thought she finally accepted the fact that I was just, *me.* Both lost and found in one single step.

And now here I am, walking in this straight file line. My hand trembles with each breath I take and every time I swallow, the air traveling down my throat feels like a ball of fire plummeting toward my stomach, but stopping at my heart as those images replay in my mind

Omar. Dead. Casket. Grave. Cover it. Gone!

Then, he would be six feet away from *my* woman, *my* backbone. I never deserved her; I can say that today. But I didn't deserve to have her snatched away from me either. She was building me up, she was changing me. She had me thinking I was God's gift to women, that's how good she was to me.

My career as a real estate agent, my two-story home – almost every aspect of my success is all thanks to Olivia. She's a true motivator, and gentle soul. She upgraded me. I planned to wife her as soon as I ended my cheating spree, but before I could stop my dick from churning she fell into the arms of my childhood best friend. **I was going to change, I really was, but Omar didn't give me the chance to.**

Yeah, yeah - I know what you're thinking: *'you don't miss a good thing till it's gone,'* or, *'one man's trash is another man's treasure,'* something along those lines.

First off – Olivia ain't never been trash. Second, I know – I messed up, and now I'm missing my good thing. But my bad, *huh*? I mean, even though she deserved to be rescued from my grip, it's foul that Omar was the one who was there to save her. What ever happened to our brother hood code? Not that Olivia could ever be called a hoe, but you get what I'm saying.

Once I lost her my life spiraled down-hill, and I lost sight of everything. With my backbone now the center of someone else's life, I feel like I'm outside of myself, and I can't think of anything else but how to get her back – that's the only train of thought I'm riding.

But she's never coming back to me, I can see it in her eyes. The way she keeps looking at him makes me wanna bust'em in his mouth, especially when I look around the room at all this *happy people* garbage.

So surely you understand why I've got beef with everybody in this joint; The bride, the groom, and their family and friends. *MY* family and friends. My heart clumps into knots of what feels like synthetic fabric - tight, bulky, hot. I'm in hell.

The joints in my knees loosen then shift behind my skin but I stand my ground, trying hard to hold myself up. As Omar positions himself then utters, "with this ring, I thee wed," he penetrates the small wedding hole with Olivia's finger, but it feels like he just finger fucked *me*.

Goosebumps trail my skin. My unblinking eyes roll pass the silver glaze of Olivia's nails and land on that cryptic symbol of eternal love. Shivering like a supernova, it's like a star fell from the night sky and landed in the perfect spot on her hand.

Something about that glow changes the channels in my mind and suddenly I'm standing in Omar's shoes. *'Now, Go over there, confess your love to her,'* Yang challenges me. In the wake of his command, my foot budges but never lifts from its spot on the floor. I just stand here, six feet away from *MY* ideal wife.

'So hurry, go over there!'
'Don't embarrass us, Al.'
'alright then - let off!'
'NO, don't shoot!'

My head is crowded with the faint sound of popping bubbles. Once Ying is silenced, Yang gets his last words in, *'fold that nigga up!'* He demands, *'do it - now!'*

This scar on my hand is now itching like crazy so I put my fingernails to it and scratch, providing myself with a soothing breeze of short-term peace. The tension drains from my body like I just swallowed a chill-pill but seconds later, Yang's voice comes back into play, *'it's either NOW or NEVER... you gonna just let him have her? She's YOURS, remember?'*

In a flash, everyone in the room except Olivia fades out of sight and instead of doing what I came here to do, I waltz up to her and I grab her hand. She shows me the sweetest smile as she spins into my arms. Together, we waltz. I take a step forward, she takes a step back.

We sway in unison, then she presses her lips against mine. When I swipe my tongue through my mouth her sweet lip balm greets my tastebuds – cherry lemonade, that's always been her favorite.

I hold her hand up and spin her around, twisting her to re-face me. Another soft kiss sends my nature rising toward the ceiling. Gracefully, she reaches out to me in a waving type gesture - the way she did when our relationship was ripe and new.

Be mine my love, touch me. Give me you

A single stroke of her hand is all I need to water my growing need for her. But instead of placing her hand over my heart like she used to, she suddenly digs into my chest and snatches it out in one swift motion.

Step, slide.... heel-toe, twist.

My heart locked in the tight grip of her fist. She spins out of my space, forcing me back into reality where again I find myself standing hopelessly at the altar, six feet away from where I *should* be.

∞ ∞ ∞

One pixel per second, the congregation of *happy people* snowball back into view and my Rage is resurrected. All the while, the minister's amplifying voice brings forth the question that sets my soul ablaze. He looks to his left, "Do you, Omar take this woman to be your lawfully wedded wife?"

"I do."

The instigator turns to Olivia but before he could finish his question to *her*, she confirms the demise of my heart, interrupting his words to insert her own

"I do."

The smile stretching across her face is so bright that the chapel becomes three shades lighter. She stands there with glowing eyes, her cheeks puffing out with the instigators next announcement, "... then you may kiss the bride."

"You iight man?" Michael whispers. A quick response is warranted, but I'm too fixated on the bride and groom who stare at each other as if no one else is in the room. In their twisted minds, standing here at *my* dream wedding they are the only two who exists.

"yea," I lie.

Hot lava, running through my viens. It makes my eyes sweat, and I could feel my brain twitch. I hate this moment and I hate this nigga. How could he faulter the peace treaty we'd made months ago, where we agreed he would *not* marry *MY* future wife. "Handkerchief," Michael whispers, winking his eye two times fast, "Scar."

SCAR - A deeply-rooted brotherhood code that means I need to chill. I flex my fists, then relax my hands. The next thing I know a single tear is stroking my cheek, then I feel the skin on my face tighten and shift. Focused on staying grounded I take a deep breath in, and slowly ease it out through my nose.

Why am I allowing this to happen?

Here I am a thirty-four-year-old man with everything I could ever want, everything thing except that one person that would make my whole life complete.

Just this time last year, it was Olivia and *I* who hosted our engagement party. *Everybody in here fake!'* Yang's voice penetrates my ear canal, causing my head to nod. After all I've been through in these last two years with burying my dead-beat mother; mourning her while feeling freed from the burden of saving her - Life couldn't get darker than it is in this very moment, on this very day.

The effort to control my breathing this time goes in vain and becomes particularly harder with the whispering voice of Ying. Here comes another storm

'He's your brother, just be hap--'

'he can be happy when this all blows up in Omar's face. Once he's suffered as Al is suffering.'

The choir harmonizes this fraud of a love connection, but all I hear is the faint sound of bubbles popping off inside my head, then my nails pierce my skin. *Breathe, breathe. Deep breath in, deep breath out.*

breathe...... breathe. My heart repeatedly thumps against my chest as I continue to walk myself through the turmoil of my existence.

After a few more deep breaths the bubbles stop popping, but I feel my eyes narrow in the trail of the two-legged snake that just walked by me. *This motherfucker needs to be deflated.* My eyes flutter as I imagine bullets penetrating his body.

thoot, thoot, thoot

Music to my fanciful ears. There he is, wrinkling and shrinking like a California raisin, his skin stretching over his bones. My flapping eyelids never fail me.

Now I see him bleeding at Olivia's feet as she steps over his body and approaches me, *"you're the one I love"* she whispers before her image glitches from my sight.

Shit! I gotta pull myself together, quick. Shaking my head, I try to change the visions displayed in my mind. I look up to see Omar easing down the aisle with Olivia curled up into his arms. The next time my eyes flick, I see an even more fulfilling pic:

There Omar is being pushed around by the bullets that expel from my burner and plummet into his body. Fire-engine red, the burst of color oozing from the holes in his stomach, his heart, and his almond-shaped head.

The next thing I see is Omar and Olivia moving out the door, on their way to the stretch limo that awaits them past the steps. Amidst the thunder of applause and whistles, there's a storm of snickering echoes bouncing around inside my skull. *Damn Omar... haha*

why

    won't

you die!?

From my point of view I see a dead man walking in the six-hundred-dollar suit he should actually be buried in. In my mind, he's on his way to his funeral, and Olivia is the demon ushering his soul to hell. It's funny if you really think about it. Of all the words that have been spoken up until this moment, the one concept that stands out to me is *Death do them part.* But knowing what it's going to take to bring that concept to fruition, my insides ball up in a knot.

Breathe...... breathe...

I can string a few words together right now to describe the pain: *The piercing gash from the knife of my bestfriend was no match for the burn of my self-inflicted wound.*

My so-called best friends never even noticed that I was injured. Who'd ever think secrecy could be an art to master. Up until this point I'd concealed my troubles within the fog of my mind, but today of all days, the secret I have held in for so long is about to reveal itself and change the lives of everyone who knows me.

Looking around, I notice so many familiar faces, and the one with the salt-n-pepper goatee is approaching me with a twisted smile. The second he's in arms reach he parts his lips, "sup nephew, how you holding up?"

"I'm smooth," I quiver, looking straight ahead at Michael as he talks to Olivia's girl crew, "you know me, just.... *Man,* just chillin."

Uncle Stan gives me that *'I told you so'* look, "Good thing It's almost over," He looks at me with sinking eyes, then he taps my shoulder and gestures me to follow him, "looks like you're handling it well."

Flexing my fists, I gather a puff of breath and hold it in my cheeks before swallowing, then I look toward the ceiling, "yeah I guess."

"You glad you came?"

Am I glad I came?! Is he serious right now?! I think for a second before replying, "oh, *tuh* - fa sho."

"Yeah," He looks over his shoulder and shrugs, "Guess its always best to be the bigger man. Besides, everything happens for a reason."

The crowd waves and cheers the couple on as they disappear in the distance but me, I stumble forward. My heart - torn to shreds, my skin - hot to the touch, my right hand - ascending from the waist of my pants... empty, shaky, trigger finger itching.

My rage is unwavering.

Michael daps his eyes with his thumb as Stan and I ease into his view and that's when I feel a single tear slide from the corner of my eye. Don't trip though, I caught it with the back of my sleeve before anyone else noticed. Once Michael is in arms reach, he looks at me and closes his eyes, his lips pressing into a sympathetic grin. Already two steps ahead of me, Stan greets him first, "Mikey *MIKE!*"

"My man Stan," They slap hands and pull into each other's shoulder, "You standing over here like you don't know nobody," Uncle Stan dribbles an imaginary ball between his legs, "What, you still mad about taking that 'L'?" he tosses the ball toward a fictional basket as Michael travels over and blocks his shot, "it's all in your head bruh, you've never balled me up."

I guess they think it's a game, if I start lettin' off right now, I bet they feel me then. My thoughts of retribution are clouded by

Ying's crackling voice, *'Allen, please don't –'*

Pop! plop! pop!

'it's either now or never.'

Out of nowhere, Toya walks past me and sticks out her tongue. Of all the people here she can get a pass, because she's the only one who had objected to this Olivia and Omar deal.

Toya and I have always been cool and even though she's Olivia's friend, she and I have a solid bond. When I don't react to her goofiness, she swerves around and peeks over Michael's shoulder, then she sticks her tongue out again. This time her eyes are bucked and crossed.

"Ole gurl still a weirdo," Uncle Stan says. Everyone in eye's view burst out laughing, but I'm burning with so much animosity I couldn't push out a smile even if I were being tickled. Seriously, I don't know how some of ya'll *'smile through the pain,'* but I just can't do it. I might be a lot of things, but I'm never fake so if I'm not happy, I'm not going to pretend to be.

What bothers me the most is the fact that months earlier, Omar and I had agreed to put this "Flaw" in our friendship behind us. We have been friends far too long to let a female shut us down. But none of that even matters, cause every time a forgiving thought enters my mind, I find myself once again, trapped in the Wright storm.

'He's married YOUR wife, at YOUR wedding.'

'He's still your best friend.'

'Betrayal doesn't come from strangers or enemies.'

'Swallow your pride, be happy for them.'

'He promised to fall back and let ya'll work it out, but he was still screwing her behind your back as you broke your neck trying to make things right.'

'Let bygones be bygones. Be the bigger—'

Pop! pop! plop!

'Fuck that bitch ass nigga!'

I swear, I cannot wait for the day I can put these two bickering bastards to sleep. The confusing thing about all of this is, I can sometimes shake off the anger, I can even overlook the residue left behind by Omar's betrayal. Sometimes, it be all good. What I can't seem to do is ignore the broadening realities of how to get away with murder.

But like always, Ying is right. Enough blood has been shed - at least for now. Anyway, for some of these people on my list a quick death would be too easy. I need to see the pain and suffering play out in real-time. Unlike these visions in my head where every time I blink my eyes, Omar dies.

I should have listened to Uncle Stan when he told me not to come here, but I thought I had gotten over it. I thought I had moved on. I didn't deserve her, I know that. But to see her looking like a beautiful queen at *my* wedding – words can't explain the hate I feel.

Now, as I participate in the union that was originally orchestrated for my first love and I, I drift on memories as I realize that I am still very much in love with her. Remembering the nights I left her crying and worried about my well being, a sharp pain overcomes my stomach line. She's the only woman who had ever shown me love and understanding, and even though I realize she deserved better, why did it have to be my best friend?

Why was *he* the one there to pick up the pieces and mend her broken heart? Just thinking about it brings fire to the pit of my stomach. I look at Mike, then nod at Uncle Stan, "excuse me, I'll be back."

"Where you going' man?" Mike wants to know. But my mouth is too wet to spit out a coherent response. I dash back into the chapel, make two left turns, and now I'm in the bathroom. As soon as I enter the stall, I spew partially digested eggs and sausage casserole into the toilet.

'Breathe, breathe.'

My clothes are so moist with sweat they cling to my skin, and the space surrounding me starts to vibrate. This is not supposed to happen. I'm supposed to be the bigger man. Instead, I'm trying to find the strength to turn this day into a tragedy.

'You'll feel a lot better after you do it,' Yang insists. No more than five minutes after releasing the contents of my stomach the bathroom door flies open, "Al," someone yells in panic, "Allen man, where are you?"

It's Mike, the peace maker. The swinging doors amplifies the sound of bubbles popping in my head. Stall by stall, Michael tries to discover my location. Finally, he finds me in the fourth stall still vomiting.

His grasp of breath echoes through the emptiness of the stall, ricocheting off the walls and stroking my heart so deeply I could feel a numbing sensation cover my palms. The cold toilet and the icy floor beneath it are the only things keeping me stable. "Allen," Mike sighs, "Man Listen, I know this is hard, but you have to accept that it is what it is, so you can move on."

wow! My stomach balls up into an even tighter knot, *you should be just as angry at dude to have damn near killed over 18 years of friendship, for betraying one of his boys and violating the brotherhood code. If he did it to me, he'll do it to you!*

My twitching guts make me flinch and squirm. The butterflies in my stomach must be doing some type of a ritual to push something out of me. Only problem is, there is nothing left to expel, nothing but the secret I've fought so hard to keep inside. My body takes on a life of its own as I fight even harder to keep that secret from escaping.

"shit, man!" I fly into a rage, unbuttoning my Armani vest then twisting my shoulders free. I feel it coming; an overdue confession. With my head nearly buried inside the toilet I try to hold in my darkness, but the vomit filled commode symbolizes the mess I've made of my life. If only I can make it all disappear with one flush.

Michael pulls tissue from the roll and hands it to me, "Come on Allen, think about the peace treaty--."

"Ion wanna hear that shit right now iight," I cough out the words, "Fuck a treaty!"

"Come on, pull yourself together bro."

Muthafucka, I'm trying to be strong, but the darkness inside me is a giant. The harder I struggle to hold my secret in, the weaker I become. With sweat oozing from my pores, I call Michael's attention to my shrinking frame, "look at me man, what'chu see?"

"What, speak up," Mike leans in with his ear turned toward my face, "I can't hear shit'chu saying." He then walks over to the sink, grabs a cup, and fills it with water. He hands me the cup and I turn it up, pouring the water down my throat hoping that the h20 would dilute the darkness, or maybe even wash it away.

The moment I take that last swallow, bubbles start popping off but before Yang could get a word in, I interject, "Not right now! Stop! Both of ya'll - shut up!" Mike's neck cocks back and he looks at me with his face twisted, then he leans into my space again, and he reaches for my hand, "Get up, come on bro you cannot let them see you like this. Is this about the surgery? Are you scared that--?"

"SHUT UP!"

While Mike stands there with his head waving back and forth, tears leap from my face and drop into porcelain toilet. Waving off my outburst he asks again, "are you still worried about the procedure?"

"I, I......I, " The wet bubbles filling my head space interfere with my effort to respond. "Al, bro," Mike leans against the wall, "it's not as bad as you think, your bros gonna be there with you every step of the way, we've already made the arrangements." Refusing to let him finish his impromptu pity-party, I cut him off mid-sentence, "I have AIDS." I finally manage to confess.

∞ ∞ ∞

"Hold up, *what*?"

Michael's voice hikes and his face melts into a frown. After a few frozen moments, the questions began to melt away the silence, and before I could attempt to repeat myself, I hurl more vomit into the toilet.

"you're forgetting to breathe bro," he reminds me with a *tisk*, "you can't hold your breath, mess around and die choking off your own vomit."

At this point, that doesn't sound like such a bad idea. "Breathe bro," Michael demands, sending me into a fit of rage, "I'm fucking tr--, I'm tryin!" Holding himself up against the wall of the stall, Michael looks up at the ceiling, "I'm sorry man, I'm, I'm at a loss for words, is this a joke? you serious bruh?"

"Why would I play around with something like that?" I flush the toilet and I look up just as Mike wipes the sweat away from his forehead, then I refill the toilet with vomit. The bitterness of the thick, green slime makes my face tingle, "I'm dying." I say with tears streaming from my eyes. Desperate to get my point across I repeat myself, and it feels like those two words have a tight grip around my throat, "I'm dying."

"Nah bruh, you're alive. Here - let me help you up." Michael reaches out his hand again and this time I reach back, latching on to his palm with my trembling fingers. The bathroom becomes three shades brighter as he strong arms me and pulls, ejecting me from the tiny hell where I'm trapped.

Now standing in front of the mirror I'm face to face with my reflection, and I can't even look myself in the eyes. Lost in the shine of my black Dior loafers, my face is blurred into a twisted image of myself. *Ugh*

Michael 's voice snatches me from my slump, "I'm sorry man, I'm sorry. Let's get to the reception before people come looking for us. Don't worry bro, this between us – you tell everybody when you ready."

Whatever makes him think I want to tell everybody is beyond my understanding. But anyway, when we arrive to the reception I manage to find some left over food in my gut, so my throat and stomach work together to force it out. We get past that, then try to sneak in without being noticed. supreme fail.

Omar spots us sliding through the foyer and approaches us, "What happened man, where ya'll been? Ya'll were supposed to make it here before everybody. He looks into my eyes then glances at my hands like he always does when he's reading people. *The ole simple motherfucker! F*rom afar I could see Olivia dancing and mingling with her bridesmaids. For a second, we lock eyes but in that very same moment, she looks away, breaking our already trashed connection.

"Come on, it's time to cut the cake. Bro," Omar looks over his shoulder at Mike as he heads toward the dance floor, "You ready to deliver your speech? Olivia's been looking all over for you."

'*That selfish bitch!*' I hear Yang loud and clear, '*She thinks she can just go and live her happy life without you, marry your best friend in your face at the wedding that she and you planned and twist shit on you?!.... You gonna let her get away with being a two-bit whore?!*'

Suddenly my lips stretch and push out the words, "Shut up!" Omar throws himself in reverse, turning to face Michael and I as to avoid making a scene, "I'm just saying man, did ya'll even stop to grab the crowns?"

"Shit!" Mike snaps his fingers, "about that - look, we'll discuss it later." Mike looks left, then right, then over his shoulders, "we need to holla at'chu 'bout something bro." Looking at Mike I feel my forehead crunch. The rage is still racing through my veins when Omar parts his lips again, "I can't depend on you two for nothing. How hard was it to –"

"Man, we need to talk," Michael interrupts, "It's urgent, let's go to your car." Omar's eyes become fixated on my wrinkled, wet collar, then his facial expression warps into a look of shame, and he starts apologizing as we approach Michaels Lamborghini. As we draw closer to the car, the mirror-like paint job reveals our matching beige and black tuxedos and the hesitant limp in my stride.

Once we squeeze inside, Omar's plea for understanding breaks the silence, "Al, I know bro, look - the way things turned out, it's all messed up.... Man, but listen, I, I—"

"That's not what we need to talk about," Michael interrupts again; his right hand firmly grasping Omar's left shoulder causing Omar to twist in his seat, look at him and ask, "alright then,what's up?"

"Allen got sick, that's what took us so long."

"Sick? again? I thought he was getting better," Omar turns to face me, "Are you alright bro?"

"Nah, I ain't alright"

bitch, you invite me to my wedding as a groomsman, and you got the nerve to ask me if I'm alright – pussy, you just married my woman in my face, the fuck you mean am I alright?!

In my head, I'm the pilot of an airplane nose-diving toward this nigga, crashing into him and shattering his body into a million bloody pieces. Shit is funny as hell, but when I notice Michael watching me through the rear-view mirror with his eyebrow arched, my laughter halts.

"You good bruh?" Mike asks

"Yeah," I cough, trying to play it off, "I'm smooth."

"You sure?"

"I said I'm good bruh."

"sh..., iight then."

Another thing that makes me sweat, is someone interrupting my train of thought. So now I'm pissed again. Just a second ago, Omar was dead in my head. Yet here he is – looking at me through the side-view mirror like I have a pile of shit of *my* face. I return his gaze, thinking how It'd be so much better if I were looking down at'em in his casket instead. I mean seriously Omar, my nigga – why won't you die?!

"How sick can you be? You just got out the hospital last week, what's wrong now?"

"I have AIDS" I snap," and I don't wanna hear shit about this coming from no one else, cause you two are the only ones who know."

"Damn, AIDS?"

Seconds pass, then Michael looks to his right, "Yeah, AIDS." The next words spoken are guided by the roll of Omar's hands as he stutters out the questions, "What?... When? *How?*"

"AIDS... about a year ago.... I fucked a dirty bitch!"

Silence evades the small space. I just know this is the icing on this bitch's cake, and the grudge I feel for him has now grown three inches thicker. The disgusted look on his face overrides his efforts to console me, but he tries to play his fake ass role of a concerned friend, "So what are we doing now?" He asks.

"We need to get'em to the hospital, quick."

"Damn man, alright, alright - I'm in. The least I can do is make sure he's straight." Just then Olivia's best-friend, Tracey rushes over. My scowling eyes watch her feet push her toward the car, then they trail the length of her body, stopping at her widening eyes as she stops in her tracks. She's another person who's already dead-in-my-head, and if I could get my hands around her neck right now, I would choke the bitch out. She looks into my eyes and stumbles backwards into her footsteps.

"Tracey," Omar pops out and yells when she turns to walk away, "Tell Olivia I need'er!" As more guests arrive, their eyes follow the trail of vomit leading from the dance hall to Michael's car. Almost immediately after Tracey disappears behind the double doors, Toya exits the building and starts to walk over, but

Michael waves her off, "Don't worry, everything is ok, we got it under control."

Seconds later Olivia comes racing to the car, Holding the front of her wedding gown and looking at her feet as she steps over the thick puddles.

"Omar, baby what's wrong?!" She says as she approaches the front passenger door.

"We need to get Allen to a hospital, like now."

"What happened, "did you guys fight?"

"No, look, I can't talk about it right now, but I will explain everything later, I promise. Listen I need you to trust me. Just stay here, enjoy the rest of the evening then see our guests off. wait for me to call you, I'll make it up to you baby I swear."

Olivia nods and a desperate look of concern covers her eyes. But she isn't concerned for me, she is only concerned for Omar. She kisses him on the lips, and he jumps back in the front passenger seat. On the way to Harbor UCLA, the ride is most uncomfortable. Michael drives in silence and I sit in the back seat in utter pain. My head, my joints and my eyes are hurting, and the animosity constantly being released by the encapsulated hate that floats inside my mind doesn't make it any better. Needless to say, Yang is pissed.

'people get happy to hear bad news, and ain't nobody trying to hear all that fake positive shit either... it is what it is, and niggas is snakes.'

I couldn't agree more. I stare at the back of Omar's head, his fresh fade blends into a swoosh, and the swoosh is telling me what I should do next – it's bullying me right into kill mode. Refusing to be ignored Yang scowls, *'On God you need to match this nigga to a suicide note!'*

And before I know it, it happens again – the drive to kill, steal and destroy is re-born inside my mind. I'm trying my hardest to practice that mindful breathing bullshit, and I just need to live long enough to do what needs to be done to this snake in the

front seat. **As I listen to Omar and Mike converse, I talk to myself**
Breathe Allen, breathe....... Breathe.'

Taking my own advice has *never* **been so hard.** Omar sits
so still, I could see the tension weighing down his athletic
frame. He must be wondering about his new wife; whether she
had been infected. See Olivia, best-friend-fucking-Olivia, is two
months pregnant with child. So in essence, the penetration of
one single bullet may have caused a triple homicide.

At least I know that's what Omar is *thinking,* because he
won't stop doing that thing he does with his lips when he's
nervous. As skilled as he is at reading people and energy, I'm
surprised he can't feel me giving him the death stare through the
side-view mirror.

Yeah – He's scared. But who cares? Maybe that's the price to
pay for the scandalous act of betrayal he committed against his
brother. I must admit, I wouldn't feel ashamed it if were true, if
they shared AIDS with me. I mean if you were in my shoes how
would *you* feel? Would *you* care?

We're now Five minutes away from the hospital. On the other
side of the window, everyone looks too damn happy. **Along
Carson Street, all I see is laughing and smiling faces. People
appreciating life.** I curse the scenery as we pass a couple hugged
up at a bus stop, embracing each other's warmth.

A woman in a blue dress with the words, *'Children should
be seen AND heard'* printed in gold letters across the top skips
toward McMasterpark with a small child wearing the same
outfit. Just as Michael pulls up to a red light a transients thrust
himself towards the driver's side window, "three dolla wash yo
windows – holla!" he sings and dances a jig. Bystanders look and
laugh as the man auctions off his red light special. Michael opens
his side-rest and whips out a few bills, "Here, take it," he says,
then swipes his fingers back in forth in front of his neck, "I'm
cool on the wash."

The transient continues to zip in and out of traffic, waltzing over to the driver of a teal-colored car, "wax yo impala – Three dolla, *HOLLA*." I look up just in time to see the driver of the car use both of his hands to press his steering wheel like he's giving it CPR, his bottom lip wedged between his teeth

HOoONnK!

"Move around dude!" he yells. Everyone in eye's view is laughing, everyone but me. When you're consumed with *this* much hatred, laughter is reserved for the sight of blowflies and maggots, exchanging vows in the rotting flesh of a backstabber, *ha!*

As I lay down on the cold leather seats, I wish for the moment that *I* could be that transient. Contrary to what you might believe, suffering is the least of his worries. Once we finally we pull into the drive way of the hospital, Michael and Omar rush toward my space; Omar pulling the door then holding it open while Michael grabs hold of my arm.

Ain't this some bullshit

Snatching my arm away I smack my lips, "Move, I got it!" What makes these two blowjobs think a person with AIDS can't get out of a car by themselves. *Damn, I'm sick - not disabled. Stupid muthafuckas.*

Pins and needles trickle across the soles of my feet as we walk inside the hospital. I can't ignore the lingering thought that an explosion to the brain would be the perfect remedy for the spreading agitation. The thought of snapping out of existence is just so self-soothing. After what seems like forever, we make it to admissions and I get checked in. The moment Doctor Joseph lays eyes on me, she reads me my rights, "You haven't been taking your meds as prescribed." Of course she's right. She lectures me for about twenty minutes, then she turns to Mike and 'O,'

"having a support system during this time is essential, you all can help him by reminding him to take his meds and just simply, being there when he needs you. Escort him to appointments –

31

offer him words of encouragement." She passes me the slip and as Mike walks up behind me, his warm breath taps my ear

"Stavudine, Zah... Zal-cita-bine?" he reads down the list, "I've seen that one somewhere before." His forehead wrinkles as he scratches his head. When he walks around and stands in front of me, a strange look comes over his face. He knows better than anybody that I never liked to swallow pills. Turning to face the Doctor he asks, "Will any of this cause adverse reactions to the surgery he's –"

"I got it Mike," I interrupt. Michael looks at me, his eyebrows meeting at the center of his forehead form the capital case 'M' with a lower case 'm' in the middle. I know what he's thinking, and I've got to think fast before he follows up with a question.

Uncrossing my arms, I look at his wrinkled nose, "....I already know about these meds, I just hate taking pills, and you know that. I misplaced a few bottles, that's all.... I'll be alright. Right now I, I just need some rest - My eyelids are getting heavy." My follow-up appointment would be in two weeks; A period of grace for which to clean my hands.

"Are you alright man?" Omar asks on the drive to my place. I return his gaze through the side-view mirror, "I'm smooth, You iight?"

"I can't call it," he utters, "I'm sorry this happened to you, I can't begin to know how you must feel."

"Dead."

After about thirty seconds of silence and head scratching, Mike speaks up, "Your'e only dead if you let yourself die, bruh," He sounds irritated, like somehow, something is eating at him, "we gonna make sure you stay alive."

What a lie to tell, I live for the moment I can put this all to an end. The only plausible explanation for them assuming I'm just about to live like this is that they share the IQ of two turds bumping heads over a spot inside of a toilet. Hell, I already have my casket picked out. Once we arrive at my house we squeeze inside, and I hurry over to the couch then flop down on it in relief. Michael sits at the dinner table and Omar stands around for a while, as if my house was AIDS and he doesn't want to catch it.

I wait a few seconds for him to have a seat, then my eyes start to flicker, "you can't catch AIDS by getting comfortable at a friend's house. Grab a seat man - relax. Do not treat me like a sick animal." Omar looks around in doubt, but he grabs a seat at the table next to Michael, "I'm sorry man," he explains, "this is going to take some time to adjust to."

"I bet," Those two words ease from my mouth with a slight chuckle. The more I talk, the harder it is to keep my eyes open. It's like I'm running out of breath just moving my lips

"I... never..... thought this could happen to me. I always .... saw it in a nightmare.... but never would I.... have thought.... this could really happen.... to *me*."

"Man," Omar flicks his wrist and looks at his watch, "how long have you known?"

"Just found out... three months ago," I lie, "But apparently it's been in my system... for some time."

Omar's eyes widen and veer towards the stairs, then they scroll the wall before stopping on the picture above my fire extinguisher. He appears lost in a train of thought - so much so that it seems he's forgotten how to blink. I make a split-second decision to answer unasked questions

"chill, bruh....I got infected after we split..... Doc Joe says the disease advanced so quickly because of.... My lifestyle – you know I like to smoke and drink and ride white horses from time to time."

"Yeah man," Omar sighs, "I'm just saying Yo, this right here isn't easy to process."

"Easy to process?" I slide out of my shoes one by one, "You know better... or *do* you? Olivia tests every six months. Well, she did when ... she was with *me*."

I could tell by the way Omar's face relaxed that the words *'thank God'* just flashed in his mind. **He scratches his head, "so, seriously - what happened? I mean - when, where, who, how—"**

Well damn - I'm glad the lizard didn't ask *'why'*. I pull a stream of air into my lungs, "I had been ....dating this married chic named... Ali'zane.... for about nine months when I became sick. I mean, out of nowhere – dry coughing and throbbing headaches. I would wake up... in the morning, shivering.....

Yet my bed sheets would be soaked in sweat...... I mean.... I guess it was sweat.... Headaches would not stop. No matter how many Tylenol I popped..... the pain just... would not stop. The second Ali'zane saw how sick I had become.... she ghosted... my ass. Last thing she said to me was.... Call me when you feel better."

I'm lying through my teeth. That's probably why I've got so many gaps in the motherfuckers. I refuse to face my truth, so I continue to lie - not about Ali'zane, but about the rest of the story that followed.

Ali'zane was just an innocent pawn in my troubled world. AIDS is a self-inflicted wound for me. I bought this upon myself the day I dove inside the deep, tight entrapment of a woman who lost at a game she didn't even know she was playing; It was a vicious game of predator and prey. But that's a story for another chapter in this twisted ass life of mine.

"Do you think she's the one who infected you?" Michael finally speaks

"....Or, I infected her... we never used condoms – and she said she was on the shot." **Stepping into character, Omar hisses like the snake he truly is. "*tsss*,"** he shakes his head, so suddenly there's an *AIDS* vaccine?" Now my blood is boiling. *you got one more time to give me that shit face, I promise you Imma rock yo shit sooner than later!*

"nah bruh," I give him the side eye, "We was worried about her getting pregnant."

"tssss, well, where she at now?"

"I don't know. I told you.... she told me to call her, when.... I feel better. I never felt better... not for a long time. But Once, I was diagnosed I dialed her number, and her shit was... no longer in service."

"but wait," Mike raises his voice, "How'd you find out you had it? What made you test?"

Thinking back to the day I learned I was in what I now know was the conversion stage I answer, "I was showering when I found a huge purple.... blister on... my ankle. I knew I hadn't....burned myself, it appeared just out of nowhere...... I popped it but.... it filled back up with pus.

Then, the next day...... I found one exactly like it on my neck. I went to a clinic, and as soon as they saw the blisters, I was referred to my regular doctor," I prop a pillow behind my head, "Long story short, I've been trying to contact.... all my sex partners since. There's still a few... that I can't find. I have tried though."

Omar checks his watch again then he looks at my front door. In a desperate attempt to change the channels in our minds, I reach over to my coffee table, grab the remote and click the TV on, hoping to send the message that I'm done with this conversation.

∞∞∞

A news reporter wearing a red dress-suit laced with white lining appears on the screen with a microphone in tight grip, inches away from her crimson colored lips. Her straighten hair falls over her shoulders and the brown tint of her nails are only a shade or two lighter than the tone of her cocoa colored skin. She clears her voice, then her lips twitch.

"We're here live at Griffin Park where the body of a male victim has been found - nearly decapitated. Detectives believe this discovery is tied to the recent string of murders that have been taking place around the--"

I click the TV right back off, "Damn."

"Why'd you turn it off?" Mike throws his voice across the room, "that's over there near '*CROWNED*' - your friend's jewelry shop, right? *Damn*. Come to think about it," Mike turns to Omar, "when went by there to pick up you and Olivia's crowns, the place looked ghosted. I hope he's alright bro - you know it's not like him to be M.I.A - that man is about his buisness."

"I know, but I'll check on'em later. I hate watching the news.....always some... shit going on. "

"Yeah," Omar chimes in, "I think I've heard enough bad news for the rest of this year." The sympathy in Mike's voice strikes my ear, "damn, but what kind of person goes around just taking people's head off?"

Omar replies, "A monster." If I don't know anything else, I know I need to take control of this conversation, so I raise my voice a bit and say with a tisk, "Ain't no bigger monster than full blown AIDS."

"Is that where this tumor in your prostate come from?"

"Yeah, it's a symptom of the disease" I lie, yet again. Staring at the doorknob, Omar asks, "so...What did you do when you found out?"

"I Passed out and woke up screaming.... to the heavens. Begging for this man ya'll.... Call God.... To tell me why. Why do *I* always have to grab... the shitty end... of the stick"

The screeching sound of a chair being forced from under the table does something to my brain. I raise my head a little and look over the couch just as my bathroom door closes. The chair Omar was sitting in is now empty, and Mike just sits there, scratching his head. He looks up at me from under his wrinkled brows, and he tells me something I already figured.

"Bro's gonna be tripping for a minute."

Seconds later Omar returns, and as though in a hurry to gather information he asks, "Do you plan on telling anyone else, or are you expecting us to keep quiet?" My response is halted by his ring tone when his phone sings a question about living happily ever after. Now I'm triggered.

"Hello?" he answers on the way to my kitchen. From the distance I could still hear his conversation, and it makes me sweat. He tries to whisper, "Ok baby, I just had to make sure he got home safe, I'll be on my way shortly. I love you too..."

The scab I had drawn over the wound from his betrayal is snatched off in an instant as he waltzes back into my dining room with a smile plastered across his face.   The heat traveling through my veins refuels the war in my mind

'kill, steal, destroy,'

'Forgive, forget, move on.'

'Karma is a bitch on her period' Yang barks as he reaches into his bag of tricks, *'so, you just gonna let him walk away unscathed? match this nigga to a suicide note!'*

I swear, he is relentless. My heart thumps against my chest. *Breathe Allen, breathe....*

The deepening tempo of Omar's voice will make the taste of his blood that much more satisfying in the end. My nails pierce my skin as my fists curl into knots of flesh, bone and sweat. Omar looks at me, then he looks away. I can imagine the conversation he and Olivia will share later tonight, how they will frown their faces at me and thank God they are not in my shoes.

Up until now, Omar and Michael thought they knew everything about me but today they learned how wrong they truly have been. Today they have learned one of my darkest secrets but soon enough, they will learn of my darkest flaw. Mike stands and pushes his chair under the table, "Bro, you were pretty sick today, you need to take your meds, this is serious."

"How you feel now bro?" Omar asks, moving toward the front door.

"Like I'm dying from the inside out.... that's how.... I feel. Doc Joe suggested I, attend this AIDS support group. Every time I go there, I look around the room, No one looks sick at all – everyone looks healthy and happy, yet I always feel like they could look at me and tell.... like I'm always the only sick person in the room."

"You can't tell just by looking at someone," Omar walks past my fire extinguisher and glances up at the picture. Once he makes it to the front door, he stands there with his hands in his pockets and his head hanging low. Michael walks over to the hook and grabs his keys, "Aids hath no face."

"And AIDS shows no mercy." They play pity pat with their two-way conversation until I intervene, "Every time I go to this meeting.... there's a bisexual man there... his name is Sam. He always stares at me, like I owe him something. One time, I flinched at'em, but he didn't budge. He just stood there, looking. I could tell he's just as angry as I am and as much as I despise his presence, it helps to know someone can relate to my pain."

"So what are you going to do now?"

"I guess I'mma die slow."

"Yo, don't say shit like that bro," Omar's palm slides down his face, "you been living for this long, don't die now."

"ain't got enough time left on this earth to be sugar-coating shit." I drop my head upon the back of the couch, my eyes landing on the bumpy texture of the ceiling, *Cringe*. I shiver as a flood of darkness waves by me but I shake it off, crossing my feet upon my coffee table.

Omar's wondering eyes find my ankles and stay there a second too long. I uncross my legs, "all those years of being a player, I was only playing myself. Now the game is over. I played the game and I played it well…. But I still lost."

The weight of the world falls upon my face and my eyelids starts coming together. Omar sucks his teeth, "I've got to get going – my wife awaits, and she will start to worry if I don't get home soon."

"iight man, let's roll… we'll check back wit'cu later my nig. Call me if you need anything, anything bro."

As the two of them exit the dungeon of hell, Omar turns and reaches back, then twists the lock as he pulls the door closed behind them. Before they could get all the way out, I've already fallen asleep to the soundtrack of my insanity.

Ploop! *pop*! *plop*!

"*kill*"

"*steal*"

"*DESTROY!*"

Chapter 3

Omar

Mike slaps his feet against the concrete as if time is fast-forwarding to the last day of his life, leaving me in his dust as we head to his car. I call his name twice, but he never looks back, he just keeps beating his feet until he makes it to the driver's side door. Flowing through the wind like a speeding bullet, it's like he's trying to beat a deadline.

On my way the passenger side, I look through the back window just as he slams his door shut, and I watch his wrist pop out in front of him with his eyes aiming for his watch. He then looks over his shoulder.

He nods his head from side to side, then up and down. His nerves must be tipped over, so I slow my pace to give him a few seconds to be in there alone. When I finally pass his fuel tank I stride to the passenger door, grip the handle, and pull. Then I drop into the seat, "Got-damn fool, are you alright?"

"Yuh, yeah."

"Could've fooled me man. What is it? spit it out."

"Man, just get in the car."

"I *been* in, bruh." My seat belt is already buckled, so I'm looking at Mike from the side of my eyes, only to see him flick his watch again, "iight let's bounce."

"You've got to start the engine first bruh," I shake my head and look out of the window. Three seconds of silence pass then my eyes sway back towards his direction, stopping on the crunch of his bushy eyebrows, "Yo, what's up?" I ask as he cranks the engine and pulls off, providing no response to my inquiry. For about thirty seconds, I look out the window watching trees, houses, and people whisk by.

Two minutes pass and Mike checks his watch again, driving under thirty miles per hour. Ten minutes into the ride he glances at his wrist, twenty-five miles per hour. *Driving under the speed limit yet checking his watch like he has somewhere to be, classic sign of anxiety - undiagnosed like most people in America.* With his head cocked to the left he looks at his watch for the fourth time just as the California Science Center crawls out of view. "Are you alright bro? I chuckle, "Yo, you're driving *mad* slow."

"yeah," he glances over at me, then changes his mind, "no."

"Man, you're killing me. Where are we going?"

"Right here." He makes a right, pulling into an empty parking spot at Ladera park, then he silences the engine. By now I'm a nervous wreck, and I've already got troubles brewing in my own mind.

The inside of Michael's ride is engulfed in total silence. Although only for a few seconds, it seems like forever. A million thoughts plague my mind; *Is Olivia sick. Could there be a chance that....?*

"What're you going to tell Olivia?"

"The truth, somehow."

"....and your honeymoon?"

"Honestly, I don't know. When Olivia finds out about *this*, she's going to push the baby out early," I chuckle while gasping for air, "This is serious. We'll have to do our honeymoon on a later date."

"Dude I was thinking, I've been noticing a change in Allen, he's our best *friend* how the hell did we not know something was wrong? And you - you're always reading people, how did you not see this coming bro. I mean, you don't miss a beat."

Aware of my talent to size people up, I have to agree, "you right man, everything had changed about him. His walk, his talk, dude – everything. He hasn't been the same Al we grew up with."

"how did you not see it bruh?"

"I... man, I kind of *did* but, I thought he was just struggling with this whole situation between Olivia and I, I thought he was just taking it hard, you know? Then the surgery and, and – wait,"

I twist in my seat to face Mike, "why do *you* seem so bent out of shape? We're talking about me, but what's up with *you*?" Michael loosens his necktie, "we flipped chicks bro - you know how we do." He pauses for a second and keeps his head stiffened to the left, staring out of the window as if trying to avoid his own reflection in the rearview mirror.

"One day we ran a train on that broad in the apartments on ninety-fifth in Broadway. And then there was this one time we were so drunk, we flipped this chick in the jungles. I can't remember if we'd used a condom man, I was so drunk." Michael's chin drops to his chest, his full-bearded face contorted with distress, "two months later, she claimed she was pregnant and that either Allen or I was the father."

"So, what happened?"

"Al talked her into an abortion clinic, and we never heard from her again."

"I tell you what bro," I nudge Michael's shoulders, "Let's make a pact; from now on we'll go in and get tested every six months. Shake on it." He hesitates for a few moments, then he finally grabs my hand, "Bet."

"Bet. In the meantime, strap it up," I adjust myself in the seat then I check my watch, "Alright man, take me to my car and let me get to the crib before the wife puts out a missing-husband alert on my ass."

Michael restarts his engine and drops me off to my car. When I finally make it home to Olivia, I walk right into a cloud of cigarette smoke. As soon as she sees me she races to my side and bombards me with questions, "baby, where have you been? what happened? what's wrong with Allen? are you okay?!" She embraces me with kisses and hugs as she scans me from head to toe, checking for damage.

"I'm good baby. Come sit down, we need to talk."

She follows me through the hallway leading to our living room with the cigarette tucked between her index and middle finger. After taking a deep breath she flops down on the couch. Feeling no need to beat around the bush, I just come out and tell her, "Allen has AIDS."

Silence and space, I've gotta help her snap out of it.

"Oli, baby - talk to me."

"AIDS, Allen has *AIDS*?"

"Yeah, and it's bad. He got sick at the wedding – hadn't been taking his meds, his doctor said." Olivia's face melts as she begins to sob. "Baby don't worry, your last test was negative right?"

"Wrong, they checked for a heartbeat, you know I'm high-risk. I didn't test for AIDS on that day. Oh my God Omar, how long?"

"He says he's known for a few months."

"Without you guys knowing?!"

"We only knew he was going through that surgery baby, to remove the tumor in his prostate. Mike and I were just talking about how we had noticed a change in him. We both assumed he was having it hard accepting you and I being together. Baby the change was so drastic, I don't know how we couldn't tell that something else was going on. I mean, he walked different, he talked different – he even started looking different."

Olivia takes a deep breath in and slowly blows it back out,

"Tracey told me that she'd noticed something strange too, she once said that he seemed to have gotten a surge of confidence from out of nowhere. It's like he had become obsessed with himself – she said the tone of his voice had even mellowed off."

One thing I've always wondered about my wife is how the hell she never knew that Tracey's constant joking about Allen being *her* man was a side-ways confession. Sometimes my wife can be the most naïve person in the world.

∞∞∞

Olivia cried in my arms for almost an hour as we put our heads together and rewound Allen's transformation over this last year. For a person diagnosed with AIDS, you'd think he would become depressed and saddened but aside the strange change in his swag, Allen was still the vibrant, active player that he had set forth to be. Not only that, but he was always laughing - so I thought he was happy.

"Does he even where he caught it from?"

"He says a girl name Ali'zane may have infected him, but if she didn't, then he infected her for sure, because they didn't use condoms."

Olivia's bulging eyes flicker, "well I'm going to the doctor first thing in the morning to be tested. And baby, let's hold off on the honeymoon."

Just as I suspected. Olivia lights another cigarette, wedges it between her lips and takes a long pull. She blows a stream of smoke through the slit in the corner of her mouth, looking at me with her face twisted.

"Michael and I made a pact to test every six months, and, I'm sure you can agree to us practicing abstinence until we both test negative, right?"

"Ya think?!" She questions, her voice elevated as if she's not sitting there, slave to nicotine. I don't mean to sound like an asshole, but I'm disgusted with the thought of touching her right now. It makes me sick to my stomach to even think of making love to her at this point.

"Ok baby, and listen - you will NOT smoke another cigarette, ever again while you are carrying my baby. Deal?"

"I'll try."

I gently snatch the cancer stick from her parched lips. as though a light came on in her head, she looks at me with her face frowned, "If I was Allen, I'd kill myself and get it over with, I wouldn't wanna wait to die slow. Is the tumor in his prostate because of the AIDS?"

"He says so, but he also says he found out he had AIDS after he'd already started undergoing surgery. Says he started right after you two split. It seems kind of strange to me, but that's none of my business."

"I know Allen," She interjects, "he's the type who never goes to the doctor *until* there's a problem. He never went in for regular checkups when we were together. When he got sick, he just stuffed himself with over the counter meds, like the time when he cheated on me and gave me gonorrhea."

What the... Gono-who? My eyes shoot toward the lil bump in her belly.

"He never went to the doctor, he bought bootleg antibiotics from a street pharmacist, and they didn't cure the disease, so we ended up passing it back and forth for almost two months."

what in the ever-lasting FUCK?

"Oh yeah?"

In my head I'm like, *Oh no.* Learning things like this makes it hard for your muscles to relax. I try hard to keep my face from twitching, but I feel my features shift as my skin warms and tightens. Then, as though having a life of its own, my body shifts left, and the private conversation continues on in my head, *you could've kept that to yoself. Who wants to learn that their spouse was once a walking talking STD?* When I notice her staring at my lips, I pull myself together quick, "Bad timing."

My effort to redirect go in vain, "Uhm hm," Olivia groans, ".... your lips were just flapping."

She squints her eyes and smirks a little. Olivia always swears by the bible that she could read my lips, but if that were true she would be down my throat by now. Instead, she reaches out and touches my shoulder, "Sorry baby. Look, let's not worry ourselves, we'll end the night on a good note and take care of things first thing tomorrow."

"Bet."

"I'll run you a bubble bath, I want you to relax. Today has been *hectic* for you. let your wife make it better - Let me make love to your mind."

Shit! Can you catch AIDS in the mind? I'm a nervous wreck - thinking mad crazy. Of course, you can't catch AIDS in the *mind*. I could really use a squig of Patron right now, because I'm *tripping-tripping.*

Olivia walks into the kitchen and twists the knobs on the sink. Something about hearing the water flow calms me. "Want a shot?" she shouts from the distance.

"A few will do."

One thing about Olivia, she's always been an expert at attending to my needs. I smile to myself and accept her offer, "thanks baby." After I take back six shots, I bathe away the troubles of the day then I creep in bed with my new wife, still pondering my fate as we fall asleep in each other's arms.

Chapter 4

Omar

I've never seen Olivia so out of control. I mean everything from chain smoking, pillow choking, the works. Today alone she's cleaned the house four times within the last hour, dusting away dirt that doesn't exist and constantly rearranging the furniture.

I've tried to get through to her, but it's like I'm talking to a statue of my wife. When she's not puffing on cancer she's stuttering out words that make no sense and repeating herself. *She's hiding something.* Her anxiety is causing the turmoil inside me to boil over.

What have I gotten myself into? I'm at a total loss of what to do. It doesn't help that Allen has had to be rushed to the emergency room twice since our wedding.

The other day he had gotten so sick with pneumonia that his neighbors called the ambulance when they heard him moaning and crying out in pain on his front steps. He stayed in the hospital for twenty-four hours, then two days later, he passed out while watering his grass. His hospital stay lasted three whole days that time.

Refusing to be rendered helpless, he tries to continue life as normal – without taking his meds and adhering to the twenty-four hour care he needs. This doesn't surprise me though; Allen has always been stubborn.

When I think back on my wedding day, he's the only one who refused to coordinate with the poses when the choreographer arranged us for the pictures. Every time I looked over at him, he was twisted in the opposite direction, laughing.

In hindsight, my entire wedding day was awry. Instead of standing next to me with poise, he obsessed over that scar on his wrist, and he only plays with that scar when he's on edge. It's one of the things that lets Mike and I know he's trying to stay in control. Most of the time he fondles it without noticing what he's doing, and the day of my wedding he damn near scratched it smooth off.

Acknowledging that scar is Allen's way of changing the channels in his mind. He always seems to scratch it only when he's out of his element. I bought that to Mike's attention years ago, and he mentioned it to Allen. Since then, he's tried to be more aware of his scratching.

He's always hated that scar, and not because it looks like a purple ground bettle stuck on his skin, but because it reminds him of when he was cut trying to free himself from the handcuffs that engrossed his arms after he was caught stealing food from the store, at only nine years old.

In his defense, my brother was hungry. His drug-addicted mother had abandoned him in an empty warehouse, leaving him to fend for himself for two whole months. That was back in the day and since then, the only time he acknowledges that scar is when he doesn't even know he's doing it, and that's when things are bad.

It's like when Dorothy clicked her ruby slippers together and magically appears back at home. When Allen rubs his scar the channel in his mind seems to change – and the transition is visible.

He would always seem to regain control after he'd rubbed or touched that spot on his wrist. Thing about it is that over time, he turned a *little* scar into a deformity. One time when he was soothing himself, Mike yelled, "Scar!" and Al snapped right out of his trance. Ever since that day, 'Scar' has been our code word for 'chill.'

But on my wedding day it was different, he never regained

control. He rubbed and scratched that scar as if he were trying to erase it. The more I think about it, something definitely isn't right. The swinging door that just flew open only amplifies my anxiety. I watch Olivia rush over to the dining room table and throw herself into a seat, "Damn baby," I chuckle, "slow down."

"How slow you want me to go bae?" She twists a bottle of water open, "how slow do you want me to go?!"

"You act like you're making things better, feeding the baby cancer sticks and all."

"Uhm, whatever."

"Yeah, whatever is right. You need to calm down." The truth is that the thin line between life and death await her, just hours away. I'm hoping like hell she doesn't have to cross that line and if she does, I pray she won't take me with her.

"you're coming with me right?"

Damn. I shake my head, "Yeah baby, relax."

"Relax my ass, don't try to act calm. Mike told me he had to drag you in there kicking and screaming."

"You know how I feel about needles. and besides, that was getting tested, you're just going in for the results. You're not getting stuck with a needle again, the hard part is over."

"What'chu mean the hard part is over?!" Olivia snaps, "the hard part is waiting to see whether you have a date with death, the hard part is the reality that someone you were intimate with for over ten years is sick with AIDS. The pain from a punk ass needle could never compare. *The hard part is over,*" Olivia mocks, "tahu, fuck outta here!"

I decide to take her advice - I shut the hell up and got the fuck up out of there. Besides, I can't stand another whiff of that cigarette smoke. An hour and a half later while driving down La Cienega, Olivia's mood changes from worried to relaxed. As soon as we enter the office her name is called.

"Mrs. Parks!" We both stand, following the receptionist to the consultation room. In less than ten minutes a tall, slim figure sways through the door followed by a scent of fresh lavender. Her hair is a black ball of cotton adorned with a yellow daisy.

She flips through pages of paperwork before she looks up and makes eye contact with Olivia, "Doctor Stokes is out on vacation, so I'll be seeing you today. I'm Doctor Joseph," She nods at me, then she flips a page on clipboard, "everything is fine, you tested negative."

Chapter 5

Allen

Life is a *bitch*, and then you die. I should be gone by now but I'm still here, and I don't know why. I just keep dragging on, in slow motion at *that*. Every second seems like a minute; every minute seems like an hour.

Time is simply not on my side. But every day, it begins anew - this horror story that people call life. Every morning, day after day. I peel my eyes open and the same two words greet my thoughts: *Not again.*

This has to stop. I'm sick of looking at the same blue sky and walking among people smiling with numbers over their heads, telling me how many days they have left on this earth. Tired of doing fate's dirty work.

"excuse me bruh, this your truck?"

I hate it when my thoughts are interrupted

"Looks like it is."

"Signs says you're selling?"

"as is"

"Perfect. I've been looking for a hummer just like this one, and black is my favorite color. GMC EV, SUV edition... about a 2022, right?"

"Right."

"Can I pick it up on Friday?"

"Absolutely."

"Cool, I'm Tim by the way. And you are?"

MOTHERfucker, make like a turd plunging down the toilet and get fucking lost

"Allen."

"Nice to meet you Allen, see you Friday."

Yet another smiling face.

In an instant my insides feel like human-body soup and my outsides are *writhing* in static. *Raggedy bastard.* I guess *Tim* didn't have time to put an iron to his clothes this morning. His outfit looks like chitterlings, and his shoes ain't even tied. I hate chitterlings, and I hate people who walk around smiling for nothing. Tim turns and walks away, a backpack over his shoulders and a halo hovering above his head, standing upright.

∞ ∞ ∞

Mike and Omar know nothing about me after all these years. They may know some things about me, but they don't know *me*. I'm sure of who *they* are though; Mike - his brother's secret keeper and Omar, full of shit

I can smell'em from a mile away. Promising to love *my wife* until death do them part? *Tuh,* yeah. Ok. Death. And so it is. He really thinks I'm happy for him, for "*them?*" yeah right!

One thing he will not do is keep waking up to the woman who's supposed to be waking up to *me*. If that's what they think is going to happen morning after morning, then she's as dumb as a wad of cum and he's as dense as the condom that swallowed it.

As if stabbing me in the back wasn't enough, the snake

had the nerve to invite me to the wedding, and ask me to be a groomsman. I guess he thought he was softening the low blow to my gut. Or he thought I would be honored. *Huh, fuh sho.*

Waiting for this meeting to start, I contemplate bringing my daydreams to life. I doze off for only a second and just that fast, a horrific scene plays out behind my eyelids

There Omar is, changing colors like a wad of tissue swiping up the crack of my ass; multicolored, twisted - bent out of shape. His insides circling the wheels of my truck as I pick up speed, and grind'em into *nothing*.

ha ha, comedy. That laugh almost made me orgasm. That is, until a police car races by with it's sirens wailing, forcing me back into a reality where Omar is still alive. To add insult to injury, a memory flashes in my head

Olivia, on top. Her hips rolling to Omar's beat as the straps
of her red silk negligee slides down her shoulders. The glare
of the window does it's due diligence in providing a 3D view
of my woman bouncing on top of my best friend.

The sight, gut-wrenching. The feeling of my boots sinking into the mud, relieving. Cold as it was, sweat oozed down my face and spread across my tastebuds as I peek past the curtains of Omar's bedroom watching the betrayal play out. Position after position, blow after blow.

Then *and* now.

The sight is always both triggering and amusing. See this here grudge, it's personal, and what I need is closure; a one-on-one interrogation with the main question to Omar being, '*after all is said and done, why in the fuck do you refuse to die?!*' The thought of him suffering always makes my dick spit.

Imagine the worse person you could think of, twisting out of existence while the life seeps from the orifices of their body. Everytime you see that person, you remember that image. Sooner or later they'll be dead to you and because they are dead in your head, they can easily die in your face.

mmm, Ahhh ... I think I just nutted.

See, as much as I would like to be that perfect forgiving person, I can't get over how he spent ten years being around my woman. The entire time he was scheming and hating on me. All I know is that because of that, he's gotta go. For now though, I'll just keep deleting smiley-faces. It's the only way I can let off some steam. As I Look straight ahead at the billboard, this time I deliver a response, *"I will."*

Tapping my middle finger against my steering wheel I wait to hear those bubbles but just as I quiet my engine, whispers start to float around in my head.

'Kill.'

'Steal.'

'Destroy.' Harmonized in a demonic tone. It's becoming all too clear that it really *is* now or never. But, not just yet. Guess I gotta keep being fake for now, just like everybody did with me.

"Come on in," Daniel waves me toward his direction as he ascends the steps, "We have coffee and refreshments." I nod my head and hold up my index finger, taking a few more minutes to gather my thoughts. Finally I free myself from the seatbelt and I exit my car, then I press my feet against the steps until I'm in front of the door of the meeting.

When I look through the window I see people engaged in conversation, smiling and exchanging gifts. Watching a fellow member, Patrick, offer Sam a red box wrapped in yellow ribbon, my eyes flutter. Once my sight adjusts to the flickering lights, I focus in on Patrick, who stumbles backward then leans out of Sam's space the second Sam flaps his tongue to say thank you.

It takes a few minutes for me to grab the door handle and pull, but I finally do. I enter the room swaying my head from right to left, connecting with a different pair of eyes with every move. Step by step I walk by the coffee maker, then the sparkling heart-shaped cookies, then the red ribbon that adorns the book shelf. When I pass the acceptance-based mirror mounted on the wall, I catch the reflection of Sam staring me down with his mouth twisted. My insides ball up in knots every time he harrasses me with face.

I've made it up in my mind that he's as good as dead - and not just in my head. Walking toward my usual seat near the back of the room, my veins pump blood faster than I can think about it. No matter how many times I stretch, shake my hands and breathe, the tingling won't subside. It feels like fire is rushing through me.

Truth to the matter is, the world needs a superhero now more than ever because I'm on a mission, and I will not be stopped. Maybe God will part the clouds and save Omar, before I kill'em. He took away from me, the only woman that ever loved *me*. If he thinks he's going to live my happily ever after while I suffer from AIDS, then his brains must be loose inside his skull.

It's *his* fault I met Ali'Zane, *his* fault I got my dick dirty. If it were'nt for him, I wouldn't have gotten so drunk one night that I forced myself inside ....

Nevermind.

Humanity is well-seasoned when it comes to misplacing blame. Let everybody else tell it, I'm the salty one though. People always make excuses for other people and what they do, talking about, *'You can't help who you fall in love with,'* and *'Everything happens for a reason.'*

So they can snake *me,* smile at *me,* do all these things to *me,* but when I start twisting heads off, suddenly, *I'm* the monster? Ok then, so be it, I'll be that. I'll be candyman like *jeepers creepers,* the devil on steroids. Hell I'll even be a hissing snake. I'll be all that from now on and I won't give a fuck.

And why should I? I don't have control over my thoughts anyway. I can't seem to silence these voices in my head telling me what to do. So, you know what they say, 'if you can't beat'em, join'em'.

'Match that nigga to a suicide note.'

Yes sir!

Truth be told I've tried to beat the bad thoughts, I've tried to ignore the voices, but every time I find a moment of peace here comes the Wright kids singing out

'Kill,'

'steal,'

'destroy.'

Yeah, there's three of those little fuckers and apparently, they're daddy's girls.

Chapter 6

Michael

There's nothing like a hot shower to wash away the residue of yesterday. All the sin, temptations, lust, and dirt melts away, ceasing to exist in my world. I like to watch it all disappear down the drain. *Yup,* a nice brisk shower will cleanse the body, mind and soul – that is, until you start a new day and once again become covered in dirt and grime.

The jazz music escaping my waterproof JBL speakers and the hot steam filling the walls of my thirty square foot shower room makes me feel like I'm in my own universe. Five minutes into my cleansing, I realize I left my razor on my dresser and I step out of the shower to grab it. Just then, an instrumental tickles my ears; my favorite artist invites her crush to join her on a long walk around the park. That sweet angelic voice always takes me to other places, sending me on trips down memory lane.

Right now, I'm thinking of a woman I dated in college. I could still smell the cinnamon from the churros I had baked in celebration of her passing the state bar exam. The sex that followed was amazing. It all happened right here on this couch, and on that table, and in the halls of that foyer and ... Hell, it happened everywhere in this house.

I could feel it like it was just yesterday; her love tunnel was so tight and warm I almost came instantly but I held back because I wanted to see her jerk and moan and lose control as she climaxed. But that didn't happen, at least not the first time.

As soon as she arched her back and twisted her hips, the warm milk erupted from my shaft and filled the condom I was wearing. That was just the first round. The second round, I felt her walls tighten and jump around my wood. Till this day, that was the best sex I ever had – That sister was a real freak.

The memory dies off gradually, and I stand around in the nude, glancing at the spoils of my success. My home is designed to my perfection – a man's world *without* the woman's touch.

My living room is splattered in purple and gold from the ceiling to the floor with an autographed moment borrowed from Kobe's first championship game, may he rest in peace. All three of my degrees are displayed in an area of my living room, that I call the *'wall of fame.'*

Bachelors in business administration

Masters in electrical engineering

PHD in research journaling.

My ninety-five inch plasma screen television takes up almost the entire wall adjacent to Kobe's moment and eggplant-purple, leather reclining couches sits right in the middle of my paradise. From afar I still hear the music playing from the shower, and after I grab my shaving kit I begin to two-step back to my personal rain. Suddenly my attention is called to the subtle sounds of whispering.

Oh snap, I forgot to close the curtains. My neighbor Tonia and her two sisters Unique and Star are enjoying front row seats to the strip show at Michaels. Tonia drops a plump avocado in her bag while Unique stops mid-reach to the branch above her head, looking through the window with her mouth hanging open. For a split second I think about being embarrassed, but I know they're getting an eye full of goodness. So I step in front of my large bedroom window and shift my frame from right to left. My eyes are focused on Tonia as I bite my bottom lip.

I didn't expect my shaft to stiffen, this thing has a mind of its own. Thrilled at the attention, I rock my erection back and forth, causing my shaft to grow two inches longer along with Toya's widening eyes, "touch it" she mouths. I stretch my palm towards my arrowhead but before I could grant her wish, my cell phone rings. It's Omar, "Yo, I'm about to hit your block right now."

"You pulling' up?"

"In about fifteen"

"iight, bet."

I've got to hurry. Instead of pulling on my joystick, I pull the curtains close then I rush back to the shower. My erection dies within seconds after I hit the luke-warm water. On my way out the door I call Allen's phone, but it goes straight to his voicemail. It's not like him to miss three sessions in a row, but I'll chop it up to the fact that he has been battling that sickness. When I dip into O's ride, I notice his outfit matches mine; we both have on white air force one's and NIKE shorts that are blue and grey, topped with white t-shirts. After adjusting my chain I check my reflection in the mirror, then I glance over at Omar, "You tryna be like me bruh?"

"Dude, you're lame," he laughs aloud and tugs at my gold link, "Take off this fake ass chain. We're about to ball."

"Come on maine, you know ain't nothing fake 'bout dis here," I tuck my thumb behind my chain and swing it from left to right, "This bling is legit. Ya boy feeling lucky today. Tonia and her crew gonna be up there playing tennis, and they lose their minds when I wear this combo, ya dig?"

"yeah, yeah - I dig"

I don't know what it is, but for some reason I feel like O's got something on his mind. He waves his head to the side to look at me, "Have you talk to Al?"

"I just called him on the way out, no answer."

"Oh."

"You know he hasn't been doing too well lately."

"Yeah, but I thought he started taking his meds again and was

59

doing alright."

"Iono bruh, you ready to get balled up though?"

"I'm ready to ball your ass up son."

We pull off and head to the Santa Monica Pier for our brotherly ritual, "I'm hungry as hell," Omar blurts out, "my stomach is touching my back."

"We can hit up Jack in the Crack afterwards. So, when's the last time *you* spoke with bro?"

"Come to think of it, I haven't talked to him good since he got back from the hospital last week. He posted a crazy ass message the other day on FakeBook, talking about *'I can't wait to introduce ya'll to my new bitch'* - bruh sounded like he was on something else."

"New *bitch*?"

"yeah man, *'new bitch'*... other than that, I talked to him briefly maybe two days ago. He said he was handling something and would call me right back, but he never did. He hasn't been answering his phone since then. He said he might be going out of town to visit family for the holiday - him and aunt Deb. I don't know if he left yet though."

"Dude," I swipe my hand down my waves, "I don't know." On most mornings Al, Omar and I usually play basketball for an hour before work. It gives us a jump start on our morning, and some days we play at night to relieve the stress of the day - It's been our ritual since junior high but for the past few days, big Al has been M.I.A, and this isn't normal for him.

Allen loves basketball and he loves a good work out. But most of all he loves hanging with his boys, his *family*. His absence here recently bothers me, but I know he's going through some things and just may need some space, so I shrug it off.

We pull up to the courts and I redeem myself from our last game, beating Omar fifteen to nine.

"Charge it to the game bro."

"Alright son, you got it – that's what up."

"So, I'll take the sour dough breakfast combo, supersize bruh – good looking." Omar opens his wallet and peeks inside, "yeah, ok."

Omar really hates to lose at a game of basketball and he hardly ever loses, but this thing with Allen has got him by the balls. Once we finish our breakfast and Omar drops me off, I head to the shower then take a nap before work.

Almost an hour later I'm bullied out of my sleep by another of my favorite artists telling me to be like a sex machine and get on the scene, ironically, depicting a dream I'd just had about Tonia. I quiet the alarm, then I tend to the ringing. My morning is ruin the second I touch my ear with the phone.

"Hello, good morning Mr. Man," The soft, squeaky voice on the other end pauses, "...I'm sorry to call you on your off hours. This is Debony, your new editor for *'Flip The Script'*. I'm here at your office – you had requested I deliver your next five episodes in person."

"Yes mam, I did."

"uh – you're going to need a cleanup crew, STAT"

"Cleanup crew, for what though?"

"For your studio, it's been vandalized. I got here pretty early, just to tie up a few loose ends as I waited for you to arrive. Sir, all the windows are busted out, and there is graffiti all over the walls. Worse of all, the inside was on fire when I pulled up. I've called the police and I hear them arriving now. I'll hold on to your scripts and you can come pick them up at my office at your convenience."

"Wait, wait – what?!"

"I'm sorry Mr. Man. Also, someone defecated on the front steps and spread it across the windows and doorknobs." Wait, did she just say someone shitted on the steps? The distant sound of sirens makes it all too real.

I feel my fists ball into tight knots. The one thing that makes my blood boil is somebody messing up my money or *shitting* on my brand. Before she could utter another word, I jump up, grab my car keys, then I head to my lab.

I get there as two fire trucks are pulling off, but I manage to catch up to a third truck and right away I start demanding answers. The only thing they could tell me is that witnesses saw a black male running away from the building right before it exploded.

'what the --'

Thank goodness for insurance. I'm not even about to sweat it. This ain't the first time a hater tried to stop my grind. I allow the cleanup crew to do their thing and I head to my nine to five.

∞∞∞

Feels like my skull is stuffed with spagetti. Something must be off in the universe, can this day get any foggier? *YEP, right away.* My mood takes another plunge as I flip through the pages of these scholarly journals and I'm reminded that society is a big boiling pot of injustice.

If my thoughts were'nt backed up by decades of research I wouldn't believe it myself. Unfortunately though, the facts my eyes just met *again* are true; hiring managers are trained to overlook resumes when the address of job applicants fall into neighborhoods where minorities such as African American's, Hispanics and indigenous people reside, and when the applicants name indicate that they are a member of a specific race.

According to this article, if your name is 'Shaniqua', or

'Mohammad,' you should be prepared to be pushed to the side by almost every corporation in America. In other words – further marginalized. The practice goes hand-in-hand with a process called 'redlining,' and it's a way to keep poor people poor, and rich people rich.

The scholars report that for the economy to run smoothly, there must be some level of inequality embedded within the corporate world. In essence, certain groups of people are meant to fall below the poverty line. Very unfortunate. My mission for this research assignment is to argue the many ways the government encodes jim-crow laws within the economy and the legal system to implement systematic discrimination.

Trip off this: Your address on a resume signifies whether or not you live in the hood, and prospects would much rather keep "Hood" applicants at bay. According to the findings, minorities who 'whiten' their resumes get more interviews and are most likely to be approved for loans. *Damn*, poverty versus wealth is a game well-played by elites, and I intend to expand on evidence showing which groups were meant to be poor, and which groups were meant to be rich.

In analyzing the statistics, the numbers seem to jump around in my head like fleas bouncing off a rabid dog – I can't focus on anything right now, all I can think of is who, how, and *why* someone set my studio ablaze.

In all the chaos of the last four hours, I manage to review enough articles to lay the foundation for the draft of my research analysis. I will worry about the numbers later. I sure can go for a shot of D'usse right now. I make it through my front door, snatching my clothes off like they're on fire, and I head straight for my third shower of the day.

It's now seven-thirty p.m. and I can't think of anything better to do than hang out with my boys to talk about this madness. When I pull up in front of the Cougar's Den, Omar comes rushing over to me as I put my car in park, "Here, hit this."

He passes me a blunt full of girl scout cookies, and we stand there getting lifted for a while before we swagger inside. As we enter, I glance around looking and listening for an all-black hummer blasting that reggaeton music to pull up, but the vehicle never appears.

We walk over to the table where our crew always hold our brother time meetings and we both sit in silence, waiting for that third brother to waltz in. He doesn't. Neither one of us crack a smile, but Omar finally pops a bottle and pours himself up. he raises his arm to take his drink back, but pauses when something in the distance catches his eye. Influenced by his body language, I glance over my shoulders.

Standing at the entrance is a slim, fair-skin woman, looking like a goddess. She has the unmistakable features of a girl we knew back when - a familiar face indeed. She sways past our table followed by her equally attractive crew. Ze'Amora, Allen's former mistress is apparently back on the scene.

Ze'Amora had crept around with Allen behind Olivia's back for their entire relationship. Omar found out and "Accidentally" informed Olivia, who reacted by using Omar to get revenge.

Oh, and by the way, Ze'Amora and Omar were best friends at one point in life - friends since pre-school. When Omar found out about the affair he nearly pushed a seven ounce baby from his dick hole, but he seized the opportunity to sway Olivia to choose the better man. Ze'Amora proclaimed her love for Allen and when it all hit the fan, Allen grew to hate her and she blamed it all on Omar. After I take a sip of the Screaming Eagle Cabernet, I chuckle in Omar's direction, "Run."

Omar slides down in his seat, causing his shoulders to separate from his Shearling Sheepskin vest, "Nah son it's cool," He glances at his watch, "Not for nothing bruh, that's always gonna be sis." The sounds of clinging glasses and light chuckles fill the room, and a sudden thought penetrates my mind. "Aye you think she got outta there in time?"

Omar's face wrinkles, "Shouldn't we say something?"

"Maybe she already knows," My eyes dance with the sway of Ze'Amora's green silk dress as she wiggles into a chair two tables down, "what if *she's* the one who hit *him*?"

"Ze'Amora would'nt do that, she didn't sleep around. If she's got it, she got it from him son, I can tell you that, no doubt."

Omar's New York accent thickens and his eyebrow arches. He glances over his shoulder at his ex-best friend who sits surrounded by her entourage. "Yo, as fine as Ze is, I know she's not a walking talking disaster," Omar comments, second guessing his original conviction, "I'm going to need something stronger than this."

"I'll take a shot to that."

After twelve rounds of Patron the conversation nose-dives into the abyss. All the while Omar keeps peeking over his shoulder at Ze. At first she seems to be avoiding him, but soon after I make that assumption, I twist back towards Omar to see her standing over his shoulder, parting her lips. Guess I was too busy scanning the room to see her approach. She leans into Omar's ear, "what, you don't know me no more?"

"You know you're my girl, Ze," Omar's his body erects in his seat, "I was going speak but--"

"it's cool," she interjects before he could finish lying, "... I almost didn't notice you, but your spaceman ears gave you away. It's good to see you," She looks at me, "hey Mike."

I nod at her, pleased at the visual stimulation she provides. "Someone's missing," she looks around the room, "Where's Big Al?"

"I guess he's been tied up. Yo, Have you talked to him lately?"

"Uh, yeah. I met up with him a few months ago. We went out a couple of times, tried to rekindle the flames. But when we had a pregnancy scare, we realized that we weren't ready for anything long term. After a few dates, he started making plans to go and visit family. Since then, I've been in Detroit on business. Today is my first day back."

Every word she spoke after "Pregnancy Scare" sounded like Charlie brown chatter. All I hear is *'womp womp womp'* as the two words stretch like flinging rubber bands inside my head. "You thought you were pregnant Shorty?" Omar asks as he straightens his collar.

"Yeah," Ze shrugs, "started feeling ill, and aunt flow ain't come 'round for two months straight. But I'm good – ain't no baby coming out of these panties no time soon."

"umph." Omar groans then calls for the waitress to bring another bottle in the same moment I think to myself, *'Welcome to hell on earth.'*

"Put my number in your phone, 'O'" Ze says as she looks over her shoulder at her friends, "I gotta get back to my girls before they start complaining."

"That might not be such a good idea."

"Oh, it's like that?"

"Nah sis, never. It's just that," he holds his left palm up toward his face, "I's married now."

"*Aww*, who's the lucky lady?"

Omar pauses, "O, Olivia."

"You mean Allen's high school sweetheart, *Olivia?*"

"Uh, yeah."

"Damn, what a round world we live in." Ze chuckles. All I could think of is how to tell her, and how could we not. But I keep my mouth closed and I order a rack-of-lamb.

'Maybe she already knows, maybe she gave it to him,' I try to reason, excusing myself from the responsibility of being the barrier of bad news.

"Alright then," Ze says as she pinches Omar's cheek, "I'll just give the math to Mike, ya'll keep in touch."

Hell, I don't want it. I'm not trying to get caught up in that madness. I give her a sideways look, "you sure about that?"

"Yeah. We can all hang out sometimes, for old times' sake."

"iight then, bet." I take the piece of paper, fold it and stick it in my wallet. I've got plans for it – dump it right in the trash as soon as I get the chance. "Well, bye ya'll. It was good to see ya." She winks at Omar and sashays back to her table.

"Yo it's like everywhere I turn now, I'm faced with this mess. The world isn't safe anymore - It's like, a new trend."

Recalling my assignment for an upcoming AIDS project, I confirm Omar's assertions, "You ain't lyin'. I was reading in an article earlier last week at work that every three out of five Americans get caught up in that new trend. The sources said that thirty-five thousand people are infected every year and that every two out of three of those people don't even know they've been infected; they either never test or are simply ignorant of the disease. Do you know what that means?"

"Nah," Omar says, looking away, "what does it mean?"

"It means that a lot of people are committing involuntary manslaughter every day."

"Why are we talking about this right now," Omar snaps, "we're supposed to be turning up." He pours the last ounce of liquid fire down his throat and slams the shot glass onto the table. Then he looks over his shoulder at the approaching waitress while holding up his index finger.

Before he could part his lips, I place my palm on his wrist, "look around you bro, like you said - it's everywhere. It's in the clubs, It's at weddings – even in church on Sundays. How the hell could we not talk about it? That's the problem, people are scared to talk about it until it catches up with them."

I don't mean to snap at his carelessness about the situation, but I mean, *damn!* If people would educate and inform themselves there wouldn't be so many new cases. Maybe the epidemic can be eradicated.

Omar's frivolous attitude makes me angry so bad, I literally yell at the waitress for three more shots of patron. Hell, truth be told, until I learned about Allen's status, I'd never been tested myself. But the day of Omar's wedding when I was driving him to his car, every girl I'd ever slept with came to mind. I thought about the girls I'd gotten so comfortable with that we'd stopped using condoms. A total of fifteen girls I took down, raw.

Two nights before the wedding I ran into one of those girls, and we danced again for old's time's sake without giving it a second thought. In the heat of the moment, I slid bare back into her wet entrapment.

Ever since I tested, my life has flashed before my eyes daily. Waiting for the results seems more like waiting to die when you've taken so many chances, and accepting the fact that a friend is sick is one of the hardest things I've ever had to do. As if life weren't already stressful enough with the acts of living and dying – along comes *AIDS*.

"Yo, everything was fine – I was getting married, about to start a new life with my new wife, then out of nowhere hell strikes. Now it's like I'm running, hiding... ducking AIDS. Wondering if it will ever catch up with me. Or maybe it already has," Omar's chin hits his chest, "I'm tired of running yo, I feel like just giving up."

"You sound crazy ass hell. What'chu mean give up?"

"I mean I should just retire my wood."

"How da hell you gone do that and you just got married?" We laugh in unison. "I'm just saying - think all the way back to high school. It all probably started with that cheer leading chick. The one who loved to do the splits when she wasn't at practice."

We chit chat for another twenty minutes and Omar yells for another shot. His trembling hand drops onto the table, empty shot glass tight in grip. He then reaches down and rubs his palms on his jeans and when his mouth starts moving without releasing sound, I poke my head forward and focus in on his lips. Unable to make out what he's whispering to himself, I throw my head back, "What's up with you bruh?"

"Nothing, why do you ask?" His look-away reaction confirms the fact that he knows I'm reading him. Hell, I learned from the best. I chuckle, letting him know his cover is blown, "your mouth is moving but you ain't saying nothing. You always do that when something's on the brain."

"Trust me yo, you're not trying to hear it."

"Must be deep."

"Yeah," he takes one last shot of patron then spins the glass around between his fingers, "deep."

"Well, look. Speak now or forever hold ya peace. I'm 'bout ready to call a cab cuz I'm faded, and if I don't stop now...."

I glance over at the girl sitting at Ze's table just as she winks in my direction. The way I'm feeling right now I'll mess around and charm the panties right off ma, she better stop playin'. Suddenly becoming thirsty, I swipe my tongue through my mouth, "I can already taste the pussy on my lips."

"Olivia's test came back negative," Omar stutters.

My lowered eyes stay fixated on that glossy plum-colored smile, "yeah man," I smirk and finally wink back, waiting for a three leaf clover of a signal

"... the article I read said that a person can be asymptomatic for ten years before even experiencing the symptoms," I put the glass back to my lips and take another sip before I continue, "... for a person who doesn't go to the doctor regularly, that can be a problem. AIDs could seem to come out of nowhere."

I don't know if ma is reading my lips, but suddenly she disconnects from me and turns her attention back to her chatting click, so I return my glass to the table and get serious with my conversation, "… that's why they encourage you to get tested, it's not that testing will cure or prevent the disease, but if you catch it soon enough you can stop HIV from turning progressing to AIDS."

Omar's face melts and his energy goes dark. I think I struck a nerve, but then I hear him mumble, "Olivia cheated on me with Allen two months before we got married. She doesn't know if the baby is mine or his. Al doesn't even know she told me and man, I just chopped it up to the game. I know he still loves her and plus, plus," Complete and utter silence for the next three seconds, "I got myself mixed up in this mess, so I mean –"

"But wait, we know Allen can't have kids because of that thing with his prostate."

"Yeah, we also know that Al knew he was living with AIDS for at least three months. That means he'd had HIV for some time without even knowing."

"Damn, how'd you find out she slept with'em?"

"She was acting strange for a few days after I told her the news. Then one day she sat me down, told me everything. I been washed up since yo."

"*tuh*, rightfully so."

"Yeah."

"They might have used a condom though."

Omar smirks and shakes his head, "*tsss- hu.*" At this point I must admit that Omar is in his right mind to worry. This situation just took a plunge downward and I am ready to call it a night. The cab pulls into my driveway at eleven-thirty pm. I stumble out, tipsy from the alcohol but drunk from the conversation at the bar. Two minutes after I burst through the door my phone rings. It's Omar, "Touch down." He says.

"You good bruh?"

"Yeah bro, I'm good – I'll call you tomorrow." On the way to the fourth shower of my day I stop to brew a pot of mint tea, then I start ripping off my clothes. The wonderful thing about living alone is never having to answer to anyone. The freedom is yours - being wild, being naked.

My compulsive need to keep my house free of the dirt from the outside world is evident in the pile of Abercrombie and Fitch design by my front door. I bathe in my personal rain long enough to wash away all the germs, and all the madness that gravitated towards me tonight.

When I emerge from my universe, I finally collapse on my king-sized bed and flip through the television channels. A news reporter pops onto the screen, alerting the world that someone was lucky enough to hit that thirty-million dollar power ball.

'That's none of my business.'

Pressing my thumb onto the buttons of my remote control I gaze at the flashing screen, but I pause when I see yellow tape and flashing lights.

BREAKING NEWS:

The sad-face killer strikes again.

Another body has been found with a sad face carved onto it's mouth. The victim has been identified as twenty-nine year old Timothy Cruise, a resident of this gated community right here behind me. Nieghbors describe Timothy as friendly and always smiling - singing, "Hi Nieghbor!" the moment he stepped out of his home. Police are asking for anyone with information to contact the Sherrif's depart--

Click

Damn, again? They need to hurry up and catch that monster. Just as I flip past BET, a Common rapper flashes on the screen,

"Wrap it up." he manages to get those words in before I click him away to be with the rest of tell-a-world. I Wonder what Al's up to...Maybe I should hit his line, because a feeling in the pit of my stomach has me feeling like something's wrong.

It could be the alcohol making me feel so uneasy. But still, I have to follow my first mind and check in on my brother. For the umpteenth time, there is no answer on his home or his cell phone. At this point I'm worried.

The last time we spoke he mentioned a trip to Memphis, but I know this dude ain't just sneak off without telling his boys something. I'll give him twenty minutes and then I'll call him back. If he doesn't pick up this time, I'm driving over to his crib. He doesn't need that much space – not from his brothers.

Through the slit of my lowered eyelids, I could see the beautiful frame of my muse rocking the boat, and I can't help feeling enticed by her. *God, we have lost so many good entertainers – it's sad.* I watch her until my eye lids cut off the view. That visual put me to bed, but it's the man with the plan who gives me the rude awakening.

I jump out of my sleep and start singing and dancing to his command; just like a sex machine, I'm now up and on the scene. This man bullies me out of my sleep every morning, and that's just the way I like it. Seconds later, the ringing phone interrupts my vibe. It could only be my boss calling me at this hour, "Hello... uh, sir, will you be in today?"

Fuck! My palm smashes into my forehead when I realize I have three researchers to interview about the AIDS project. And I forgot to call Allen back. I'll give his phone a ring on my lunch break. I grab my robe from my walk-in closet then start out for the first shower of my new day.

Rushing out the door, my brief case is locked in my palms, following me as I exit my home. The Uber driver pulls up the moment I reach the curb and when I swing the door open he asks, "Cougar's Den, right?"

"Right."

"I heard it was poppin' in there last night."

"I couldn't tell you, I was too drunk to notice." After a ten minute drive he pulls into the parking lot, "This good?"

"Yeah, this is my car right here." I flip a twenty dollar bill toward his ear and wish him well. Once inside my car, I send a text to Omar's phone, *'No jump start today.'*

Chapter 7

Olivia

Sleeping with an AIDS infested dog top's the list of the stupid things I've done in life. The words continue to echo inside my head, *'Allen has AIDS.'* That's all I can seem to think about here lately. I can't even focus on the case load ahead of me, pondering that information. I mean, I know he likes to throw his dick in any open hole he could find, but I mean, *AIDS? ALLEN? - DAMN!*

Fifteen cases to review by six p.m. and I'm sitting here stuck on that thought. So many things plague my mind that I can't even attempt my job assignment. The phrase, *'sleeping with danger'* takes on a whole different meaning in the acknowledgment of my infidelity. Yes, we used a condom, but not even those things are one-hundred percent reliable.

I mean, Omar and I have been trying to get pregnant with no real luck, but as soon as I sleep with Allen, boom! I get pregnant? Forget about the years Allen and I tried while we were together - the moment I *cheat* with him I get knocked up? Omar forgave me when I told him and even though my test was negative, it's like he's making me experience the ordeal all over again.
He accuses me of still loving Al and insisting that the fact I cheated with him was proof. He does it in very subtle ways as if I don't notice.

Our relationship has shifted drastically since we found out about Allen's status. I can see the disgust in my husband's eyes when he looks at me sometimes. I don't really don't blame for it; I'm carrying a baby that may or may not even be his - A baby we are not sure if we want to bring into this world to serve as a permanent rip in our bond.

"Hey girl," my new co-worker Ze'Amora walks up and pulls me out of my thoughts. My lips twitch and I try to be cordial but really, I can't stand the bitch. She's one of Allen's old flames, or should I say one of his old side-bitches. It seems she has been following in my steps, trying to be *ME* since high school.

I never sweated her though, even when I first found out Allen was screwing her behind my back, I always kept my composure when she was around. I never let any of his lil thots think they'd won when it came to Al. Yeah, he was screwing them, but he was coming back to me. So that for me at the time, was enough for weak bitches to know who was winning.

Now that I've moved on, I couldn't care less about what she does with him. As long as she doesn't touch Omar, we're good. As she inches closer to my desk, the bounce of her honey-blonde lace front catches my attention. it's the exact color and style I mentioned last week at our potluck. I'd asked our associate bleu if she could hook me up with that style this weekend but you know what, nevermind.

"Good morning," I say without a smile, trying to prevent my eyes from trailing the contour of her face. This chic's make-up is usually on point, but this morning I see she didn't have time to fix that blotch of foundation caked up on her cheek. The way her makeup is crunching around the bumpy, ragged edges of a spot above her lip, it almost looks like she's trying to cover up a wart. Although it's barely visible she's standing over my desk, giving me a close-up view of her blemish. Reminds me of a ringworm, *so freaking cringe.*

"We're doing a lunch poll at chipotle's, you want in?" She asks holding her pen, ready to scribble onto her notepad. "Yeah," I reach into my purse and grab a fifty-dollar bill, "I'll take the wet chicken burrito with some bean dip and chips, keep the change for gas."

"Ok, ok, anything to drink?"

'Hell no, I don't need you breathing on my drink with that thing on your face. It might piss all over my cup.' Those were my thoughts, but the words that leave my mouth are, "yeah, bring me back a bottled ginger ale, please and thank you."

"Got it." she says, transcribing my order with a smooth swerve of her wrist. As she walks away, I notice another one of those caked up blotches on the back of her neck.

I remember when another associate had a similar lesion. Everyone was worried that whatever it was, it was contagious. The sores seemed to have grown on Donna out of nowhere and when the boss pulled her to the side and asked her about the blister-like bumps, she said that it was a condition called hidradenitis, where the sweat glands fill with waste and become infected, yet it's not contagious. Donna had agreed to let the boss explain her condition to the firm to put us all at ease, and everyone soon relaxed. Looking at Ze'Amora, it seems like the condition is more common that I thought.

"Come on Lexi, let's roll." I hear Ze'Amora say from a distance, her jingling keys irritating my soul beyond belief. Sitting behind the desk of my office chair, I go over the details of my life, then I take a deep breath in and I release it. A wave of relief overcomes me, although my troubling thoughts won't go away. Twelve cases and four hours later, I'm stuck on the same thought, *Allen has AIDS.*

As bad as it may sound, that thought translates in my mind as, *the player got played.* Even though I hold fast to the fact that I may still have been put at risk, my negative test gives me a little comfort, so it's safe to allow myself to wallow in that thought. Huh, imagine that, *the player finally got played.* Out of nowhere a soothing, familiar voice comes through the ceiling speaker and sends me spiraling into a blissful memory.

It was the night before our wedding. Omar had called me just to say, 'I love you'. He was out with his bros, and he said he couldn't wait to marry me the next day. Before we hang up, he told me to look out the window. When I looked over the balcony in my bedroom there was Omar, standing with his broad chest high and a fresh bouquet of colorful tulips – my favorite flower. Smiling from ear-to-ear, he sang along with the music that was coming from his car speakers.

There surely was something in the sky for our love. I'm not sure if it was a ribbon, a guardian angel, or a guardian angel *wrapped* in a ribbon. Only thing I knew right then was that the sky couldn't even place a limit on our love.

A smile tickles my face.

What am I thinking? Why am I feeling so insecure?

I have no real reason to be worried, Omar cherishes me like I am his life, he is all I could ever ask for in a husband, a friend. He is my soul mate

I know it was wrong, how we got together. But sometimes it just happens like that. You can't help who you fall in love with, and I love my baby. In fact, the thought of him sends chills down my spine right now as I gaze at him wearing his space suit, floating over my desk in a moment frozen.

God knows I love that handsome, humble man. Just as I finish reviewing a breached music recording contract for the group *BitterSweetHearts*, a voice rings out, "Mrs. Parks, can you stay till seven, Shana called off last minute and we have five cases to process by the morning."

"Sorry, I can't – gotta prior engagement, already running late. I was suppose be outta here fifteen minutes ago."

"Can you take some of these files home with you and process them from your workstation there?"

"Uh, ok – sure." I grab the stack of files and flee before she could hand me the other stack on the file cabinet next to her, and I race to my car overwhelmed and excited, horny to be straight forward. Hey, that's me - always straight forward.

The craziest thing happened on my way to the store to pick up some strawberries; my phone rang, and you would never guess whose name flashed on my caller ID. Allen. Yes - *Dirty Dick* Allen, as me and my girls learned to call him.

I have no idea what the hell he could have wanted so I ignored his call. After everything he'd put me through, I wouldn't accept an apology from him, even if it were dipped in chocolate. My man is on my mind and all I can think about is getting laid. On my way to my paradise, I stop by the mall to pick up a silk negligee and with my hormones bouncing, I head to our bedroom to prepare a love cave for my honey. but then that's when it hit me, the pact that me and my husband had made.

Damn! I could sure go for some of that good dick tonight. All my life I'd believed that the female milky way was a myth. That was, until I first made love to Omar and he sent me right to it. My husband's sex always sends me into another dimension. That's another thing I'll never forget, the first time we made love.

It was truly a night to remember. My dirty thoughts are interrupted by my vibrating cell phone, which rested in my lap so close to pearl that it made her smile and drool. When I hit the button on my steering wheel the baritone blasted through my speakers, "sup shorty" my husband says, "Tell me something good."

"I was just thinking about you."

"Oh you miss me?"

"I want you."

"can't have me right now." He says to me in a teasing manner. "I know I just remembered." The whining pitch of my tone must have turned him on because he pauses, and his voice mellows. I know my baby, when his voices changes to a mellow tone it means he is turned on. Anyway, when I finally make it home, I rush to the bed with Omar still on the line, "You on your way home zaddy?"

"Actually baby, can I hang out with the boys."

"Two nights in a row?"

"I know baby, I just –"

"Go 'head but stop by the house first so I could sign your trip slip." Translation: bring me my kiss. We both giggle in agreement and within the twenty minutes, I'm tasting my husband's lips.

∞ ∞ ∞

Amid my kiss-down with Omar it slipped my mind that my girls would be here at seven. Every Friday we throw ourselves a bubble bath and yeah, we made that up. It's just like a bridal shower or baby shower, but we link up to wash away our troubles and to talk about what had been bothering us up to that point.

You know how the characters of that one TV show get together at the bar to talk about their day? Well, that's me and my girls at our bubble baths. We take turns hosting at each other's houses and we always have a different theme. Mary Jane and bottles of Moscato always accompany us at our shindigs.

Our bubble baths are a time for us to counsel each other and vent about things that we don't trust other people to know. This week I'm the host, and I know the perfect theme for our soul cleansing – sex! Something I have been deprived from for what seems like months. For dinner, I'm making fried fish and shrimp with Hawaiian bread and French fries. Hey – somebody around here has to keep it hood. For dessert, a banana pudding pie with graham cracker crust and a small mountain of whip cream on top.

I finish setting up then I realize I don't have enough strawberries for the pink panties, so before I fry the last batch of fish, I rush to the grocery store. Everyone everywhere knows that I make the best pink panties, so I won't be surprised if a few extra heads show up tonight. When I pull back into my driveway, I hear Tracey's loud voice blasting from her car. She sits across the street, two houses down, arguing with someone over the phone. With my body slightly folded forward, I tiptoe to her car then jump into view, "Hey!"

"oh hey gyal, nu waak up pan mi me like dat. Yuh nearly give mi heart attack."

"where's the rest of the click sis?"

"mi talk tu Toya earlia. She cumin', ha sister cumin' too. Shi hear yuh making de pink panties ey?"

"Which sister, Champagne or Lisa?"

"Champagne gyal yuh kno Lisa nuh like yuh."

"I was just making sure I don't have to thief proof my crib," I laugh, "Come on sis, I got one more batch of fish to fry – you can help me."

Tracey ends her conversation with a blast of anger. When she's pissed, I never understand a word she's saying. She slams her car door while screaming into her phone, "Fuck yuh! mi try tuh tell yuh but yuh neva wan fi kno. Mi neva gi it tuh yuh yuh tek it. Mi kno yuh nuh wa mi tuh sey nuhting suh mi neva say nuthing!" Tracey ends her calls then throws her phone into her purse and waves her hand wildly as she walks toward my porch, "Boodclot bumbohole!"

We enter the house and Tracey fries the last few pieces of fish while I start the pink panties. Twenty minutes later everything is mastered, and I add the finishing touches by lacing the end-tables with toys I'd purchased from Adams and Eve's.

Tonight's game – questions. We'll play that once we have had our drinks and everyone is tipsy and victim to the truth. I'm just about to pour myself a glass of my specialty drink when I hear a commotion stirring at my front door. Then the bell rings

"Open up this got damn door before we kick it down!" That's the voice of Toya, the self-proclaimed hoe. Toya has always been sexually liberated, and proud of it. Hey – she's single, she's sexy, she's free and well, she can do that. Before I could pull the door open they're already pushing themselves inside. Shay, the bisexual closet freak, MoMo the motivator and support system of our click, Lady the pimp, and Pa'Trice – the nymphomaniac.

Tracey, the man-eating slut steps outside to suck on a cancer stick while Mo-Mo squeezes by and heads for the kitchen, "oooh girl, I smell cat fish and French fries," she rushes over to the fish sizzling in the fryer, and she swipes a piece from the dish next to it.

"nuh touch mi fish gyal, mi wi kick yuh ass." Tracey yells from the doorstep as she blows a stream of cigarette smoke from the side of her pierced lips.

"I haven't eaten since breakfast, I'm hungry bish." MoMo waits until Tracey turns back around before she swipes two more pieces of fried fish from the silver dish and passes one piece to Pa'Trice, who eats the fish in two bites. Pa'Trice then turns her attention to the box on one of my end tables. "What's this?" She asks as she opens the small velvet box and peeks inside. Her eyes widen, "Oooooh, it's *that* kinda party."

"Alright," I ring our tea-time bell, "enough, I'm ready to get it cracking." Pa'Trice swipes another piece of fish from the dish and whispers in my ear as she passes me, "you ain't 'bout dat life." She then flops down on the couch next to MoMo and devours her food.

"This my kind of party though," Says the self-proclaimed hoe. I laugh out loud, "we know."
Shay grabs one of the vibrators on display, turns it on, and smiles when it hums pleasantly.

"Aye Pa'Trice, let me use this on you," She yells across the room. Pa'Trice smacks her lips, "Bitch please, get a dick." Thrilled and humored at Pa'Trice's response, Shay rushes over and grabs the twelve-and-a-half-inch dildo then hurries over to Pa'Trice, "Got one, bitch lay down."

Laughter fills the room, and I turn on the radio to amplify the fun just as Tracey pulls out a bag of trees and prepares it for *"Medicinal Purposes."*

"Let di mada fucking rotation begin," She demands. The lighter she holds matches her nails perfectly, showing the colors yellow, red and green with a black leaf in the middle. She rolls her thumb against the spark wheel and looks at me, "Dis dat real fiyah."

"I'm cool on it, I'm still with baby."

"Olivia, you with baby?" Mo questions

"Shi might not be fer long." Tracey sets the trees ablaze and passes it to Pa'Trice who sucks on it with passion.

"I've been waiting all day for dis here," She puffs out a cloud of smoke then passes the blunt to the left, but Toya is too busy examining my many toys from the silver bullet to the magic wand. Toya looks surprised yet impressed. She raises her voice, "Damn sis, 'O' ain't handling his biz or ya'll both some freaks or what?"

"nah," I sigh, "we're just waiting to see what we gonna do about this belly bump, that's all." The room grows silent. I really don't want to talk about that low down dirty dog called AIDS. At this point, only a few of the girls know. Plus, today is lady's night and guess what - AIDS isn't invited. At least I hope not. Toya quickly takes the conversation back to the theme of the evening, "boo, your sex drive must be on *over*drive."

"Hell yeah Toya, Girl. I have to take cold showers every night and Omar has caught me masturbating thirteen times already." Laughing out loud, Toya asks, "what did he do?"

"Nothing, he stood there and watched," I told her a straight face. "Bitch what did you think he would do, get mad?" Pa'Trice asks as the blunt comes back around to her and she wedges it between her lips.

"Hell, I thought he would join in" Toya's facial expression droops as she must have realized how slow she is at catching on. For her to be a hoe, I swear – it's like sometimes, she doesn't know anything about catching a nut.

"Oh, he joined in alright. He took out his meat and stood there swinging it back and forth and then he long stroked himself." The girls all laugh, but I sigh out of frustration, "It ain't funny ya'll, I'm going crazy here, having withdrawals from my own husband. I see him, I smell him, I shower with him, but I can't have him. And ya'll know how much I love to have my husband."

"Yeah, wi kno dat gyal." Tracey gives me a side-eyed glance and when her favorite music artist comes trickling through the speakers demanding to get bodied, Toya obliges. She cranks up the radio and immediately starts twerking.

Ten minutes of dancing and partying then there is a knock on the door. It's Toya's sister Champagne, "Where dem pink panties at?!" She holds an empty champagne glass up towards the sky. With her eyes scrolling Champgne's body from head to toe, Tracey frowns and hisses, "Yuh late gyal, di party start an hour ago."

"Late?! no more pink panties?!" Champagne whines. "Girl, they haven't even started drinking yet, the pink panties are in the freezer and the Moscato is in the fridge - go 'head and pour it up." I nod toward the kitchen. Without hesitation Champagne dances over to the freezer and fills her glass with the liquid pussy holder.

Champagne has always been the envy of all women. She possesses all the qualities of a good woman, plus she has the brains to compliment her beauty, and her flawless hourglass shape is to die for.

Pa'Trice's eyebrow arches, "pour everybody up since you late," she says to Champagne, irritation distorting the natural tone of her voice. I feel the tension in the air, so I decide to change the mood. You know, break the ice. "Let's start a game of questions" I suggest.

"How do you play questions?" Champagne asks as she parted her lips with the crystal glass. "Yuh just aks a question," Tracey subtly snaps as she rolls another blunt, "eff sum'ady lies dem haffi tek a shot. Di one drunkest by di end of di game haffi host di next bubble bath."

"bet" Champagne sang out, "Can I start?" Tracey sets the trees ablaze and looks at Champagne from the corner of her eye, "Di host aks di fos question, chill." At first, I glance around the room searching for my first victim. After careful consideration, I target MoMo, who is still dancing in the background.

Although her life is not as exciting as the rest of ours, the mellow, quiet kept individuals are the ones with the most to hide. MoMo notices my gaze on her and her eyebrow arches as she swivels her hips to the beat.

I ease into her space, then I tilt my body towards hers, "Girl, you dancing like you horny as hell, when is the last time you got some dick?" Champagne jumps up and co-signs, "yeah girl, all these years I've never heard you talk about a man."

"And I know somebody poking you, the way you moving those hips." Shay insists as everyone focuses their attention on MoMo and waits for her answer. Mo smiles and looks away, "two weeks ago, but I just got ate out." She says that as if still satisfied.

Every girl in the room responds in shock and amazement. MoMo is so gentle and innocent looking, no one could imagine her spreading her legs. A tornado of voices storms through the room and Mo finds herself bombarded with follow-up questions.

"For real girl?"

"With who?"

"Exactly... and how good was it?"

"Anyone we know?"

"You mean, you're *not* a virgin?!"

"Aye, it Mo's tun tuh aks a question unu settle dung." After being saved by Tracey, Mo scans the room looking for her victim, but the girls are still fixated on the fact that innocent Monique is not so innocent after all. After a few seconds of contemplation Mo decides on a victim.

"Pa'Trice, this is something I've been wondering about for some time now. Have you and Shay ever been intimate with each other?" Pa'Trice pauses for a second, then she responds, "no."

"Aw take a shot bitch," Shay interrupts, "remember on your twenty-first birthday - me, you and Ronnie? Take a shot you lying bitch!" Shays bursts out laughing, and Pa'Trice's face wrinkles then folds.

I look at her and see her hands clench into fists. She gazes at Shay and frowns. Seconds of silence whisk by, the tension could be cut with a knife. Everyone knows that Ronnie is Pa'Trice's step-dad. I swear, you could hear a spider spin it's web until Pa'Trice crosses her arms and blows out a loud roaring sigh. It's clear that this secret was meant to kept and not thrown around in a game.

"You want to play dirty bitch, let's play." Pa'Trice pours her shot down her throat and slams the glass on the hardwood table. I could literally see the liquid fire ooze down her throat as she swallows. Her eyebrow is cocked, and she bites her lip, looking directly at Champagne who's now bouncing on her toes with her mouth hanging open.

"Wow, wait Trice, what happened with your best friend and your mother's husband?" That question leaks from champagnes mouth and sends Pa'Trice into rage, "I'm asking the questions now."

Champagne throws her hands up and flops back down on the sofa, disappointed at the lack of details Pa'Trice offers. Pa'Trice looks at Shay, then she turns her attention to her arch enemy, "It's my turn, right?" she sips her drink, "So Champagne, what's the name of the last man you slept with?" Pa'Trice asks her with one hand on her hip and the other resting on the dining room table as though she's holding herself up.

Champagne sips her pink panties as she answers with no hesitation, "Big Mike." A collective gasp of breath travels through the room and then another tornado of questions follow.

"What!?"

"You and Mikey - Mike?!"

"When?"

"Where?"

"Was it good?"

"you heifers speaking out of line," I remind them. Everyone shifts their body towards Champagne and wait for the details, but they are never spoken. Champagne and Michael would make the perfect couple, and everybody knows it. Champagne being the envy of all women and Michael the envy of men - they would surely complement one another in the most explosive way.

The problem is that MoMo has been crazy about Michael for years now and everyone knows that too. She's had a non-dying crush on him since high school and she never let it go. Most of her innocence was rooted in the fact that she's been saving herself for big Mike, in hopes that one day she would win him over. But it seems that Champagne has beat her to him. The corners of MoMo's mouth drops, "it's cool, I knew the bitch was a slut," she says, staring into her glass of wine.

"Well," Champagne shrugs her shoulders, "it was gone come out one day and yeah, FYI – the dick was fire." she takes back the last of her drink then walks over and refills her glass. The entire time, she avoids eye contact with Mo, who is now staring her down to hell.

"Pour everybody up, slut," Pa'Trice demands, walking over to Shay but never speaking a word. From the way Pa'Trice cut her eyes at Shay, I know she's about to get it cracking. I also know that whatever comes out today is Shay's fault for spilling Pa'Trice's biggest secret. Shay has never been the one to hold water, and *that's* no secret. When Champagne finally looks up, her eyes connect with Mo's eyes, "it was a foursome anyway, it wasn't just me." She clarifies, then looks at Shay as she takes another sip of her drink.

"Bitches been hoes since day one." Pa'Trice proclaims with a chuckle. Champagne sucks her teeth and cackles, "and the dick was good too." I really want to slap the taste out of Champagne for being so careless. She never shows a bit of remorse. Even though MoMo looks like she's about to cry, '*The dick was good too,*' *is* all she has to say. MoMo's head hangs low and the chain reaction ripples through the room.

Everyone is feeling their drink and tongues has become super loose. There's no turning back now, and the best part is yet to come – I can feel it. "It's my turn, right?" Champagne asks with a salty smirk on her face, "Latoya, what's the freakiest thing you've ever done as a hoe?"

Toya jumps at this opportunity to express her sexual liberation, "One night I squeezed four dicks in at once, well – not all at once but at the same time. They took turns trying to see who could make me squirt. That was some fun sex ya'll, I was handcuffed, tied up and blind folded. They pounded my lil twat that night. I still have the tape if ya'll want to see it."

"Bitch we're playing questions, not show and tell," Shay says laughing out loud. Toya is the most sexual woman I have ever known. Everyone loves her sex stories, especially me - I find them embarrassingly entertaining. She brushes the imaginary dust from her shoulders, "ok, it's on me now right? Tracey - I want you to be my victim." Everyone chuckles and let Toya finish her question, "have you ever slept with any of your friends' man or someone they were intimate with?" Tracey's eyes pop wide open and freeze inside their sockets, "no."

"Take a shot bitch you're lying," Toya yells. Now everybody's attention is on Tracey, but Tracey's attention is fixated on the wall in front of her. and the wall? Well, if the wall could talk it would tell Tracey to pick her mouth up off the floor. Tracey snatches her glass from table and tilts her head back. She pours the drink down her throat and swallows so hard, the sound of her throat opening and closing travel through the room.

It's a known fact that everyone here are the only friends Tracey has. She doesn't fool around with females because she considers them fake. The last female she tried to befriend ending up setting her house up to be burglarized when she was at work. After that, it was a wrap for any female outside of our close-knit circle. So uh, who in the hell's man did she sleep with in here and when? Toya's question takes this game of questions to a whole new level. Suddenly, the close-knit circle is unraveling shred by shred.

"Latoya," Tracey says with so much base in her voice that it makes my heart jump, "Ave yuh eva had di herpes?" Toya's smile glitches then twists upside down, "yes," she murmurs, "but how did *you* know that?"

"Mi nuh kno mu just aks a question," Tracey says while laughing out loud, "Yuh pan blast der gyal? Yuh blast yuhself, mi neva blast ya. Mi just aks di question." All around the room, lips are pressed together. My guess is that the same thing is running through all our minds. Herpes has no cure, so there's no such a thing as you *had* herpes. Once you got it, it's in your blood stream forever.

"Okay then, let's blast away," Toya says with her eyelids wrinkled, "Tracey, who's man was it that you slept with in this room? cause we all know you don't have any other friends."

This is the question that we all want to know since everyone in this room has or has had a man somewhere along the lines, someone we care about, someone we loved or love - and we all know she better not have touched mine. Tracey's chin hit her chest and in a low, murmuring tone she whispers, "Olivia's."

Chapter 8

Allen

If Sam had kept his head cocked to the side with his eyeballs turned away from me, he wouldn't be laid here, bleeding out on my floor. I'm sick of looking at'em, and the sound of him breathing is starting to make my mouth slippery.

Every time Yang's voice pushes me in his direction a wave of heat whips me and my heart explodes. I always thought sweat was your body's way of cooling you off but for me, it ignites my rage like gasoline poured over stagnant flames.

Step by step, I ease from the dark corner and back into the light. Burdened with nothingness my fingertips sting, tingle, tickle. I roll my fists open and look down at my hands to see red slime, covering my joints and fingerprints. The outer layers of my skin, coated in a peppery static, causing goosebumps to sizzle and pop. The heat brings third-degree burns to my soul. So deeply I feel the urge to destroy.

Tick, tick, Tick

Not just yet

Rage. Begging. Pleading - it's sending me over the edge quicker than I could jump. As the Wright storm starts to brew, I crash my shoulder into my ear, "Not right now, fucking dummy!"

A ringing silence fills my head space, *'Do it,'* Yang commands. I could barely hear myself think with this bastard constantly ordering me around. Fed up with those popping bubbles, I crash my knuckles into the wall then snatch my fist loose, "Aaarrggh! Stop fucking with me!" My screams are so automatic, it feels like I'm just a bystander in this circus of a life. Using my wrist to clear my nose of the draining snot, I smell blood - and I'm thirsty for more.

The numb feeling that has come alive in my toes is now moving towards my heart. AIDS is supposed to stop you, right? It's supposed to make you weak, and vulnerable and fragile, right? Well guess what, AIDS AIN'T STOPPING *SHIT*! It's only motivating me to keep going until I kill *everybody*.

And this picture hanging above my fire extinguisher, it's giving me all the strength I need to see things through. It reminds me of when I was in my prime, when I was still a lady's man. Olivia snug tightly in my arms, as if she would be mine forever. Every time I walk by it, my heart balls up like a sheet of paper containing words void of value.

I remember the day we took this picture, she acted like everything was cool, like we were going to work things out. The whole time she was screwing my bro, and she had that smile on her face as we entered the Queen Mary. *God I hate a smiley ass face*!

My mother smiled when she sat me on those steps and told me, "I'll be right back." My guts had been roaring for two days, but that didn't stop her from walking away from me, never stopping for a second to glance over her shoulder.

Then Olivia smiled. "You're everything to me," she said, her gaze fixated on something past my ears. She was was focused, she didn't notice my heart practically bulging from my chest, pleading for her to come to its rescue.

But back to the picture fading behind this soon-to-be broken glass; It tells the story of the day I proposed; Olivia was wearing her favorite yellow sweater with her hair pulled up into a ponytail. I remember it like it was yesterday, and I can't forget the feeling in the pit of my stomach when I first sensed that she was with someone else. It was the day I had told Omar to hold her off until I can get Ze home, and now looking back on it, *he* was the one up in'er. You know what, *FUCK* that nigga and *this bitch!*

ugh...

arrgh!

Watch how I crack every bone in that snake's face the same way I just shattered that picture frame - into a million pieces.

See, what people don't seem to realize is that I already accepted the fact I'm dying, and I anticipate my last breath. But there's just a few more people I need to bleed before I leave this earth, and I've got something for everybody – me and my *new* bitch. She's on her way to town, and she's coming to blaze shit up!

Why should I be the only one to suffer?! We all fucked up somewhere along the lines. So if *I* gotta go, ya'll gotta go. I no longer gives a fuck about the who's, when's, where's or how's.

'Just do it.'

"Ok!" I tilt my head to pour more of the liquid flames down my throat. Gazing at the ceiling, my skin crawls at the sight of the crumby texture. I swear I just saw a face protruding from that corner.

You watching me, huh? With your stupid eyes?!

Staring back into nothing I empty the rest of bottle into my body.

Viola! an entire fifth of vodka - gone. My soul is now a silhouette of smoldering flames. My muscles relax. The bottle drops to the floor with a piercing *clack*.

Looking past the hallway and into my guest room, a mountain of snow awaits my approach. Three quick sniffs and gone! But you know what isn't gone? These irritating ass voices floating around, ordering my steps.

'just do it,' is all I hear time, and time again. I line up another row of the snow, this one thicker than the last three put together, and I, *inhale.* Flash-flood, incoming

'The time has finally come. Claim him Al, he's yours.'
'kill,'

'steal,'
'destroy.'

That whole family gonna catch one, I swear. But right now, my attention is called back to this pile of waste on my floor. It's like his body changes form every other second, and now he's looking back at me, talking like I give two fucks. I **never thought** the sound of someone begging for their life could be so annoying.

"SHUT UP!" I hear myself scream. Next thing I know, my steel toe boot goes swinging through the air. I watch it crash into Sam's mouth as words leap from my voice box, "this is what you wanted!" He must think I'm a damn fool, like I don't know he's been running his mouth to the people at those meetings.

"Yuh, you don't have to do this, I'll give you anything you want." The blood leaking from his mouth sends a chill down my spine, and it makes me laugh out loud, "Look *Sam, Sam-I-Am*, your God *gave* you to me," I remind him.

"I, I'll geh you anything you wanth, just pleasth."

"Sam...are you choking, are you fucking dying?" He spits out another clot of blood and a tooth pops out, "there's thoo-hundred dollars in muh wallet mah, take it pleasth. leh me go."

"I don't need yo money!" Stumbling over the mess I'd made, I think twice. Then I snatch the wallet from his back pocket and I grab the money, "This all you got?!" Sobbing Sam, that's what I feel like calling him right now, is *mine*.

I kneel beside him, "Sobbing Sam, you tried to cross me, pussy. Tried to rat me out. Now you gonna pay with your life, bitch!" I spit in his bleeding face. The more he begs for his life, the more sweat oozes from my pores. What makes this leaping-lemur looking bastard think I'mma let'em go after what he tried to pull? Inching closer to his face I ask, "Why are you always smiling at me!?"

"Pleasth just tell me whath you want Al."

"Don't ever say my name!"

Right now, I'm not even sure if I'm me. I feel like somebody - or *something* else. I grab another butcher knife from my bamboo block then I bring it to eye's level, and I glance at my reflection in the blade.

Who the fuck is this?!

What the fuck is that?!

My once flawless face now looks like a nestle crunch bar, twelve years past its expiration date. All I see is a cocktail of boils, bruises and new sores that come out of nowhere. The sight of it makes my skin moist and hot to the touch, but it takes more than just a few moments to snatch my gaze away from it.

The gurgling sounds coming from my victim's throat calls my attention back to the floor. When my eyes roll towards him, I notice that the bitch has changed form, again. "Stop moving!" I warn. I can feel my arm weighed down by the handle of the knife and as I struggle to ignore Ying, Sam asks again, "Wuh do you wanth from meh?

"Your soul," I inform him. Sam swings his head upward, his eyes almost completely swollen shut. I watch as he tries to force them open, but the blood oozing from the gash in his forehead seeps into his purpled eyes, sealing them. Just a hot mess, looking like rotten flesh with his body odor calling for maggots - his limp torso covered in red.

Wait, did his mouth just twitch?

Standing over him, I stare at the rainbow carved under his nose, "You like to smile right the fuck at me, I see." A hot flash of darkness consumes me in a instant. I feel as light as a feather.

there I go again.

There's me, I crash my thumb into my chest then point toward the ceiling, *and then there's me.* I don't know which one to believe; The *me* hovering above singing out, '*walk away*,' or the *me* swaying back and forth on unsteady feet whispering, '*it's now, or it's never.*'

My face starts moving and my eyes flicker, but my voice trails off into the distance. I can no longer hear myself, *feel* myself. Desperate to get my words across, I keep talking to Sobbing Sam, "People smiling in your direction is like saying fuck what you're going through."

"It nah like that."

"So why did you smile?"

"Pleasth..."

"Why are you always looking at me!?"

"juh hear me ow."

"No you hear me ow," my words sound foreign, and my jaw is like that of a ventriloquist dummy, falling open then popping closed repeatedly, releasing the words, "you don't always have to play with fire to get burned."

Gradually, my voice becomes loud and clear. With my head held high I stare into the apparition of my own face, and my lips stretch toward my ears when I finally hear myself say, "This is what the devil looks like, in the *flesh*."

$$\infty\,\infty\,\infty$$

A smirk caresses Allen's cheeks as he turns to walk away, laughing aloud at his victim's wobbling head.

hyuck, hyuck, hyuck

He blends into the darkness, warping into his grandiose delusion of lucifer himself like - Jeepers, creepers

"God please, help me," Sam cries. The weight of his skull mixed with

the spinning going on inside it is too much to bear. he drops his head back onto the floor, causing a subtle thud to echo through the room.

With the life slowly draining from his body, his instincts kick in. Using his chin, elbow and his shoulder he begins to drag himself across the floor. Once he reaches the hallway, he glances to his right and see's Allen digging his head into a large pile of white powder on the table in the guest room before disappearing behind the door.

The walls start closing in, and shadows of death surround him. Determined to survive, something tells him to stand up and run for the front door. His thought of escape is halted when he feels the soft carpet beneath him move in rhythm with the footsteps that slowly approach him from behind.

"no way out," The words slur from Allen's mouth in a demonic tone, "..... you wanted to fuck with me?" Al pulls out his penis, "Open your mouth, you slut ass nigga."

Sam does what he's told, in hopes that if he cooperated, Al would spare his life. But what Big Al has in mind is a crime so horrid, it makes Charles Mansion look like a saint.

"Listen," Sam cries, "yuh dun have to do thith mah, I suth your dick whenever you want just pleasth.... leh me go."
Al laughs are monstrous, "shut the fuck up."

"Al," Sam cries

"I told you never to say my name, not even after you're dead bitch. Keep my name outta yo mouth and put my dick in it," he drops to his knee, cramming his penis straight to the back of Sam's throat, "suck bitch, and I better cum."
Al grabs a hold of his balls, making sure his pubic hairs doesn't get caught in the zipper of his jeans, "yeah..... aaahh.... Yeah suck, suck." He thrusts his pelvis with each demand, "suck."

In his struggle to survive, Sam puts in a few exaggerated neck thrusts in rhythm with Al's movement.

"Aahh," Allen sings as he thumps on Sam's tonsils and covers his tongue in warm, bitter silk "...that throat is extra active tonight.

You ain't never made me cum that fast," Al chuckles, then he stands up and kicks Sam in the face, "swallow it."

He didn't even have to make that command, because the slime had catapulted down Sam's throat the second Al's boot met his lips. "Now it's time for the real fun," Al says as a world wind of voices takes over the space in his head. The Wright family sang out in unison, 'do it...'

'Kill'

'Do it...'

'Steal..'

'...Do it!'

'DESTROY!'

"Shut up!" Al shakes his head and slams his palm onto his forehead, "I mean it's----it's not---time, not yet." Al changes his tune and suddenly starts talking in a calm voice, causing Sam to look at him

what the fuck?

Slave to the Wright's commands, Allen relocates the butcher knife and he walks over to Sam. He then bends over, snatches the twelve inches of golden locks in Sam's hair and pulls his head back, exposing his well-pronounced Adam's apple. Then a distinct ringing comes from Al's back pocket, and Sam's life is spared by seconds. Allen reaches in his pocket and when he sees Omar's name and number appear on the screen, his muscles tense back up.

He calmly ignores the call and slides the phone back into his pocket. Looking down at mixture of colors bubbling from Sam's mouth, a rush overcomes Al's body and he tilts his head back to enjoy it, "Aaaaaaaahh," he let out an involuntary moan. When the tickling ends, he kneels down once again next to his victim, and places his lips upon Sam's cheek.

"The kiss of death," He laughs aloud. Big Al is now ready to comitt to his cosplay as the play grim reaper, but when his phone starts singing again Sam is tortured through a few extra seconds of fear. Al stands up, traces of white powder scattered across his lip, and he reaches into his pocket. With sweat leaking from his pores, he aims his index finger at the ignore button on his phone when out of nowhere - he's tackled to the floor...

Chapter 9

Olivia

Staring into Tracey's eyes, I pull a deep in a deep breath as the thought of slapping the teeth from her gums dissipates like a puff of smoke. I'm focusing on her lips so hard that everybody else in the room fades out of view.

"Snap out of it," Shay yells. A second later Tracey starts talking, "Let mi explain, it nuh wah yuh tink. Mi sleep wid Al, Nuh Omar," Shaking her hands wildly she continues, "it did a big mistake. Mi feel terrible 'bout it sista. Mi neva mean tuh hurt yuh."

Her words travel in and out of my ears at the same speed of the stagnated flow of blood easing through my veins; slow and steady; almost stuck in a stand-still as my emotions shoot from anger to concern for my friend. The thought travels through my mind that she may have been exposed. Most of my girls know that Omar and I was tested for AIDS but Just two of them know why. I never mentioned to the other ladies that Big Al, the man we had all crushed on from the day we laid eyes on him, had been diagnosed with AIDS.

After a few moments of silence, I walk over, and I embrace her for the bad news that I'm about to bear. MoMo and Shay look at each other, then they look at me. Everyone else stands around shocked and amazed. The look of confusion distorts their faces in such a way that they become hardly recognizable. Not even Tracey understands the decent of my anger, she gently pulls away from the entrapment of my arms and looks at me with her face twisted. A few more seconds of total silence and my lips finally part so that I could inform her of how deadly her mistake may have been. "When Tracey? I need to know."

"You're speaking out of turn hun." Shay reluctantly interrupts. I ignore that truth, and continue, "Tracey, I need to know when." Tracey drops back into the seat. The force from the weight of her body causes the small fold away chair to shift. Suddenly the game of questions become a two-player challenge with the other girls acting as spectators.

"Wah mek yuh nuh mad?" Tracey asks, hiding her face in her cupped palms in shame. "Sis, I realized long ago that Allen is a male whore and besides, I have a good man in my life now – the past, well, let's keep it in the past. Tracey, this question is important, so I need you to think hard ok babe." Before I ask the question, I glance around at all my girls. The vibe and the fun has completely went south. Hesitantly I turn my attention back to Tracey and manage to ask, "When is the last time you were tested for AIDS or HIV?"

"Huh?" she frowns. I suck in a big gulp of breath before I give her my explanation. "I need you to listen to me sis, what I'm about to tell you may or may not change your life. Tracey... Allen has AIDS."

Tracey rises from the chair, her thick Jamaican accent blasts from her voice box, "A mi fi tell *yuh*."

Total commotion stirs as everyone tries to speak at once. Tracey stands at attention, mouth nearly hitting the floor.

MoMo runs to her side and tries to console her, taking Tracey's hand in hers and easing Tracey back into her seat so that she would have some leverage. Shay flops down on the couch and Champagne hurries over to Tracey, kneels down in front of her and begins caressing her leg, right above her knee. Toya's mouth hangs wide open allowing the pink panties to spill from her maroon-colored lips. "Oh my God, Oh my God" Pa'Trice repeats in a weeping tone.

"mi gud." Tracey tries to convince herself but fails terribly as a tear escapes her eye. "You should test anyway," Champagne advises her, "you're supposed to test every six months. If its detected early there's a chance you could prevent HIV from progressing to AIDS."

"Look, mi kno yuh concerned and me love ya fer dat gal. Me don't sleep around like dat. Yeh know me, me mess up but me don't mess 'round like dat. Me only sleep wit Marcus four months ago, he honest man, he no harm me – he good man." She speaks so fast I could hardly make out what she had just said. Her accent becomes thicker and faster, and that's what let me know there's something she left out, something else she didn't say.

"A person who doesn't know they have it can give it to you without meaning any harm, Tracey," Shay tells her frankly, "someone could have the virus and not know it because they don't test. Yet they keep having unprotected sex and sharing needles - things like that," Shay's tone becomes more authoritative as the argument progresses, "there are a lot of people out there committin' involuntary manslaughter right now as we speak, because they have HIV or AIDS and don't know it.

Then some people are angry that they have it so they spread it to as many people as they can. Remember – misery loves company and ain't no misery 'bout ta find no company right here bump *dat*. People use sex as a weapon in a lot of ways, that's why I always wrap it up, I don't care what kind of good man he is or *how* good he looks."

Lady had been quite up till this point, but she reaches into her purse and grabs a cancer stick, then she steps outside to light it. She takes a long drag and blows out the smoke. Then, with her back turned away from us she asks me when Allen was diagnosed. I stare at the back of her lowered head while my lips twitch out the answer, "soon after we split, I've already tested negative."

"Um," Lady grunts as she blows out another puff of smoke. Tracey sits there in silence, trapped in her own personal hell. Then a voice drifts from the dark corner and everyone listens to it attentively. It's the voice Toya, the self-proclaimed ho and she has a story to tell about the deadly killer AIDS.

"I read this article in the newspaper the other day where a man raped a woman. She begged and pleaded with him to put on a condom. Her request pissed him off, and he put tape over her mouth to silence her. Little did the bastard know, she was trying to save his life - The woman had full blown AIDS.

The article was written by the woman herself; she published it in the newspaper as a letter to her attacker. She started the article with

'Dear Mr. Rapist, I bet you don't know that you stole death from me that day, when you knocked me down and forced your penis inside me. I tried to save you, but yo didn't want to be saved..... sincerely yours, AIDS.'

Got to me so bad, I crossed my legs after that. Hell," She gawks at Tracey, "I'm already dealing with *enough*. I haven't gotten laid in three months because of crap like this and ya'll know me – I love to get laid. But that dude could be *anybody*, so I'm cool on meat for a while."

Tracey, stares at the wall and starts roll tapping her fingers on the table. The red tint of her eyeballs gives away her level of sorrow. Toya is such a sex fiend that her opting not to have sex means that hell must have frozen over. Nothing ever got in the way of Toya and wood.

The severity of the fact explodes in Tracey's face, and she becomes visibly shaken. Her eyes flick repeatedly as she heads outside, a Newport wedged between her index and middle finger. Whenever Tracey is worried or scared, she blinks more than three times in a matter of three seconds.

I've always thought of it as her trying to see a different picture than one that was presented to her. The added base in her voice and her amplified accent only confirms my suspicions. She takes one more pull, then she flings the cigarette, "Mi had enuff of dis day. Just chrow mi inna hole an cover mi wid dirt."

∞∞∞

Once everyone parted there's still a little bit of pink panties left, so I pour it in my glass then lay in bed and sip on it as I scroll through YouTube, until I come across an episode of Michael's podcast.

I'm so into the conversation he's having with his co-host queen-im-unique about the *'Bro's before hoes'* narrative, that I don't hear Omar creep through the door. "Hey baby," he says as soon as he steps into our bedroom. He walks over and gives me a kiss, "Is that pink panties I taste?" He kisses me again, this time he sucks my bottom lip, "Gimme some."

"I want to, so bad." I tug his earlobes softly. Omar looks at me with bedroom eyes and he licks his lips, but I kill the moment without thinking twice, "baby did you know that bitch Tracey slept with Allen behind my back?"

"yeah, I knew."

Omar stands back to his feet and walks away, disappearing behind the door. The sound of streaming wazz makes my skin shrink, then I hear the toilet flush. "Baby, I've asked you a million times to close the door. You know I hate the sound of piss hitting water."

"ha," Omar's voice blends in with the sink water, "Sorry babe, my bad."

I'll admit I'm deeply humiliated right now, but when my husband steps from the bathroom I become excited as I watch him undress. The smooth tone of his brown skin caresses my eyes as I watch his bold erection poke out through the front opening of his boxers. He swings his heaviness back and forth with that *come get it look* in his eyes. "let's make love baby please." he says in a desperate tone.

"we can't baby, remember our—"

"I just want to feel you."

The trace of silk that oozes from the tip of his swollen penis makes my mouth water. He crawls into the bed and climbs on top of me then whispers, "I want to make you say my name so bad." I look down to see my beautifully shaven vagina resting against his long shaft. The sight of it turns me on and my southern lips began to drool upon his heaviness.

I want him inside me so bad that I could feel his imprint diving towards my G-spot. But I can't have my own husband, and my husband can't have me. What I can do though, is reach down and stroke his manhood. I do just that, and my palm gets filled with the perfect massage cream. It makes me call out to him, "Omar."

"Shh, don't say another word – you hear me?"

"Yes baby."

Omar reaches down and strokes my clit; *Slow, circular inward motions, wiggle. Slow circular outward motions, wiggle.* My vaginal lips blow kisses as he continues to please me. *Inward motions, wiggle* then a soft, gentle *tap tap tap* as he pulls back on hood of my clit and exposes the pink bulb that hides inside. Rubbing his fingers back and forth, he makes me sing, "Ooh baby."

"Thought I told you to be quiet." He says through clenched teeth, biting the tip of my ear ever so gently. The feeling is explosive, and our connection is even more powerful. Without penetration we make each other throb and moan and expel liquid pleasure. Every time he makes me orgasm, I fall in love all over again.

For at least an hour after, I'm always blushing and giggling and feeling as shy as I did on our first real date. The way he touches me is like art. He's so skilled at what he does that I'm scared for another woman to find out. He has me totally sprung on him in every way, and I would never share him.

The fear of someone else connecting to him in that way scares me to death. After we fondle each other into orgasmic bliss, my husband kisses me on my back softly and repeatedly until we fall asleep. I'm definitely sprung – there's no doubt about it.

I turn around to face him so that I could watch him sleep and the next thing I know his Slow, gentle kisses are caressing me out of a deep slumber, "time to get ready for your meeting, beautiful." he says as he passes me a tray of breakfast with an ice-cold glass of orange juice.

Chapter 10

Omar

Chocolate-caramel kisses have been a ritual for Olivia and I since we first started spending nights together. When the alarm clock sounded off, she was still in 'the coma,' So I sent my trails all over her body.

I could remember going to sleep at night looking forward to those wakeup calls. From the first kiss she placed upon my lips my nature would rise. Those kisses are my reasons to wake up every morning. Sometimes I'd be already awake, but I'd lay there pretending to be sleep just to receive them. When she first started it, I loved them so much I began to return the favor to let her know how much I liked it, in hopes that her kisses would never stop. Now, whenever I wake up first, I deliver trails to her sensitive areas and she melts upon my lips the same way I melt when she kisses me.

There's no way to put into words, the way I feel for her. I dream of her at night, even though she's laying right next to me. Last night I saw her floating toward me, reaching out heavenly as he blew me a kiss. That was my cue - I woke up and headed straight for the kitchen. Once I make sure my wife would wake up in perfect peace, I crawl over her to deliver my caramel kisses – that's what I call mine. Olivia calls hers, *chocolate kisses*. Olivia finishes her food, then she hops out of bed and dashes toward the bathroom, "wait, baby what's the rush?" I grab her nightgown but it slips from my fingertips. "I'm supposed to be in an hour early, I have three reports to prepare before the hearing starts at ten."

Olivia's drive matches mine, and that's one of the many things I love about her. She has dreams of owning her own Law firm, and once I satisfy this contact to design Nasa's new single-rotor telescope drone, I'm going to make her dreams come true. She truly deserves it, she's nothing like the women I've dated in my past. A lot of people think it's foul that we're together and, in some ways, they're right. But *somebody* had to save her. Olivia, she is a true Queen, she didn't deserve the heartache Al was putting her through. Besides, I got tired of lying to her for him.

Killed me every time. Just knowing how good she was to him, and how badly he dogged her. I *had* to save her. I mean, that night, the first time we made love – those were not my intentions. But how could he just leave her stranded the way he did? I really just wanted to make her feel better at the time. She needed reassurance that she was desirable, so I gave her that. Never did I mean to cross my boy, but I mean he was crossing his woman, his good woman - so really, what was the difference?

Shit, it's a dog-eat-dog world out here, in case you didn't know. Our love grew so deep over time, there was no way I could turn back. It was something about the way she received me that pulled me in even deeper. One night before it got **solid**, she was at a deposition for an extortion case, and I had a meeting with my fellow engineers from Nasa. We ended up at the same hotel and agreed to have lunch after wards.

It wasn't until then that I realized she was truly made for *me.* On that day we really connected, and I knew that she would be mine. One of my biggest accomplishments is taking her away from the heartache and showing her what love really feels like. *That's* what she deserved - not lonely nights and tear-stained pillows.

"You doing any work today babe?" she asks me as she buttons her blouse. "Yeah, I've two meetings and another contract to negotiate. After that I'm all yours – maybe I'll cook dinner, if you're a good girl."

"Maybe?" Olivia's eye arch in seriousness as she kisses me and rushes out of the door. I watch her squeeze into her car then check her rearview mirror. The tail of her zebra print skirt is caught in the door, it blows in the wind as she speeds off. I laugh and shake my head, then I walk into to the closet and grab my outfit for the day. After I dress I feed myself, I grab my car keys and dash toward the door.

Five minutes into my ride, my mobile calendar alerts me that my results are four days away. *Damn, time flies.* The thought brings Allen to my mind and something in the pit of my stomach tells me to drive by his house.

I know he's dealing with some heavy stuff, but there's no way to explain the fact that he hasn't been answering or returning my phone calls, or responding to any of my emails. So, I make a mental note to go by and check on him. Maybe I can finally pull him out of that dark world he's buried himself in. As a matter of fact, between projects I'll take him to lunch. One thing Al could never say no to is the strawberry Cheesecake at his favorite restaurant. I know if I mention the Cheesecake Factory, he'll be on his steps waiting for my return with his feet bouncing.

As I turn the corner, I make a quick detour to my bro's house. Two blocks from his paradise I hear sirens and helicopters swarming over the block where he lives. The weight of my foot drops onto the gas pedal and before I could form my next thought, I'm already racing to the scene.

I pull up to the corner, my eyes met with shock from the flashing red and blue lights that jump from house to house, illuminating the gloomy morning ambience. Then a fire truck zooms by, causing my car to wobble and jolt toward the direction it's headed.

What going on?

I look back and forth, then over my shoulders. Allen's **neighborhood never gets this much action.** In an instant my phone magnetizes to my hand and my fingers start tapping the screen.

In what seems to be a new ritual, the call goes straight to Al's voicemail. I wait a few moments, and I call again. With my head swinging back and forth I watch the scene stretch. A deafening silence thumps around in my ears, then I hear *Beeepp*! After the third time, I call Michael.

My hands are shaking, and my lips twitch. I can't even tell you why, but something isn't right. In the pit of my stomach, a rolling thunder strikes my nerves. Finally, a voice comes through, "sup bro what's g—"

"I need you to stop whatever you're doing man and get to Allen's crib pronto."

"what's up my guy?"

"I was stopping by to check on'em – police cars, yellow tape, firetrucks - everywhere. Allen nowhere in sight. His truck is in the driveway but he's not answering his phone bruh. Something went down." Suddenly there's a click and the phone on his end goes silent.

My head starts spinning at such a high speed - I don't know how much time has passed, but I look up to see Michael trying to get past the yellow tape that surrounds the area compassing Allen's castle. I hurry to join him and the both of us rush over to the crowd of Officers near Allen's front porch.

"What's going on man, this is our brother's crib." Michael exclaims to the police officers as we approach. The only thing I could think of is that maybe Allen stopped taking his meds and just allowed himself to die, that the disease finally claimed him. The gathering crowd looks on and from the corner of my eye, I spot Allen's uncle Stan - Deputy sheriff. Stan holds a grudge against me, and I know it.

He despises me for *"stealing"* Olivia from Allen, and he's picked bones with Michael for *"Allowing it to happen."* Stan moves over to where we're standing and approaches Michael, "all bad." He comments, hands in his pockets.

Before he could explain, a white van pulls up in front of Allen's house. Stan clears his throat and excuses himself. Walking toward the van, he leaves Michael and I standing in a puddle of anxiety.

Two men emerge from the van carrying a large, empty black body bag. Michael and I stand there, frozen in despair. I try to lift my feet, but my whole body becomes so heavy and stiff that it feels like my shoes are glued to the concrete. Just as I break free of gravity's strong hold, the coroners emerge from Allen's house carrying the bag, now filled with pounds of death. My knees hit the ground at the same time Michael bellows, "what the fuck?!"

"I need to ask you two a few questions" The voice sang out in sorrow. Uncle Stan has managed to pull himself together and is now heading our way with his emotions under control, yet his face damp with tears. He's almost directly in front of me but he stops in his tracks, pivots and faces Michael. He removes his walkie-talkie from in front of his mouth, "When is the last time either of you saw or talked to Allen?"

"tell me that's not him in that bag unc."

"Yo, that's not my brother," I complain, "that can't be him."

"I need you to answer the question so we can pee, piece together what happened." Stan chokes those words out, the entire time his eyes are fixated on the concrete while my heart feels like it's about to drop out of my asshole.

I grab at my chest, "I talked to him about two weeks ago. He, he said he was going out of town. I've been calling him since then, but my calls go straight to his voicemail."

"So you haven't spoken to him in *at least* two weeks?"

"That's what made me stop by here today. Nobody has heard from him."

Just then, another police officer approaches and takes down

our names and numbers, then he hands us two small cards, "If you hear anything, or if you come across any information please call right away. You can remain anony---"

"Yo wait, what --" I blurt out, and then Michael verbalizes my thoughts, "*Who* or *what's* in the bag?!"

"We cannot confirm nor exclude the identity of the victim, but we will have more information once we get a positive identification from a relative." **The officer states it flatly. I look up just in time to see the headlights of Stan's cruiser disappear around the corner.**

"So there's nothing you can tell us, the man who lives here is like a brother to us man, come on bro," Michael pleads, "Officer Stan, he knows us man – just ask him. He knows who we are."

"Look, I'm sorry – all we can tell you is that an African American male, seemingly thirty to thirty-five years of age, was bludgeoned to death."

"*Bludgeoned?*" Michael and I say simultaneously. I clear my throat and ask again, "Bludgeoned - the victim was *bludgeoned?*"

"Beaten beyond recognition." The office clarifies. Without warning Michael jams his fist through one of the police cruisers and he let out this loud, roaring moan that not even a lion could mimic.

shifting back and forth on my feet, my sight is overwhelmed by the array of shadowy figures outlined in window frames as neighbors try to get a good view of the crime scene that rocked that normally quiet neighborhood. Desperate to snap myself out of the daze I'm stuck in, I try to focus in on the shine of the Officers badge, but before I could blink my eyes I feel my chest hit the concrete.

Three days fly by with the speed of light and before we knew it, Allen's body had been identified. The only thing I can do at this point is grieve as I listen to Uncle Stan's voice come through speaker of Mike's iPhone.

"He was so badly beaten, I could hardly identify him. Had it not been for the *'bug'* on his wrist, I would not have been able to tell it was him. It was so bad, the mortician had trouble putting his skull back together. Early stages of decomposition suggests that he had been dead in his home for five days to one week."

I crumble in Olivia's arms and I sob for my friend, my brother. Thoughts race through my head like a wave of heat on a hot summer day, the type of heat that drains all your energy and leaves you powerless. *What kind of friend am I? I should have been here for him. I should have gone by sooner.*

My soul outweighs my flesh in this very moment. How could I not have known that something was wrong? He hadn't been answering his phone and he had been a no show to our jump starts for months. That wasn't like Al. I should have worried the third time he missed our boy's night out. In my defense, I assumed that he needed space. I mean, I knew how sick he had gotten, and I didn't want to put him under any pressure to hang.

Over the next week, Michael, Olivia and I managed to pull together some friends from high school, college and a few of Al's distant family members to give him a memorial, and to plan a proper burial.

"Big Al ain't have no insurance?" Marcus, a brother from our fraternity asks. I pause before responding, "Insurance policies don't cover a person with AIDS. They feel you're non insurable, like you're going to die before the ink dries on your signature."

"Big Al –*AIDS*?" Marcus questions with his eyebrow arched. Silence had never been so loud. The only thing that could be heard is the contagious gasps of breath that whips through the room.

"Dat rite?" Lamont, an old neighbor of Big Al questions with his chin between his index finger and his thumb. His are eyes fixated on a figure in the distance whose red hair almost completely hides a pair of cupped, manicured hands, that cover her face. Other than the tears dripping from the sharp triangular shape of her wet chin, the rest of her features are hidden from plain view.

"it's iight ma, ain't nuttin' wrong wit cryin.'" Lamont says on his way to her side. He swipes the tooth pick from his mouth and tosses it into the trash as he moves toward a seat next to the distressed woman, and tries comforting her. His effort to dig her face from her hands go in vain when she turns away from him. "You don't understand," she cries, "I was sleeping with him. We stopped using condoms about a month ago, he said they irritated him." Lamont drops his weight into the seat, "Jesus."

All eyes are now on her as she cries her truth out, "I've been feeling sick for about a week now, and I'm scared to find out what could be going on." I could feel Sympathy ricochet from heart to heart, although at first, no words are spoken. Olivia breaks the silence, "What's your name?" she asks, bending down next to the crying woman.

"Elle" the woman manages to say between sniffles. Olivia touches Elle's knee and bows her head, *"Father God, we come to you today, to ask that you grant Elle with strength, courage and healing. Father, we pray that you purify her spirit, her body and her heart - make her whole and be her savior as you have been to your faithful followers. We ask this in Jesus's name, Amen."*

"Amen" the rest of us repeat in unison then raise our heads and look at Elle. "it's ok," Michael assures her, "I'm sure you'll

be fine." We end the small memorial service with hugs, kisses on the cheeks and sympathetic disclosures. Once everybody else has left, Michael, Olivia and I stand there for another minute, capturing a moment of truth.

The red head had said that she stopped using condoms with Allen about a month ago. It's been almost four months since Allen told us that he found out he had AIDS. If suspicions serve us correctly, and I am sure that in this case they do, my old friend Big Al didn't plan to suffer to death alone. It seems he made sure that his misery had some company. But exactly how much company did he manage to find? I mean, first the pregnancy scare with Ze'Amora, now this?

"He must've gave that shit to someone, and they killed'em." Olivia states with a blank gaze painted across her face. I'd have to agree - her assertion would explain the overkill and the amount of hatred it must have taken to beat someone's head into a meat ball.

I swipe the back of my fingers across Olivia's cheek, and wipe away her tears, "now's not the time to worry, we gotta start funeral arrangements. Ya'll know we're the only real family he's got left. There's a few other's we need to find," I look into Olivia's eyes, "baby, you alright?"

"yeah" Olivia says as she looks up at the ceiling and another tear oozes from the corner of her eye. We exit the building, heading back to our separate worlds. On the way home my head starts spinning and a sharp pain pierces my side. As soon as I force my way through the doors of our home I collapse on the floor and stay there for a while, staring up at the chandelier.

Thirty minutes into my breakdown, Olivia collapses beside me and whimpers, "Michael's been trying to call you ever since we left. There won't be a funeral, Allen was cremated."

At nine o'clock in the morning Olivia glances out the window of the Doctors office to see the sun hovering over Ladera Heights. Normally the leaves of the oak trees would wave at the slightest breeze of wind but today they stand so still, it's like Olivia is looking at a picture of the forest. Gazing past the glare of the window she sucks in a gulp of air.

'Today is going to be a very long day,' she thought.

For reasons unknown, she starts to feel uneasy. With no idea of what she's about to hear, she takes in a deep breath, and she prepares herself for the worst. After experiencing two failed pregnancies within the last year, she had had it up to the top of her head with it all.

The door swings open and in walks a tall, bronze colored Doctor. His eyes are contorted with a look of concern. He walks over, followed by a bright ray of light which seems to dim with each step he takes in her direction.

By the time he's six feet within her personal space, Olivia's world is dark. Her heart has now broken free and is on its way out her chest. Palms sweating and feet tapping, she takes in another deep breath and exhales. The Doctor offers his hand to her for a shake and looks into her eyes simultaneously, "Hi, I'm Doctor Paul E. Stokes," he says.

Embracing himself for the bad news he is about to deliver, he takes a seat and rolls close to his patient, "I'm going to have to refer to our specialist."

Olivia takes note on how those words seem to fight their way from his throat. Paperwork in hand, he flips through several pages of notes and he carries on, "How long have you known?"

Olivia's eyes widen, "known what?"

As though he'd just received a death threat, Doctor Stokes glances up at Olivia and he gives her a look cold as ice. Olivia would never forget the darkness in his eyes when he places the paper upon the examination table then asks, "You mean, you don't know?"

Chapter 11

Olivia

The alarm clock snatches me out of the darkness, and I wake up in deep, cold sweat. Still a little shaken from the dream I just had, I move my trembling hand over to check the time. *Shit!* I overslept. Why does time seem to be moving super-fast, in slow motion.

I've been trying to piece the events of the last two years together to figure out how I failed Allen, but I keep drawing a blank. It kills me to know how things went down between us, but my conscious won't let me blame myself for his destruction. Instead, the same tune keeps playing in my head; *the player finally got played.*

My heart is now thumping against my chest as I ponder the irony. It's been three weeks since Allen's murder and the police still have no leads in solving the case. Through my mourning for Allen, it kills me to know he had to die so suddenly.

Parts of me feels as though he should have been kept around to suffer a little longer, so he could finally grasp on to the concept that this is a round world, and what you dish out, it comes back around.

I mean, I have some love left for him in my heart, but somewhere in that open space I wanted him to live longer to suffer Karma's raft. Whoever killed him must not have known that they were just taking him out of his misery. But then, maybe they did know.

Even worse than my dark thoughts is my reality; I can't help but notice how things have changed in my home. Omar hasn't said much in these past three days. He's become so distant; I can hardly even see him half of the time. His sudden addiction to nicotine has gotten the best of him and bought out the worst.

He's an emotional wreck, but he's not the only victim in this collision. The worst thing about it is that he keeps blaming himself for everything that has happened. I want so badly to be his support system through this tragic time, but whenever I try to comfort him, he pushes me away. I know he doesn't mean to disconnect from me, but he is overwhelmed in guilt. The only time he allows me to comfort him is when he's at his absolute worse, and he *can't* fight me off.

Yesterday I found him in the corner, crunched into a fetal position. My instincts pushed me over to him and ordered my words, "Baby, how long have you been down here?" I kneeled to his level and ran my hand over his back. He never responded, he just cried out, "My brother, my brother." He unraveled his body then started rocking back and forth, "My brother," he cried, "I messed everything up."

"Baby, we're not gonna blame ourselves, remember? This is not our battle."

"I messed up," He repeated.

I sat down next to my husband and relaxed my body. When the skin of our forearms touched, I could tell that he was tense. I squeezed so close to him that our bodies were literally pressed together, and I whispered in his ear, "relax." I said that to him in my softest, calmest voice, "relax" I whispered again, this time stretching the five letters in the shortest song ever heard.

Finally, Omar's muscles loosened, and he let the weight of his body fall onto mine. "We're going to get through this together baby," I reminded him, "I'm here for the long run." Omar came out of his spell slowly, then he followed me to the bathroom where I had a warm silk-bubble bath waiting. Once he dipped inside, I lit a candle and turned the radio to his favorite mix of jazz and R and B, then I went to prepare dinner. Normally at a time like this a wife is supposed to be the strength for her husband. But all I can do is pray and keep reminding him that I'm here for him when he needs me.

Preparing him for today, I walk over to the window and pull back the curtains. The sun illuminates his athletic frame, exposing the tears that had dried upon his face. Then his mobile calendar beeps, and I swipe the phone from the loose grip of his hand. Omar doesn't budge. The reminder on the screen reads *'results tomorrow'*. Out of love and concern for my King, I press number three on Omar's phone and Mike answers on the first ring,

"hey Mike."

"Hey sis, how ya livin'?"

"It's kinda, all bad. Omar hasn't gotten out of bed. he's sunken into a downward spiral and I can't seem to pull him out of it. He has completely shut me out. I was hoping you could get through to him."

"I will shoot by there before my meeting if that's okay. I'll help him move around a little. Separate'em from that bed for a while."

"that'd be great. I was thinking maybe you can take him back to your house, and he could spend a few nights there. You guys can go from there to get your results and-"

"Ooh snap," Michael interrupts, "the *results* – I almost forgot. Most def – we can do that. Pack him up some clothes, I'll be there *after* my meeting instead."

"We forgot too; his calendar just reminded him. I know if someone doesn't take him, he won't go. So can you be sure that he goes in Mike, please? Ya'll are already what, like months late going for these lab results?"

"Yeah, *over* three months. The office kept rescheduling us

'cause Covid 19 hit. I figured if anything was wrong, the Doctor would have called us in. You know what they say, *'no news is good news.'* But no doubt. I will see you soon sis, love you and take it easy." I hang up with Mike and go into the bedroom to check on Omar once again and find him on his knees praying – the clothes he had been wearing are scattered on the ground surrounding him.

Chapter 12

Omar

Early this morning I'm up, trailing a line of fire across the carpet on Michael's floor as I pace back and forth, fully dressed in a pair of old ragged jeans and a crisp white tee. Desperate to ease my anxieties, I step onto his patio, light my cigarette then I take a long pull, inviting a tornado of smoke into my lungs. Once my cancer stick is down to the butt, I thump it into the sandbox near his garden, then I step back into his dining room.

To be honest, I'm trying to find a reason to skip out on my results today. I'm just not feeling it, and I'm sick and tired of always having to wear a mask everywhere I go. "I ain't trying to go there maine," I interrupt Michaels' phone conversation to coward away from the upcoming trip.

"*ain't trying to go there?*" Mike mocks, "We're using Ebonics again?" Everybody has always known me as one of the most well-spoken men in town, but amidst of all this disaster, I always seem to forget how to speak, how to think. "I ain't gone – I mean, I'm not going to make it yo, I just got called in for work. I have to —"

"Dude, you're basically your own boss, you can show up when you want to. Lemme see your phone bro" Michael manages to snatch my phone from my hand, "we need to stay two steps ahead of the rubbish. After what happened with Allen, if your'e not convinced you're already as good as dead."

"Yeah man, whatever."

"you're going in for your results even if I have to drag your punk ass down there, here." He tosses my phone into my hand just as my favorite neo-soul mix starts playing from my Pandora app.

"mmman, what time we gotta be there?"

"Any time after nine, but we ain't trying to spend our entire day in that bitch so let's get there at nine-0-five. Michael stretches his arm toward the ceiling, "what time is it now?"

"Almost ten."

"sh, I over slept. Aye, I'll hit'chu back." Michael ends his call and then he rushes to the bathroom. The sound of running water and his toothbrush scratching his teeth travels through to his hallway where I now stand. The wall holds up my dead weight as I gaze at the picture hanging on the wall; in it, Allen held Olivia tightly in his arms from behind, wine glasses in hand, as they pose next to the dining room mural of the Queen Mary. Michael, MoMo, and I sprouted out from behind them with our funny faces on.

My chin falls to my chest, and I feel my face wrinkle. *Only a bitch would steal happiness away from his own bro*, I think to myself.

The guilt inside my heart only adds a soundtrack to my already washed up morning. Michael emerges from the bathroom pulling his gray Armani sweater over his head. We arrive at the doctor's office at ten-fifteen, and at only ten twenty, the doctor appears in the doorway that leads to the back rooms, "Mr. Man?" A receptionist calls out and waves her hand, "The Doctor will see you now."

Twenty long minutes pass and then Michael reenters the waiting room smiling from ear to ear, almost skipping to the tune of his AIDS and HIV free status. "I'm good," He says aloud and proud and relieved, "I'm good." The receptionist reappears in the doorway, "Lynette Tyson."

A tall, thick Brown-skin woman arises and follows him to the back - she also returns with a smile painted across her face. For the next thirty minutes four people enter and exit the double doors. *come on man, I'm ready to get this over with.* Michael walks toward the exit, "I'll be right back, gotta make a quick phone call."

I nod my head, never taking my eyes off the knob on the door leading to the back. Just as I start tapping my foot against the floor, I see the knob twist then a middle-aged man appears in the opening, "Omar Parks."

He watches me stand then he waves me to his direction and as he walks off I follow him to the back. After about twenty seconds of flipping through paperwork, The Doctor finally speaks, "everything is fine, your test is negative."

"It, it's negative?"

"Yeah, you're clean."

my palms slaps against my chest "whew."

"Mr. Parks, your test is negative. Do you understand what this means? There are no antibodies found in your blood. you *are* AIDS and HIV free, but --"

"whoo!" I sound off in relief before the Doctor could finish his statement.

"Mr. Parks" The doc says with his face wrinkled, "Your reaction troubles me, do you think you have been exposed to the virus in any way?" His question catches me off guard, so I look at him sideways, "huh?"

"Before today Mr. Parks, when was your last test?"

I draw another blank. I can't remember when I was last tested but I know it was right after I had graduated high school, when I was thinking about joining the navy. That was over ten years ago. "Well," The Doctor speaks, "you know it can take up to six months before the virus shows up on blood test, so there is a possibility that you are testing too early. If you feel you have been exposed recently, there are more comprehensive tests that we can perform."

At first, I hesitate. I no longer want to acknowledge my brush with death. But being that my test came out negative, me and Olivia can move on with their lives. I want to start anew, and I know that means confronting the past head on. There is no revolution without a resolution, and I know that. I decide to filter out the old to make room for the new, I clear my throat and admit, "uh, my wife's ex was recently diagnosed with AIDS."

The Doctor shifts in his chair and begins to write notes, "AIDS is the number one killer of minorities in your age group, you'd be surprised at the rising number of patients we diagnose here every month."

"Every *month*?" I question, feeling my eyeballs widen.

"*Every* month. People often misunderstand the concept of testing for AIDS and HIV. They think that because they test negative, they are in the clear. But testing only determines whether you have it. If tested early enough, proper treatment can be administered, and the disease will not progress to AIDS. Testing is *NOT* a preventative measure, as people seem to think." I look past the Doctor's shoulder, my eyes landing on the plaque on the wall. It reads, '*Doctor Paul Edward Stokes, taking care of patients since 1975.*' Translation: He knows what he's talking about, and I'm sure he' seen enough in his time.

He continues his lecture, "every six out of ten people infected with HIV won't know they have the virus until it becomes AIDS. They then become vulnerable to opportunistic diseases such as cancers and pneumonia. The symptoms of HIV can go undetected for so long because they mimic the symptoms of the common cold, and people wave it off as having the flu. Have you been feeling sick within the last year?"

"No, not that I can recall."

"I want to have you and Mrs. Parks back here together in a couple weeks."

"Doc," I look around the room for a second or two, "How long does it take for HIV to turn into AIDS?"

"There's no one-time-frame-fits all answer that I can give you. It really depends.

Some people have underlying conditions they don't know about that can speed up the progression of the virus. This can be particularly troublesome if the individual isn't testing regularly." Doctor Stokes rests against the counter and places his hands in the pocket of his scrubs, "Generally speaking though, if not detected early, a person with HIV will lose white blood cells. The more white blood cells lost, the faster AIDS approaches."

"So, when it's detected early, what does the doctor do to stop HIV from catching AIDS?" The doctor chuckles and repeats, "Stop HIV from *catching* AIDS?" He looks under his glasses, "treatment is provided to save and replicate the remaining white bloods cells in order to keep a high enough count so that the disease goes undetected, and the infected person could live a healthier life. Also-"

His statement is interrupted by screams echoing from down the hall. The eerie cries make me shudder. It sounds as if someone just lost a loved one, someone dear to their hearts. Doctor Stokes looks over his shoulders then he looks back at me just as my lips part, releasing only a muffled sound. The young girl's painful roars nearly cause the building to tremble.

Her voice drowns out my words and as they bounce off the walls, my chest tightens and my palms begin to sweat. The room is suddenly quiet. "You and wifey, back here in two weeks, alert the attendant at the front desk and she will schedule the appointment." The doctor excuses himself from the room, and rushes toward the direction of the commotion.

"I assume you're free from hell." Michael laughs aloud.

"Yeah man, finally." In the same moment our fists meet, Michael tilts his head and looks at me with a grin. We open the car doors and drop in, "I asked so many questions he handed me two extra boxes of condoms."

"Did you remind him that you are married?"

"Nah but I guess now, we've got a reason to celebrate"

"Hell yeah."

"iight bet."

"Cool," Mike checks his mirrors then pulls off, "we're hitting up the Cougar's Den - there's an event popping off tonight, and I'm trying to network. You know me - money is always a priority." Michael flips through his business cards like he's flipping through money.

Better known as 'Mikey-Mike,' he's one of the best business men in town. He knows how to get money, and all his hustles are legit. Using his podcast as a platform to promote independent artists and small business owners, he takes entrepreneurship to another level with his expertise and ambition. I look out of the passenger side window, "I'll have Olivia to drop me off this time. Let's turn it up!"

"Bet."

As soon as Michael drops me off at home, I start craving my wife. Her hourglass shape and her cocoa brown skin imprint my mind. I start thinking about her chocolate kisses, and the way her tongue dances on the head of my penis when she has a taste for some hard candy. I can feel the bold curve of my wife's hips upon my fingertips as I imagine touching her. I miss the way my arms would wrap perfectly around her tiny waist as we lay in bed at night.

Lately I've been distant to my precious wife, and she's been patient and understanding enough to give me the space I need to come around. It's bad enough She's been cheated out of the perfect wedding that she deserved, and she still hasn't been invited to her own honey moon. Each day she just smiles and tells me everything is going to be okay. Feeling my love tool stretch and tingle, I pick up the phone, "Alexa, call my baby."

$$\infty\infty\infty$$

"Hey honey, you home?"

"Yeah, I just came back from my appointment. It's all good."

"aww baby," Olivia purs, "but we knew that from jump."

"Now come home, so I can thank you for being my Queen, what do time you get off?"

"at *right now* o'clock."

Within forty-five minutes, Olivia is racing into the bedroom, ripping off her clothes. I can just imagine sweet warm honey dripping down her thighs. Looking at me in amazement, she starts undressing me while kissing me on my lips.

Just as I reach out for her hips, she salsa's backward and sways her hips from right to left, her thumbs tucked into the sides of her pink thongs as she wiggles out of them. By the time she sways back into my space, the rhythm had charmed her out of all of her clothes.

Now she stands completely naked, and I look on pleased at her curvaccous body. Even though her belly protrudes from the life she carries inside of her, she is sexy none the less and I forget about everything, just long enough to enjoy the love my wife is providing me at this very moment.

She runs her fingers through her hair, parting her curls as she throw her hips to the left. When I reach out and touch her, I trail my cupped hands from the center of her collar bone, over her belly bump and down to the crease of her shaven vagina. Then I separate the thick lips with my middle finger, and it disappears between the softness as I slide it up and down inside of her drooling lips.

Every time I caress downward, the tiny pink tongue licks my fingertip. The tingling feeling that comes with that radiates to the tip of my shaft. I'm so hard that my jerking penis takes on a life of its own as it flinches at my wife's watering flower, "You want this?" I grab a handful and aim it at her.

"Yes."

"Yes what?"

"yes, I want it."

"Then beg for it."

Her facial features droop, "baby, please."

"Please what?" I bite my lip and give her that, 'I'm about to do you good' look. I ask her again, this time with more authority, "please *what?*"

"Can I have some baby?"

"I said *beg* for it."

"Omar baby, give it to me, *please.*"

Her whimpering voice sends my wood aiming toward the ceiling. I lurk in her space, stalking her to the bed until she crawls upon it and slides towards the headboard. Her legs are open for me, and I use my fingers to lure her pearl tongue back out of its hiding spot. *Slow circular inward motions, wiggle. Quick circular outward motions, wiggle and then a gentle tap tap tap.*

When I look down, I see her pleasure palace throbbing, then her body slightly jerks forward. Olivia has always had strong sexual urges, especially since she's been pregnant. At six months her hormones make her horny beyond control and if she doesn't get one off at least once a day, she's a ragging bitch by the morning.

That's why I bought her that rose toy but now, daddy's home and rose has to go. Knowing that I can go back to satisfying her every need makes me feel like that much more of a man.

"Can I taste it?" I kiss her protruding belly button and then trace it with my tongue. dirty talk always drives her wild. Before she could answer, I dip my stiff tongue between her southern lips and paint gentle flicks across her clit until her back arches and she creams all over my tongue.

"You love me?"

"*Yes*"

"Yes what?"

"I love you baby."

She says that as I swing my heaviness up and pierce her. Inside, she's so tight and wet that I almost cum instantly. but I slow the beat down just as I feel the first pleasurable jerk of my rod. We make love passionately and the deeper I go inside of her, the tighter her love grips me. After more than two hours of heavy breathing, biting, scratching and moaning, her pleasure palace starts to throb around my shaft and her leg kicks out for the third time.

She moans and sheds a tear just as her southern lips hawk and spits all over my lower abdomen – the whole time, I'm still jerking inside of her wet, throbbing perfection. I cum so hard inside of her my love spills out and oozes down her thighs. We drift off to sleep with Olivia laying on my chest, but as I look at her reflection through the mirror on the dresser, a familiar change happens in my brain.

∞∞∞

"Damn, what time is it?"

"Time to get'cho ass up, *dude*."

"Mike, man what the-"

"*What time is it?*" Michaels mocks, "*what time is it?* you sleep? It's nine pm, time to turn up."

"Aww man, my wife put me to bed, I'm getting up now."

"Have her pick me up, we need a designated driver ya dig? Wake sis up," He demands. So I send caramel kisses trailing all over Olivia's body as soon as I hang up. Her eyes flicker, but she doesn't budge. "Baby," I roll her onto her back and kiss her lips, then her belly bump, "wake up."

"Noooo, why?"

"I need you to drop me and Big Mike off at the Cougar's Den and then pick us up." She yawns then presses her lips against mine, "Ok handsome." Another tradition of ours; a kiss upon the lips is the signature on a '*trip slip*'. When Olivia first started that, she would sing, "if you don't get the lip, you can't take that trip.'

One thing I love about my wife is that she is very trusting. She never questions me or argues my need to live my own life outside of the one I share with her. Wifey always give me space to be a man first and foremost.

"Let me sign again,"

I put my mouth close to hers and she nibbles on my bottom lip for a second, then she delivers her kiss, "we better hurry up bae, there's a detour building up somewhere on Rodeo, I saw them setting up on the way home."

"There's always a detour on Rodeo. But alright, I need a quick shower."

"Ok."

"There's some money in the dresser, so you don't have to touch yours. Just make sure you get that shirt autographed for Mike."

"Ok, Thank you *daddy.*"

We kiss Once more as I rise from the bed then head for the shower. We leave the house at exactly ten o'clock and as soon as we turn down the third block from our home, the construction workers sit the sign down and waves us toward a U-turn right past the line of Palm trees on Carmelita Way. *Damn!*

I start a text to Big Mike, '*on our way, might be a few...*' Olivia pulls off and swerves the curve, causing me to sway into the passenger door window and the phone to slip from my hands. "Damn bae." I look at her sideways and finish my text, '*... may be a few minutes late, gotta get past a detour.*'

"You sure you're not running from the cops?" I laugh, glancing towards my speeding wife. "No baby, my bad." She hits the gas and makes another sharp turn. Before I could hit 'send', she makes another right, then takes off straight as I look up.

"Why didn't you turn left at the light?"

"It was blocked off over there too."

"Damn, at least they finally fixing these potholes." I look up from my phone again as Olivia is making yet another right, following the long lane of cones. With the swerve of the car, my head turns to my right.

Shit!

We end up right in front of the house where Allen lived. I could literally feel the hair on my skin wave back and forth. What is it that truly led us this way? It's been weeks and I've finally been able to move on, get things off my mind. But here I am, facing it - *again.*

Chapter 13

Michael

The party had already started at my crib, but I two-step to the door and peek through the hole when a knock interrupts my groove. I see Omar looking away, signaling for Olivia to pull into the parking space that just came available across the street. When I open the door, he turns around, a weird ass grin painted across his face. I greet him with sarcasm, "good to see you smiling again bro."

"Man, these past few weeks has had me by the balls, and I'm ready to let off some steam."

"You iight my nig?"

"Yeah, but hell nah."

"Who pissed in your lemonade?

"Life."

"Bro stop trippin', you gone be iight."

"Just drove past Al's house man, kinda got me in a fog."

"That's bro, and may he rest in peace. Tonight, we are not going to think about Allen or anything else other than the turn up. It's our night bro, we shinin'. We gone celebrate FOR Allen, remember him when he was in his prime. Let it go man, let that go."

Omar huffs and shakes his head, then he shifts gears. Hell, truth be told, I'd been making it a point to avoid that block since Allen was murdered. But it doesn't matter how hard we try to avoid the obvious; every time we hang out, there's a presence missing. The Equinox swallows us whole then growls as Olivia speeds away. When we arrive at the club, the parking lot is crowded with Escalades, Lexus trucks and Benzes. I sway with the car, "Damn sis."

"my bad, ever since we got the brakes done, the whip been pushing me in all kinda directions," Olivia looks over at Omar, "stop acting like Imma kill you," She laughs out loud, "Which way should I go?"

"pull up right at the entrance baby."

"Nah sis, let us out at the corner - we'll walk up."

I chose this club because it's far from the hood, and the crowd is sophisticated – the kind of people I could talk business with. Omar and Olivia always insist on driving this car, talking about *'we'd rather ride the wheels off this one until we can't ride it no more. Then we'll pull out the Lambo.'*

You'd think they'd wanna flash just a little bit, since between the two of them, they're basically rich. After the car regurgitates us, Omar kisses Olivia then we walk up, flash our ID's and bam! We're in there. "Where O and her girls headed out to tonight?"

"House of Blues. Jill Scott is scheduled to perform; Tracey came across tickets at the last minute."

"well, those women are going to be living golden lives tonight. You know how Jill Scott put it down, making a woman feel all empowered and what not."

"I get it dude, you're sprung on Jill Scott."

"Sorta, kinda."

Jill Scott, in my eyes, is still the baddest chick alive. The most beautiful woman I've ever seen, and just because we don't share the same views doesn't mean I won't take her down. If ever given the chance, I'd wife Scott, Jill that is. I wait for Omar to make his usual assertion, *'She's not as bad as Olivia,'* but this time, those words never emerge from his lips.

I find that kinda strange because every time I mention Jill's name and her excellence, Omar would mention Olivia in comparison. I decide not to speak on the sudden change in habit.

"What can I get for you two today?" The waitress sings out as we sit down in our seats. When I look at her, my heart damn near jumps from my chest. She's thick with big breasts, penny-bronze colored skin and her hair is short with curls that bounce with almost her every move. She has this familiar smile, and I want to compliment her. But Omar can't wait to get drunk. "D'usse" he demands before I could part my lips.

"Dude, for real?"

"For real" Omar replies.   The waitress turns to me, "Will you be having the same thing he's having?"

"Nah beautiful, bring me a bottle of Rozay, please."

"Got it" she scribbles on her notepad. She must have noticed my reaction to her because her smile widens and she winks as she walks off. Slightly bamboozled, I run my fingertip across my eyebrow, "*hu hu*, did we talk her up or nah?"

"There you go bro, closest you gonna get to the real Scott."

"man, she's *bad*," I shove my fist into Omar's shoulder, "but not as bad as Olivia, right?"

"Right. Well," He hang his head, "not as bad as Olivia *used* to be." A few seconds of silence pass with me looking at Omar with narrow eyes. He sits here, twisting his wedding ring around on his finger. I give him a few more seconds to gather his thoughts.

Omar has always kept Olivia on a pedestal, even when she was with Allen. He always felt like Olivia was too good for big Al, he felt Olivia deserved better and he fell in love with her when he saw how devoted and loyal she was to Al.

He'd confessed to me how he felt about her way before her and Al had split. I kept his little secret, and I didn't blame him. I mean, Al kept putting us both in situation to lie to his Queen about where he was and who he was with. It was only natural for Omar, being the mama's boy that he is, to feel that eventually, he had to save her. And to be totally honest, that's exactly what he had done.

He saved Olivia. Had it not been for him taking her away, who knows – Olivia would probably be dying slow from sickness. His comment caught me off guard and even though I want to ask, I'll keep my mouth shut for now. He'll talk about it when he's ready. The waitress returns, holding a tray in one hand and a bottle in the other.

"Here you gentlemen go, enjoy your night" she leans in and empties her hands onto the table, smelling like rosemary and cocoa butter. I can't resist shooting my shot, "excuse me miss, may I ask you your name?"

"Jill" she says with a smirk. I sit back in my chair, my eyes trail her body from head to toe, "Jill Scott?" I ask with a light chuckle. "No," she giggles, "but I get that all the time."

"*This* nigga." Omar says and he takes back a shot. I wave off his comment, "I'm not surprised at all. You are beautiful, *Jill.*"

"Thank you."

"You think before I leave, I can get a dance?" I look at her with puppy dog eyes. She opens her mouth to object, but before she could deny my fantasy I beg, "just one?"

"Um, it's against my code of conduct, I'll get in trouble" She looks over her shoulders, "But maybe another place and time?" she winks and walks off just as another waitress approaches her, "You got tables seven and nine." I hear the other woman say before they're out of reach. I watch as Jill squeezes through the crowd, her hips swaying from right to left. She looks back at me as she enters the kitchen. I wink at her, then turn my attention to Omar – he's on his fourth shot already.

"You drunk yet maine?"

"Stop. You know I'll drink you under this table."

Omar takes back another shot and swipes his goatee with his index and middle finger.

He twists his mouth as though he's trying to keep in the words that come out next, "she don't look the same bro." he says, staring into his glass.

"*BrUh*, of course. You're drunk, that was Jill, not *Scott*."

"I'm talking about Olivia, dumb ass." he takes another shot, "I don't what happened but... It's, It's like - she changed right before my eyes. Seriously, I blinked, and something changed."

"Foo, you drunk."

"For two months straight? I been drunk? Naw man, It's not that. Truth is, since Allen's death, Olivia has become less and less attractive with each passing minute. I can't explain it. I been trying to hold on to my love for her. I mean, it's still there, but it's not the same. It's like my love for Olivia died when Allen died. I can't explain it man, it's killing me. I tried to overcome the descent of my affection, but, but – it's eating me up. The more I think about it, the more I look at her differently."

"Stop thinking about it then."

"Easier said than done. I've been feeling my love for her get better in the last few days, but passing my bro's house today man, that was a slap in the face. It feels like Al's reminding me that what I did was wrong."

"So what're you going do, leave?"

"Man I can't leave, she's in love and she's pregnant. There's no way that I can hurt her like that. I mean, I'd just be causing her the very harm I rescued her from, and man.... It's like making a mockery out of my loyalty to Al. Like, why would I even make her fall in love with me if I wasn't going to go through with loving her back?

Allen would probably shift in his urn if he knew I did all that, jeopardized our friendship just to do the same thing he was doing to her. Remember what he said to me that day when we had that talk? He said, *'man, don't take her from me if you don't love her, don't break her heart like I did.'* You remember that?"

"Tuh, yeah - I remember."

"I told him that day that I love her but wouldn't marry her, then I turned around, married her – and now I don't even think I love her. Bro gave me such understanding, he forgave me for all that, and here I am, married to her. But yo, I don't," He swipes his hand down the waves in his hair, " I don't even think I love her."

"You tried to."

"Yeah – maybe."

I will never forget the day I staged the intervention between my brothers; Allen's normally arrogant attitude fled him with the desperation that carried his request. Whatever it was that made Omar rebut on their pact is now pushing him into some type of shell.

"I've been meaning to ask you man, what was it that made you got back to messing with her anyway, after you told him you'd leave her alone?"

"It was her, she wouldn't give up. She fought and she fought. No one had ever fought for me bro, and the way she was on me, it was a wrap. Now this is eating me alive, and my love for her is dying with each bite."

"She still fucks the same right?" I try to lighten the moment. Omar exaggerates his chuckle, staring at the shot in the glass.

"Give it some time man, you'll come back around. Just give it some time, it'll work itself out. It's just that, remorse is messing with your head and it's all because our brother is dead. But I'm sure your love for your wife will come back full force."

"I'm not sure I want it to." Omar throws the shot back and slams the empty glass onto the table.

"Chill B, you're tense."

Tonight is smooth Jazz and R&B vibes at the Cougar's Den. Beautiful women of all colors fill the open space. I scope the room, looking for Jill. I see her waltz over to table nine, then she returns to the kitchen. "She ain't finna dance with you tonight son."

"ain't *finna*?" I tease, "Wow. There you go with your street slang again. That ain't like you my guy. Now I know fa sho your mind is gone."

I sit back, look over my shoulders, and rotate my head as I scan the room. My eyes stop on a thick, dark-skinned goddess across the way. In case you haven't picked up on it yet – I love dark skin women. They do something to me, and as soon as I see a woman with penny-bronze skin, I get a sweet tooth. I study her for a second, watching her move her body in ways that made my wood stiffen.

I wonder if she moves like that in bed, my mind wonders as she bends over and rocks her round booty from right to left, showing me a preview.

Damn, I lick my lips and imagine her inviting me inside. A crowd of women dressed in the same color dress she's wearing cheer her on as she takes over the dance floor. She must feel my energy calling for her, because she stands up and spins around, stopping in a pose with her right hip up and her hands in the air.

Then her right hand slowly rubs down her hip as we lock eyes. "Go get it bruh." Omar teases and laughs. After I take a sip of the Rozay, I slide to the end of the bench. But my view of her is blocked by the silhouette of a silvery hourglass figure. She approaches our table with confidence, swinging her hips from right to left. Her round backside follows.

"Hello gentlemen."

"Hello sistah." I stand up to greet her, stretching my hand out as I peek over her shoulder. The melanated goddess is now walking my way, so I prepare myself to be blessed with her presence just as Omar is greeted by the diva in the silver dress

"can I borrow a few moments of your time handsome." she says to him. This woman is assertive, and she looks familiar as hell. I leave the two of them alone to talk as my hand finally reaches the soft touch of the beauty who had come for me.

Chapter 14

Omar

Silver dress, red lipstick - pink finger nails, taking long even steps when she walks. Hair curled to perfection, and focused eyes. She's reinvented herself and she's anxious to try out her new, *spark*.

I've never been approached by a woman before, but I rise to the occasion and kiss the back of her hand, "I wouldn't have it any other way gorgeous." She has all the features of a model; Her smile is encompassed by a set of parentheses that compliment her high cheek bones, and her skin is flawless. When I smile at her, she flashes her pearly whites, "do you dance?"

"I two-step ma."

"Hmm, well, I like what I see, and I would love to see how it feels to dance with you, to have you hold and squeeze my body against yours - if only for one song. I would love that, would you?"

Damn this chick got game. I stand without a second thought and place my hands around her hips, following her to the dance floor. My grip on her waist never loosens as we move through the crowd. The speed in her stride nearly makes me stumble over my own two feet. *It's been long since she's been this close to a man, yet she's assertive and confident. hmmm, interesting.* I chuckle aloud, "Slow down ma, we got all night."

"Oh, do we? I'm sure you'd have to get home to your wife after a while." she looks over her shoulder and exaggerates her glance at my ring finger.

"Smooth talker huh." I chuckle softly while whispering in

her ear, **Countering her charm with a dose of my own,** "I can be all yours tonight."

I then spin her around to face me. Yeah, you guessed it. The D'usse is kicking in and it's got me by the balls. After tonight, if anyone ever asks me if I'd ever seen an angel I'd honestly answer yes. I'd tell them how she walked right up to me, standing about Five-seven with copper-bronze skin and exotic eyes. I'd tell them how she approached me with such charm, as though she was asking for my hand in marriage. The sway in her hips depicted the life of two rainbows playing keep away with the sun.

She's just what I need at the moment, an escape from my troubles. I take a step back and look at her, "you bad ma, what's your name?" She giggles almost nervously, then she steps back into my space and whispers in my ear, "April."

"Nice to meet you, April." I two step in her space, trying my best to keep up with her rhythm. The way she moves man, her body swerving to the beat – everybody in the club is caressing her with their eyes. She's the hottest sight at the moment, and by far, the prettiest girl I have ever laid eyes on. Even prettier than Jill Scott, and right now I'd beg Mike to differ. April slides around with confidence. I have to pause every other step just to look at her.

She is the rhythm, and the rhythm is *her*. She has me so completely mesmerized that my troubles dissipate into thin air. I have never been the shy type, but something about her makes me blush.

April grabs my hands and puts them upon her hips as we cha-cha, and then she pauses right before she starts to slow wind against my frame. Nothing too trashy or ratchet, but saucy and seductively becoming. Just enough chemistry to make a man beg the DJ to play another slow jam.

She twists her body to the melody, "You like that handsome?" moving my hands from her hips to her perky breasts, she purs like a kitten. I'm feeling her energy, and I'm mesmerized by how the shade of her cloudy-grey irises change with every flash of the party lights. But although our energy is undeniable our eyes never really connect. It feels like I'm falling under her spell but, I can't read her. When my eyes scroll the features of her slim face, I get a glimpse of pure black Tourmaline every time she looks away. *Social anxiety*

However, she steps into my space, forcing me to step back as we dance. *Dominant in bed. Maybe not aggressive enough to be a dominatrix, but spicy enough to attend to a man's needs, noted.* She then spins around and looks at me with begging eyes as I reach for her hand, but she shakes her head and steps backwards while loosening the belt around her dress, "I love the way you stare at me, you're turning me on." After a connection like this there's no way I'm going to let her get away that easy. I step towards her and bite my lip, "you lookin' for trouble ma?"

I slide my hands around the curve of her backside and gently squeeze. Then I run my fingers up her body until I reach her hair. Aprils turns around, bends over and starts clapping her cheeks while twirling her hips and holding her ankles. Her straightened legs are topped with the arch of her rounded ass.

Still completely under her control though, I stand back and watch her tease me. Two songs later, she excuses herself to the ladies' room and just as she walks off I spot Mike parting the crowd, heading my way with another bottle of Rosay in each hand, "didn't know you had it in you."

"you and me both."

"Enjoyin' yaself a lil too much, bruh."

"that's what we came to do, right? turn up."

"Yeah, but bro - look at you, you look like you just came back from Nutville. what, you just got some ass on the dance floor?"

"Lil bit," I look over my shoulder, don't see April anywhere. One more dance is all I need to get me there, then I could go to the men's room and let one off. Mike nods towards our table, but I ignore his gesture. There's nothing I want more at this very moment than to have April in my space again. As I scan the club, Michael's voice comes out of nowhere, "Come 'on man, that girl is poison."

"Yeah, you know'er?"

"Nah, don't need to. I've learned a lot from you over the years, on how to read people. From the way she walked right up to you, she's either preying on you, or she's just, easy."

"you're stupid bruh."

"I'm not stupid bruh, you're just lame. Suddenly you're sleep? wake up bruh. How many women do you know confident enough to approach a man like *that*?"

"Aye, some women just know what they want."

"... and some women are just as doggish as some men."

"Damn, we just danced."

"Yeah," Michael says as he walks off, "That's what *you* think," When he passes me we brush shoulders and he tilts toward my ear, "....by the way you trailed her every move when she walked off – I see you're looking for something more." Michael points his pinky finger towards our table then stroll-bounces in that direction. I look over my shoulder again but there's still no sight of April. I then walk over and meet Mike as he's pouring up two glasses.

We sit back and finish the bottle, absorbing the vibe as the DJ prompts a severe case of the cha- cha. Everyone on the dance floor is inching forward then backwards, then spinning around to switch partners

"What time Olivia gone be here?"

141

"I told her I would call her. You ready to go already?"

"Nah, I'm just trying to decide if I have enough time to go get some'mo head in the bathroom real quick." Mike chuckles

"Aww you good bro, go ahead and bust one."

I look over to see April grooving my way, "You forgot something," she whispers in my ear as she walks up, slides the folded napkin into my hand and then glides off. Michael tilts his head as he watches her walk past him, "Sum'n ain't right," He says in a drunken but sure tone, sliding around in his seat to watch April disappear into the dancing crowd, "There's something about her, something familiar. It's like, I've met her before somewhere in time. I can't quite put my finger on it. I mean, beauty - yeah. Sex appeal, yeah. But, but.... her vibes are giving me goose bumps," Mike takes a gulp from his cup, "Maybe it's the Maybelline cause, I'm telling you right now bro, she wasn't born with it."

"What's that you're drinking?" I peek into his glass with my eyebrow cocked, "Hateraide?"

"Hateraide? I'm not hating on it, I'm trying to help you keep your eyes open."

"Yeah, yeah - jokes. You're a comedian now. Her makeup isn't as bad as that chick's you were just dancing with." I swoop my head around the small cluster of tables and catch the dudes to my left laughing out loud at our conversation. "Man," Mike reiterates, "she's hiding something - behind all that makeup, is a cum guzzling clown."

"Cum guzzling huh?"

"Yeah."

"Clown, right?"

"Right. There's something hiding behind that fake ass face she's wearing. Pay attention fool, she's predator - you're prey." Mike looks back at April who is now dancing with a man sending bills filliping off her ass. He takes back his shot and scuffs, "*tuh -* by the end of the night she's gonna have *all* of his money in her pocket."

The Rico Suave-looking brotha from the next table laughs out loud and proclaims, "That's real talk maine, that's why I don't put my dick in females with pink and purple faces, them be the pretty thirsty ass bitches."

"Pretty thirsty and pretty broke," his homeboy cosigns, "they paint themselves to look like dime pieces, but they be the dustiest ones out there."

Between the three tables, there's a rolling wave of laughter. A couple at a table nearby giggles, then the dude playfully covers his girlfriend's ears, "bruh," he mouths in my direction. I shake my head at him then check Mike, making his goofy ass an example for the rest of these lames, "ya'll cappin' bruh, she's bad."

"Yeah she bad, I'll give you that." Mike counters, watching me as I pour another shot.

"don't give it to me, give it to ma. Shorty a dime piece."

"Oh, you want *me* to give it to her?" Michael laughs and shoves me, then looks at me with that, '*but I'm serious though*' look in his eyes. I smack my lips and confirm, "nah. I mean, I don't care - do yo thing."

"Well let me know cause I'll find out exactly what type of creature it is. I'll do the investigation for you, and we can find out what's going on."

Everyone in ears distance bounce their heads to the music while at the same time, they nod in agreement to Mike's empty rhetoric. In the very next moment Mike looks at me sideways, then he stares off into the distance as he stands and head towards the dance floor, "so what'chu gonna do with that number, *Mr. Married Man?*"

"Toss it."

"iight then, toss it ova here." I look at Mike sideways, and I shake my head, "nah."

$$\infty\infty\infty$$

Watching her from a distance, her every move makes my dick jump. The sensation flowing through my body feels like something inside me coming alive, something *powerful*. Yeah, I've had a lot to drink, but this isn't my first time getting this lit, I turn up bottles. You could never drink *me* under the table. So trust me when I say, it's not the liquor drawing me to this woman. There's something else going on here.

Could be something in these burning candles. T*ranquilizing*. Smells like a mix between mint and citrus, like grapefruit or orange. The combination makes me feel like I'm free, riding some type of eternal wave.

I can't figure it out, but this chick got me in some type of trance. Mike says she's preying on me, and maybe he's right. Maybe some type of voodoo is at play because I swear, no matter how hard I try, I can't take my attention away from her. I can't see anything but her, I don't feel anyone but her.

"Excuse me, can I have this dance." A voice snatches me out of my trance. "uh huh," I murmur, never moving my feet.

"Why are you sitting over here all by yourself?" She asks then she grabs my hand, "come on."

Is it me, or are the women in this place aggressive as hell? Moving below the speed of her satisfaction, I remove myself from my seat with my eyes still glued on April. Gradually I hear a voice increase in volume, "...girl, something is wrong with this one, I think it's broken. Come on let's find someone else."

"You ok brotha?" The first girl asks.

"Uh huh,"

"Look, he's slobberin'." one of the girls say as they tease and walk away, finishing me off, "don't be so lame, damn."

"And close ya mouth."

"huh," I use my thumb to swipe the drool from my bottom lip. That feeling that was making me lose my grip, it travels to the tip of my stiffening wood every time April blows me a kiss, or even looks my way. It pulls at my wood hard. I flick the piece of paper she'd handed me around in my hand for a few seconds, then I fold it four times and stuff it behind the battery compartment of my phone, watching Mike return to the table.

"Look," Mike says, nodding toward April as she blows me another kiss, "the chick who handed you a first-class ticket to hell," Michael slides back in his seat shaking his head, "your'e making *love* in this club."

"Dude shut up, you were just asking if you could take a test drive a few seconds ago."

"I was jokin' around."

"Yea, right. Niggas hating hard in the club."

Mike adjusts himself in his seat and replies, "whatever weird ass nigga. Call Olivia, I'm ready to go."

"You mad bruh?"

"Hell yeah," he laughs and huffs, "I just had to fake a bust cause the slut ain't know how to suck. I got tired of the heffa scrapping her teeth against my nuts." I look away and laugh, "Bro."

While we wait near the entrance, Mike is still speaking his piece. All I hear is *whomp whomp whomp* as visions of April continue to dance in my mind. I can't stop thinking about her – the way she moved, the way she grooved. Everything about her is unforgettable. She's a sparkle of perfection from head to toe. I won't lie, I think she hypnotized me on that dance floor. I bet she's really good in bed, and it's like – I want to find out exactly *how* good.

Increasing in luminosity, the approaching head lights force Mike and I into view as we walk towards the parking lot. Finally, I snap out of my trance, shaking my head as a lecture myself, *yo I'm fucking up.*

∞∞∞

"Help him baby, he's drunk."

"Since when has a drunk been able to *be* a drunk and *help* a drunk?"

"Aye punk," Mike laughs out loud, "what month is this? *April?*"

"We're in March bro," Olivia laughs and informs the idiot. I can't even crack a smile, I'm busy digging into the wet burrito she had picked up from Chipotle. Olivia knows the only way to sober me up is to stuff me with food. She turns off the engine and exits the vehicle, then we help Michael into his home. He staggers up the steps and stands in the doorway as we head back to the car. Once back inside, we fasten our seat belts and look up just in time.

"Aye," Michael yells as he turns around, pulls down his pants then asks again, "what day is it, *APRIL?* Olivia shakes her head from left to right, but I nearly choke on my food. After I catch my breath I yell back at him, "bruh, get'cho ass out the air." Olivia and I laugh aloud as she pulls off. We finally make it home and Olivia immediately goes to work.

"It's ok baby, relax." she guides me to the daybed and props my feet upon the pillow. I feel the blood flow through my feet and to my toes as she loosens my monk strap loafers, then slides them off my tingling feet one by one.

"Daddy had too much to drink?" she purposely lets her belly rub up against my feet as she slithers towards my lips and kisses me. Pleased at her commitment to take care of me, I lean up a little and allow her to pull my shirt up over my head.

"Thank you baby."

"You deserve it," she whispers, "I'm going to run you a warm bath."

"Can I have some green tea too."

"You can have whatever you like."

"Hurry up then," I command in that deep, authoritative voice she likes. She looks at me sideways, but she blushes and gives me her passive voice, "ok baby."

Yo, she hooks it up so all I have to do is dip, and drop; dip in the bath, then drop in the bed. After my brush with a close-call entanglement, my soul is caressed; I'd had my dose of lust, and now I'm getting my dose of love. I don't know if I've lost my mind or if I have gone straight crazy, but the candles Olivia just lit is tickling my manhood, reminds me of the citrus- mint I smelled burning in the club. Now I'm thinking about the way the soft, curves of April's bottom filled my hands, and how that soft, sweet voice had warmed my ear.

'you feel so good,' she had whispered as she grinded against me.

"Baby."

"Huh?" I blink away the sight of April dancing in my eyes, and turn my attention to my wife. She walks over and runs her fingers across the top of my head, "your bath is ready." I stand to walk into the bathroom and the moment my feet touch the water I feel the tension start to cease. That feeling spread over my body as I lay back in the warm, bubbly river.

"Here handsome."

"Thank you baby, you're so good to me," I grab tea cup by the handle and blow away some of the steam, then I read the fortune that adorns the tea bag, hanging outside of the cup. Olivia sits on the edge of the tub, "what's it saying?" Per usual, I read the quote aloud, *'the only real thing consistent in life, is change.'*

"ain't that the truth."

"Baby you forgot my slice of lemon."

"I didn't forget, we ran out."

"Bad girl."

"Nah, bad boy."

"I *can* be."

"I brought myself something nice like you told me." She stands and spins around, then looks at me from over her shoulder, "it's your favorite color."

"It looks good on you too love." I sip the tea, "now turn back around." I bow my head to sip more tea just as she starts to spin. I then raise my head slowly, scanning her body with my eyes starting from her green toenail polish and stopping at the sway of her gown. Her feet are smooth and freshly oiled, making her skin glow with the flickering flames from the candles.

"um"

"You like it?"

I look up at her mid-driff, her hands are resting on her hips and her fingernails are curled upon her skin. She opens her brown silk robe, revealing the matching negligee.

"I love it."

"I knew you would."

"You wanna join me? I'm starting to feel lonely in here."

"Yes baby." She undresses and starts walking towards the tub one step per second, sliding her toes across the carpet with each move. Now standing here naked, she gives me a few minutes to enjoy the view. Out of left field there's a flash and suddenly, I'm looking at April. I want to touch her so badly, but I shake my head and look inside my cup. *Something must be in here.*

"what's wrong baby?"

"Noth, nothing. You just look so good."

"Oh, do I?"

"You do." I look into her eyes, and my wife comes back into view. She dips into the water from the opposite side, then she presses her feet against my chest. We soak and talk for a while, then we both stand to exit the tub. When we walk into our bedroom, that flash happens again, and now April is in my eyes.

"Touch me" she whispers. She then grabs my hand and places them on her breast, "feel me," she glides them toward her hips and slips my fingers into her panties, "touch me, here."

Man, I'm tripping. What did she put in that tea? I ponder my reality as I ease to the floor, using my fingertips to slide her panties toward her ankles. I stand back up slowly, letting my hands run up the length of her body. When I get back to my feet, she guides my head to the center of her breasts and moans out loud. Then she leads me to the bed and straddles me, lifting her waist before she eases down on my erection. It feels so good, and I'm lost inside of her.

She rocks back and forth, driving me into another dimension where this rush of euphoria waves through me, and I get trapped again in a trance. That is, until I hear her scream out, then I feel her crash onto my chest. With my head in mid-roll, I open my eyes to my surprise, I'm face-to-face with my wife.

Chapter 15

April

Two things that keep me grounded are sunrises and sunsets. I like to think of them as my personal slices of heaven, just to be in the peace of it all. So, there's nothing I love more than spending the night at the beach. The sand between my toes, the cool air brushing against my skin, and the sound of waves crashing along the shore.

It provides me with spiritual and mental rejuvenation. I always bring my 'hoe bag' just in case a dick with legs comes walking by. But of course, I never get *that* lucky. Still, the pleasure of staring at the sun and watching it disappear below the horizon, only to rise again the next morning brings me close to climax. It's such a rush, it makes me feel superior to anyone who lacks the experience.

This has been my ritual ever since I decided to finally live for me and set out on a journey to find a deeper connection with *self*. I always find my release at the exact moment the sun blends into the cold, awaiting waters below. It's that connection that helped me embrace my sexuality; the feeling that comes over me when the sun kisses the water is what bought me out of my shell, so every time I find myself overly aroused or overwhelmed, I race to the beach. Last night was no different from any other; I was all over the place with my emotions. I wanted to feel my anxieties disappear like the sun into the water. So here I am again – anticipating that release. Looking straight ahead, the orangish-red globe flickers like a ball of fire.

I focus on that glow, and as I take in a deep breath it starts to dance through the sky, committing a slow plunge towards the depths of my imagination. I watch patiently, indulging in every flick as it changes the color of the orange-tinted sky. But unlike every other night, today my release is halted by a nagging thought, and I can't seem to shake it.

'*Why hasn't he called?*' It's been almost twenty-four hours and I know I left an impression. The feeling of rejection overcomes me in the exact moment the sun's warm glow is interrupted by a cloud. Just like a true warrior, the sun defeats the puff of water and continues its downward spiral. Watching the sky fade through shades of orange then purple as my muse merges into the horizon, I feel my tensions gradually disappear into another world.

My roommate doesn't know what she's missing. She's always too busy trying to pick out her outfit for the next day. Either that, or she's somewhere playing in makeup. Anyways, I could do without the interference of her constant nagging. I need this time to sort out some things in my mind. Right now, I'm rewinding the conversation I'd overheard at The Cougar's Den.

'*My love for Olivia died when Allen died.*'

That statement caused me to freeze in my step, and I decided to halt my approach. *Hmmm, wonder what that means,* I thought. Luckily, I know exactly where to find *him* - at the fitness center on third and Van ness. Yeah, not only have I done my homework, but I just *know* things. See Omar, he's an easy target, and that was apparent in the fact that I was able to control him on the dance floor.

Everyone knows that a man is supposed to lead. But Omar followed my every step, allowing me to push him away from his position as a strong, good willed man. A married man at that. I'm sure I left him shook, and that's why I was expecting my phone to ring that same night. So I can't lie, I do feel rejected. I've never had a man not call on the same night, begging for even the smallest taste of *this* sweet wine.

Focus April, Focus. The sun sinks a few inches lower and that anticipated euphoric feeling rocks me. I let my body relax and with my eyes still fixated on the diminishing glow, I inhale and exhale in a purring moan.

Juicy-orange, that's what I call the dome once she's sitting at the edge of the horizon, stimulating my imagination as I envision myself swimming toward her. My nipples rub against my shirt, and then I feel my southern lips floating in a puddle of my own juices. I can't help but to touch myself; I run my fingertips slowly up and down the length of my collar bone, grinning as I gaze at the marigold-colored streak along the currents. *'Do it,'* I whisper.

My muse grants my wish, finally dipping below the ripples of water and turning my world completely black. Gazing up into the distant, illuminated face of the orb that replaced the sun, I close my eyes to welcome the darkness, sealing the moment inside of my mind as everything around me disappears.

∞∞∞

A familiar glow warms my skin as the sun returns to reclaim her position on her throne. She was mid-flight when I first peeled my eyes open, and now she sits high, mighty, and strong - delegating superpowers among her kingdom. I gather my things and once I make it to my car, I crank up my engine and back out of the parking space. Feeling light as a feather, a huge weight has been lifted off of my shoulders.

My body is pleased with the rush that the sunrise provides and that feeling of rejection ceases to exist. I shake my head at myself for doubting my perfection for even a second. *He's a married man, his wife must be on his dick twenty-four-seven.* As bad as I know he wants to, he'd never be free enough to call. I drive back to my new duplex and as soon as I open the door, hot steam and a whiff of cocoa butter rainbath tickles my face and nose.

"Hey Bes Fran," Justin shouts from around the corner, "You was having sex with the moon again?"

"You know it," I walk into the living room and fling my bag onto the couch, "You always gotta shower with the door wide open?"

"Bitch yea."

"Got it smelling all sweet up in hea."

"bitch, *YEAH.*" She reiterates before I change the subject, "aye, let's go get membership at the gym, I need to get back in shape. Found cellulite on my thighs."

"I'm already in shape, I don't need no gym." A leg swings out from behind the fog of the shower curtain and it wags back and forth, "I'm straight."

"you sure about that?"

"Hell nah." We laugh out loud before I respond, "bitch I need a workout partner, screw your perfect body."

"Alright then, I'm game."

"We gone leave as soon as you done in there."

"Bitch I'm on my way to the salon."

I walk over to the bathroom and position myself within the door frame, "we're just going to grab the membership, we not gonna stay today. Bring yo ass on and shut up."

"Ok bitch, and that's ALL I'm finna do today. now close the door and mind ya business." A swerving hand waves off some of the steam, sending another whiff of the sweet smelling body wash directly toward my face.

I turn my head away as I pull the door closed. Although there's no need to rush, I'm so ready to go a 'haunting and avenge the loss of a dear friend of mine, and I can't wait to show Omar what I've got up my sleeve.

Chapter 16

Omar

About three weeks ago I danced with an angel, and I still can't get her off my mind. Is this what obsession feels like? I don't know, but I've been questioning myself since that day. The way she touched me, the way she talked to me with that sweet soft voice. My wood is thumping against my knee right now just thinking about her.

The wait until my training hours at the gym seems too far away. I need a quick release, so I hop out of bed and rush to the restroom. After a cold shower I start dressing in my gym clothes. As I'm pulling my shirt over my head, Olivia twists in the bed, "where you going baby?" I bend my leg back and grab my foot from behind, "I need to hit the gym, let off some steam."

Olivia picks her phone up from the nightstand and looks at the screen, "*This* early?" she questions with her eyes squinted, "And what *steam*? You *ok* daddy?"

"Yeah, I'm good. Just had a nightmare about Allen."

"What happened *this* time?"

"Baby he walked up to me, bloody - brains hanging out of his head and all. He had a box in his hand, and he handed it to me," I mock the action of Allen handing me the box, "He said, '*this is for you*', then he crammed the box into my chest, damn near pushed my heart out through my back. He said, '*I forgive you for fuh....*" baby, before he could finish his statement, his mouth fell apart and landed right at my feet. You and I know I could always tell when Allen was lying, because he would always interrupt his own words. He'd be like, '*I'm not mah-*' then he'd change his tone and say, *'I'm smooth, I'm not even tripping.'*"

"so, what you think the dream means?"

"He never really forgave me for not ending our relationship like I promised I would, when I told him I'd stand down, and let ya'll work it out." Olivia's face melts, "well babe, we can't live with that guilt for the rest of our lives. I mean, it's not like he was a good man to me."

"He was a good brother to me though, and I, I just..." I flop down on the ottoman, crashing my forehead into my palms, "I can still feel it. my chest, right here - It hurts." I turn towards my wife and tap my fist against my heart. "I'll be back soon, just gonna burn this feeling off." I stand, then I walk over to Olivia and aim my lips towards hers, but she turns her head. I know what she's trying to say, but none of that matters.

I mean, yeah – that dream had me gased, but truth is, I need to retract some of the temptation of love's arch enemy. Fifteen minutes and two pit stops later, I'm programming the treadmill, ready to run the urges of lust out of my brain. Per usual I start slow to get in a mild warm up before I heat the track up, then I dive headfirst into a power work out.

An hour and a half later, I'm close to tapping out, dripping sweat and barely able to catch my breath. Michael and I had skipped out on our last three jump start sessions, and my obsession with chipotle isn't making my energy level any better. I try to coach myself, *thirty more minutes...fifteen more minutes.* the music coming from my earbuds is my only motivation, but then a flash of art comes to life, in my imagination.

There she stands in a sexy negligee wearing no panties or bra - posing like a sex God. Then she sways in my direction. With each step her hips sway gracefully from side to side, and the secret hidden between her thighs reveal itself with each gliding sway. The peach fuzz covering her vagina is a golden-brown tint that blends in smoothly with her skin, making it appear her thick lips were completely bald. Her perky breasts, topped with Hershey's kiss drops.

She moves closer to me with sex in her eyes and passion in her voice as she whispers, 'Fuck me.' Once she's in dick's distance, she runs her finger nails down the length of my arm, 'Taste me.' Her demands almost send me over the edge.

I lean back a little, trying to resist the temptation. but she pulls me back in, and I fall into her soft breasts. She then puts my earlobe between her teeth and gently scrapes my skin, 'Omar' she whispers in my ear as she runs her lips across my cheek, 'I need you.' She sniffs my neck, then suddenly shoves me out of her space, and back into reality

"Omar, excuse me - *Omar?*"

I snap out of my daydream to find April standing in front of me in an all-black, tight suit. *Did I just think her up?* It appears my fantasy just warped into my reality, right before my eyes. I don't know whether I should grab her and give her what I know she wants, or if I should just play it cool. I stop the treadmill and step down, reaching for her hand, "sup ma."

"wow, it's really *you*. good to see you again."

"My thoughts exactly."

"You following me?"

"I was just about to ask you the same thing." I gently remove her hand from her hip, then twist her wrist and kiss the back of it, "the pleasure is all mine." I wipe the sweat from my face using the end of the white towel draped over my shoulders then I ask, "what are *you* trying to work off?" Standing back and looking at her from head to toe, I feel my nature twitch. "This ass," April says, grabbing the bottom of her butt cheeks with both hands and making her huge booty bounce, "it's weighing me down."

I lick my lips, "Naaah," peeking around her waist, I give her two thumbs up, "it's perfect." I swear, a hint of something sweet spread across my tongue - It's like I can taste her. I rub my tongue around in my mouth as to savor the flavor.

"Well, I want to tone it up a bit"

"For what, you trying to be a model?"

"Maybe," April throws one arm at a time up and over her shoulders, then she stands with her legs spread apart. Tucked between her thighs - a perfectly shaped, upside down heart. I can't take my eyes off it as she bends and stretches. When she kicks her leg up to stretch on the weight bar, the heart rests on her inner thigh. I swear, I just saw it blow me a kiss. The visual almost sends my penis gravitating towards the ceiling. I tilt my head and give her a sideways glance, and I watch her lips mouth," *Can I have some?*" she nods at my lap.

Am I stuck in fantasy land.

Anyways, she steps on the treadmill and starts off on her artificial jog. There's nothing funny about the way I shift in my boxers when I turn to step back onto my treadmill, but I laugh. April chuckles too, side eyeing my pants as she increases her speed. *Maybe I should ask her if she liked what she saw.*

Before I could part my lips two of Olivia's friends walk past. I lock eyes with Quanny when I look back. She breaks eye contact, then the two women hurry to the front desk and greet a man who is jiggling his keys to grab someone's attention. I'm glad he stepped in when he did, because I need Quanny and Shay to go back to minding the business that pays their nosey asses.

I need to be as discreet as possible if I want to recharge my player card. I don't need Olivia to find out I could be lucky enough to have even a pending affair with someone like April.

You know how women get; if you cheat with someone less attractive, they get over it fast. But cheat with someone like *April*, they'll cry for days and weeks and months – looking to you every day for reassurance that the other woman isn't better than *her*. Women like April make wives like Olivia change up their whole image, and even after dying their hair, losing weight, and trying to dress sexier, they still feel as though they can't walk in the shadows of such A-list beauties. They will never admit it to you, but that's how they think.

Glancing around the room, the only familiar faces are Quanny and Shay. Shay is standing at the counter, "this is for the gram," She holds up a peace sign next to her widened smile, looking up at her phone as she spins around in slow motion.

Everyone else is caught up in their normal routines. A Hispanic woman hands Quanny her ID and Quanny starts typing on the computer, glancing at the card every couple of seconds. *Now's the perfect time.* I push the button on the jogging machine, and the speed slows. To capture April's attention before eyes could turn my way, I hop off the track before it makes a complete stop.

"Careful, don't bite the dust." April laughs

"Bite the dust? I'm too quick for that."

"Too quick to bite the dust, maybe. But what about if you slip and bite me on your way down?"

"Who said I was going down?"

Her follow up statement flows from her mouth like the raging waters of the River Nile, "since we're talking about biting," She hops off the treadmill, "I've been craving you since that night."

"yeah?"

"Yeah, so what do you think about that?" Just then, Quanny walks by with her eyes fixated on my lips. Prompted by her sudden presence, I think fast, "The treadmill is the best place to start, especially if your'e just getting back into the swing of things. Rona virus has made us all a little lazy."

"Got that right," Quanny seconds, "Get that heart rate up, right 'O'? Then balance it out. And where is your water bottle?" Quanny peeks to my left, then to my right as she walks over and wipes down the unattended treadmills nearby, "you're slipping today."

"Nah, I'm not slipping. I'm just –"

"Trippin," Quanny picks up my phone and hands it to me, "Must have dropped it when you hopped off the ride like you was a jack rabbit or something."

"gotta be moe careful, thanks sis"

"You're welcome. April, how's it going? Mr. Parks ain't ova here giving you no sweat, is he? Cause I'll make'em drop and give me fifty."

"Nah he's good."

Quanny is a handful, but she's cool. She's the one who helped me pick out Olivia's ring. Then she helped me hide it from her until I was ready to propose.

She even kept Olivia distracted while I set up the surprise proposal party. "Alright then," Quanny teases and walks away in a pimp stroll, "just let me know if we get some action up in hea."

"Ha ha," April clears her throat, "She's funny."

"More like she *looks* funny, ole '*bitch I'm a cow,*' lookin' ass."

"She was right about one thing though," April looks over her shoulder, "maybe I should call'er back."

"Quanny is never right about anything."

"I beg to differ."

"Why, what's up - talk to me ma."

"You trippin.'"

"How am I—" before I could finish my statement, I notice April's gaze at my lap. I follow her eyes, looking down at the tent of my pants, "excuse me." I turn to walk away.

"What, you can't get'em to calm down."

"Apparently not." I ease to the side and try my best to keep everything hidden between the length of my legs. Realizing I'd stopped directly in front of a man, I pause in embarrassment, staring blindly at a name tag that reads, 'Cliff'. Before Cliff could object to my presence I swivel around, stopping right in front of April.

"You need some help with that?" she asks. I could see from a distance that Quanny is approaching from the opposite direction. She hypes up the people she passes as she heads our way. At this point, I'm thinking of what to do or say. April stands there, stretching as she waits for me to respond, "you know..." she throws her leg upon the bar to her left, "I think it's getting harder, because people are watching."

"Huh?"

"You know what I mean," she switches legs and bends over, looking at me through her parted thighs, "Grab it. Control it. Stop worrying about whose watching."

"Uh ok."

"Sometimes you just gotta hop on and enjoy the ride." She nods towards the bike. Luckily my hand is already on the wall right next to it, so I grab the handlebar and hop on in one swift motion.

"Yeah, you're right, it feels good."

"Tastes even better."

"hmmm," I start slow, then increase the speed and look over at April just as she licks the sweat from her top lip. She stands about twelve feet away, but it seems like she's still so close. I could still smell her as though she's standing right next to me, and I can taste her as though she's right on the tip of my tongue.

She walks over to the ab cruncher, spreads her legs, and reaches up for the bar. From the distance, she gives me this deep, seductive stare. The way her cat sits so pronounced upon the seat makes my mouth water. I smile then bite my lip, she giggles and bites hers.

"Come on, let's turn it up!" Quanny claps and walks by, shouting at everyone she makes eye contact with, "Turn it up, let's get wet!" she yells to April when she passes her. April's lips push out words that I could see, but can't hear, *"I'm already wet."*

We both chuckle, and my dick grows two inches longer. It's almost like this woman has me right where she wants me, but does she even want me at all, or am I just tripping, again? Since she danced with me at the club, she's literally been on my mind day and night. In between home and work, there is April. When I'm in the shower cleansing my body, there she is, and somewhere amid my marriage - there is April.

I have tried with everything in me to hold on to the loyalty I promised Allen I would have for my wife, and not only for my wife but for Allen. I can't get over the thought that if it weren't for me, he'd still be here. If I had just stepped back and let them work their problems out like I promised, Olivia would have made sure she built him back up. I don't know about the AIDS part, but I know for sure that Olivia would have eventually gotten him together. That's the type of woman she is.

But see me, I'm not upgradable. I have built myself up to be on top of my game. Allen though, he needed that extra push from his woman, and when he knew that Olivia was gone for good, he fell hard and fast.

Now I don't want you to get the wrong idea about me; I have always been a stand-up guy, but everybody messes up sometimes. Whether you admit it or not, you've made a mess somewhere down the line because everybody; single, married, child or saint – everybody who is *anybody*, makes mistakes.

The joy of making someone happy is an everlasting accomplishment, a thrill that only a person good at heart will experience. But to make someone hurt? Well, the guilt from betrayal is a life sentence for someone like me. Even though Al overlooked the fact that I was marrying the love of his life, the truth remained that part of the friendship was a fraud, and I was the perpetrator.

Him agreeing to be one of the best men at my wedding, I guess that was something he had to do to prove to himself that he was strong enough to move on. He had told Michael that he wanted to prove to himself that he could take such a low blow from his brother and keep his cool, said he wanted to see if our friendship had any chance at being resuscitated.

Looking back, marrying Olivia was the biggest mistakes of my life. I can't even explain why I let it get this far. I just wanted to save her, and I knew that Al was destroying such a delicate, precious flower. Though in my defense, I had been raised that way – to protect black queens by any means necessary; I just never thought I'd have to kill my friendship to save a woman.

It doesn't even matter that I had thought for sure Allen was going to be leaving Olivia for Ze. I mean, that's what he had told me – said he had one foot out the door. So I thought the whole fiasco was fair game. I didn't plan to fall in love with her just as well as I didn't plan to fall *out* of love with her. *Shit,* everything happens for a reason, ya know?

I'll never forget those words Allen spoke during our last sit-down about the whole ordeal, *'Just don't hurt'er like I've done man, she deserves somebody better than me.'* He spoke those words with moist eyelids and a bowed head as he pumped his fist into his heart. My obligation to keep my word to Allen is what makes me shake my head at April when I see more words that I couldn't hear seep from her lips

"Can I be with you tonight?"

I stand, grab my towel then head for the weight room. All

types of thoughts crowd my head. Like, finding out that Olivia slept with Al behind my back just months before our wedding. I don't even know why it's still a factor in my mind, I charged it to the game. Olivia and I cried together that night and she agreed to have a DNA test once the baby is born, even though she claims she used a condom.

It's just strange that she got pregnant around the time we stopped having sex because we wanted to save something for our honeymoon. Damn, when I think about it, it's like, who can you trust? *Mind boggling,* but then again, I guess I'm looking for an excuse to cheat.

Allen would shift in his chamber if I were to hurt Olivia, especially since she's pregnant with child. In three months our marriage will have escalated from a family of two to a family of three. With our careers blooming, there is really no room in my life for an affair. I tell myself that while I stare at April and watch sweat drip down her neck as she steps into the weight room. She then stands over a pair of barbells and adjusts her zebra-print weightlifting gloves.

She moves almost in the same way she did at the Cougar's Den that night; in a sexual, yet sensual manner. I stand from afar and watch her through the mirror. Every now and then our eyes connect, and I give her my undivided attention while pretending to admire my physic through my reflection. When she looks my way again I see the words leave her lips, *"When can I see you again?"*

"tonight."

"What time?"

I hold up my ten fingers and stretch them apart as I grab the bar to the shoulder machine. April nods, then bends over and starts her squats by curling her arm, pulling the weights toward her shoulders with each bend.

I bet she can ride real good.

When I feel my face moving, I shake my head at myself. April must have read my lips because a slight grin grows across her face. I carry on with my routine, periodically glancing in April's direction as she moves through the gym perfecting her hourglass figure, and when I see her heading towards the sauna I decide it's time to wrap it up and head home. I walk over to the locker room to retrieve my belongings just as she double-backs and speeds toward her locker. After she opens it and grabs a towel, she walks past me then continues on her path, "The Cougar's Den, Top floor. See you at ten." She confirms as she switches past me and exits the locker room.

My good conscious jumps out the window, and every word I had spoken in effort to talk myself out of having an affair went into one ear, and flew out the other. You know a man is washed up when he can't even follow his own advice.

"Aye, Omar." a familiar voice calls out. I look around and notice the Dark skin, the bright colored clothes, and those long obnoxious ass nails. I throw my head back, "Sup Tracey."

"Mi si yuh keeping dat bady right." she compliments
"Yea, you know a brotha's gotta stay in shape. When you look good you feel good ya dig." I twist to the side and flex my muscles, ending in my superman pose. Tracey laughs aloud, "Holla at mi before yuh lef bredda."

"Alright sis." I confirm, never really hearing a word she said. On the way home I call Olivia to give her the story of Michael and I trying to locate Allen's long-lost family to inform them of his passing. *Functional rhetoric.* She bought the lie as nonchalantly as she would purchase deodorant from a drug store. I end the phone conversation just as I move through the front door, then dash for the shower. Within two minutes the shower curtains are sliding open, and Olivia is stepping inside.

I will always love the way she hums while she satisfies me with her mouth. The way she uses her vocal cords to stroke me with the back of her throat is amazing. Afterward she always challenges me, "name that tune." The rhythm of the sucking vibration always gives the song away.

Anytime, anyplace

Just as Olivia slurps my juices into her mouth and swallows, a vision of April enters my mind. I grip the shower rod and look down at my wife's bobbing head, but when she looks up to connect with my eyes - April's face appears.

∞∞∞

I pull up to valet at The Cougar's Den at nine forty-five PM. At nine fifty-six, a grey Mitsubishi pulls into the driveway and out walks the sex symbol of a goddess. She motions for me to follow her, and we make it to room one-twelve, seven minutes later.

Immediately upon entering, April begins to undress. The crazy thing about this chick is, as confident as she seems, she keeps avoiding eye-contact. She peels off her shirt, staring into the corner of the room as she bites her lip. I still can't figure her out, but something about the confidence she exudes changes my body chemistry, makes me forget everything I know about love, marriage, and loyalty.

She appears to be driven by some unknown force and whatever that force is, I can't deny it. No matter how hard I try, I just can't resist providing her with the undivided attention that she so obviously wants. I know some women like to take charge, so I let her.

Easing onto the bed, I sit back and watch as she peels off her clothes in a tranquilizing dance ritual, using my own tactics against me: Tease, then please. She walks up then leans into my ear and whispers, "There's something I want to give you." She takes hold of my hand and places it between her thighs, causing my fingers to grace her honey pot.

"You feel that" she moans, "So wet."

"Yeah," I sniff my fingers, "I like that."

When she positions herself upon my lap and straddles me, I bury my face between her perky breasts. She then slides her panties to the side and returns my fingers to her inner thigh. Overcome by her energy, I growl into her ear, "Who is this for?"

"You," she purrs as she starts to wind her hips, "taste it."

I hesitate, but only for a second. After mentally preparing myself for the challenge, I pull my hands from April's panties and sniff my fingers again, and the sweet smell of good pussy makes my lips curl. Now if you ask any man, they'd tell you there's nothing like that new pussy smell. April's new pussy smell is like no other. I can't put it together in my mind right now, but it reminds me of something. I savor her evocative scent, never realizing it would subsequently become my obsession.

When I lick her juices from my fingers, the tang that meets my tastes buds sends a rush of adrenaline running through me. I can't believe how sweet she tastes. My brain goes on an involuntary mission to match the taste to her smell, and my mouth starts to water. *she's got cheesecake in her panties'* I think to myself. Gradually I lose complete control.

"Wait, *Ape*.... Hold on."

My plea is ignored, she runs her fingertips along my collar bone, then glides them toward my belly button. *Hmmm, seductress. Passionate, and attentive to every single one of my zones.*

It's almost as if she's studied my body and she knows exactly how, where, and when to touch me. Void of instruction, she reaches into my pants, grabs my jewels, then she to massages a spot underneath. It catches me by such a surprise, that I squeeze my butt cheeks together and I suck in a gulp of air. I guess April finds my reaction to her discovery of a g-spot I never knew existed amusing, because she chuckles through a purr, then moans in my ear, "You like that?"

Now let's get one thing straight, I'm only squirming because the feeling coming alive at the tip of my penis is foreign, and It feels so good, my eyelids become moist. April takes my face in her hands as if she wants to kiss me, then she massages behind my ears.

My lips quiver in anticipation, but instead of putting her lips to mine she bites my earlobe and whispers, "I want you, *bad*." Her begging makes my wood stretch to lengths that it never has before, and I look down to see my sweatpants peeked to the height of Mount Everest.

The tingling trace of my spine is pleasurable and intense, a sensation that sends waves of euphoria rolling over my body. *What a rush*. With my balls controlled by my hormones – there's no turning back.

Usually I'm stronger than my erection but this time, that's not the case. The right inside of me keeps trying to fight its way out, but the wrong on top of me just feels so good. *Hold on, I'm a married man. I must fight the forces.* Grabbing April by her wrists, my mouth finally opens, "wait."

"what is it?" her moist lips tap my Adams apple, "what's wrong."

A trace of silk oozes from the tip of my penis as my erection stands its grounds and a flow of electricity travels from the base, to the tip and back. Maybe if I change the channels in my mind, my dick will go soft and I could just walk out of this hotel room with my morals intact.

"Please," She begs like a damsel in distress. Something about those pleading vocals make my anal opening twitch. April gazes to her left as she wraps her palm around my neck, "I want you deep inside me."

Now most people know that mental orgasms are so uncommon in a man, many might call it a myth. That is, until you're experiencing one like I am in this very moment. My

Psyche is torn between the push of a strong, sexual magnetism towards this woman, and the pull of my conscious. Exhausted from the tug-of-war, my hands pop out in front of me and gently ushers the horny woman off my lap, "I'm married." I remind her.

"so why are you here?

"I don't know."

April lowers herself to the floor while tugging my sweatpants towards my knees, "I'll tell you why," She looks up at me and smiles as my meaty sword pops out and greets her with enthusiasm, thumping ever-so-lightly against her nose, "He sent you."

In slow motion her tongue glides around the tip of my shaft. *flick, flick, slurp.* A few more flicks of her ambitious tongue and a deep dive down her slippery throat - My penis cocks back, then spit down her windpipe, and she opens her throat to welcome me, *GULP*

Two hours later, calm - An app Olivia installed on my phone to help me sleep and lessen the nightmares. The soothing binaural melody pulls me from the slumber April put me in. Some people call it a nap, but honestly it was some type of outer body experience. Mellow sounds of running water coming from my phone only adds to the Astral projection-like trance. Then a rude awakening; my phone starts to rattle and ease along the dresser.

Shit

I look over at the sleeping beauty to my left as I slide my finger across the screen, "Yo."

"Hello, Omar? Omar Olivia is at the hospital. we think she's having a miscarriage; she's been calling you for the past hour and she's freaking out."

Now I'm speeding to Cedars Sinai Hospital, cursing myself profusely. See, I'm not the kind of man who is absent when his wife needs him. I have always been there for my wife; I've *always* been a good man – my real ones can vouch for that.

'*What came over me?!*' is all I can think. Seventy-five miles per hour doesn't get me there fast enough. I arrive just as Olivia is being released. The second I squeeze through the double doors, Shay rushes over, "she lost the baby Omar, I'm so sorry."

My reality is void of the shock I should feel as I look over at Olivia and notice the subtle look of relief on her face. Everyone else fails to notice, but I know my wife. In the little time we'd grown close I have studied her like she was my college major. She's relieved.

"Come on baby, easy." I hold her arm as she lowers herself into the wheelchair. Shay and Tracey kiss her left and right cheek, respectively.

"Call ya later love," Shay says, and they head toward the exit. Following their trail, I wheel my wife to the passenger side of my car and help her in. Then I buckle her up and I place my hand on her knee, "You ok baby?"

"I am," she says as she takes a breath, "are *YOU?*"

"I'm ok, as long as you're alright."

"hmmm," Olivia stares out of the window and sucks her teeth, "so, where have you been?"

"Had a few loose ends to tie up at the office."

"umhp," I feel her side-eye me, "and you couldn't answer your phone?"

"Baby, I was in a meeting. I'm sorry I wasn't there when you needed me."

"That seems to be a new trend for us these days."

My heartbeat starts racing with that dose of reality and I lean back in my seat, hoping to not only calm my nerves, but to reassure my wife, "come on now, April."

"Huh?" Olivia's eyes veer towards me with the speed of a flying bullet. I take a gulp of breath and readjust myself in my seat, "*April,* we should finally have our honeymoon in *April*. I'll make it all up to you baby. You deserve a Vacay and besides, I owe you."

Chapter 17

April

The first thing I do every morning when I twist out of my sleep is reach over and grab my phone. I usually lay there for a few minutes, scrolling through social media until I find something funny to start my day. But today, the smell of sauteed onions and bell pepper calls for my attention, so I throw on my robe then I walk through the hallway. Intrigued by the sizzling sounds of perfection as I make it to the kitchen, I walk over to the counter and swipe a slice of bacon from the pan.

"Smells like heaven in here," I flop down in a chair, "what got you up early cooking *today?*"

Justin smacks her lips, "I guess I just woke up on the right side of the bed, girl. Besides, what better way to start the day than with a hearty breakfast?" I swear, her drama is always on full blast. I swivel in my seat and look at her sideways, "Do I smell homemade hash browns?"

"Yyeeeah girl. You better get it while the getting is good." One of the many things that Justin and I share is the love of food. Nothing floats my boat like a full course, home cooked meal. Justin, a well-respected and highly reputable culinary artist, is my favorite friend.

Somewhere between earning her master's degree and discovering her own identity, she realized that she and I also share the love for men. Justin came out of the closet when she was in her last year of college. I would always tease that the woman in Justin had taught her how to cook. Oh, and by the way; if it's not already clear - Justin's pronouns are 'she' and 'her'.

To this day, I've never met anyone who could cook as good as *her.* Justin slides a plate in front of me and it's filled it with the works: bacon, grits, country-style omelets, crispy hashbrowns glazed with a topping that she calls *butter de la crop* – and wheat toast. A tall glass of orange juice to wash it all down is in arms reach.

That first forkful hit the spot so good, I coud feel the joy stretch across my face right after I swallow, "you expecting company? you cooked so much."

"um, girl, I don't know. I was hoping your lil friend had finally come back with you and spent the night. He's like a star to me." I side-eye Justin as I slice the omelet with my fork," He's married, chances of him spending the night - slim to none." When I push the food pass my lips, the smooth texture of the gravy warms my tongue.

"Giiirrrl, please." Justin waves her hand through the air, "being married don't stop no man from cheating, or spending nights out. Trust me girl, I know."

A few moments of silence whisps by and the only thing that could be heard is the chewing, smacking and the click-clacking ritual of forks and plates clashing. But that type of silence is always too loud for Justin. Being the overly dramatic house-Queen she is, when she has something to say – she's going to say it. "Did you tell'em aunt flow didn't flow this month?"

I roll my eyes and put a twisted curl to the corner of my mouth, "Did you tell your *new* man he's wearing your *old man's* shoes?"

"Psst," she adds two more slices of bacon to her plate, then douses them with red rooster hot sauce, "I'll tell him *that,* when you tell Omar *YOUR* secret."

"Never gonna happen. He'll find out by fucking around and *finding* out."

"damn, so you not gonna even throw the bitch a hint?"

"He's ignored every hint thus far. I mean, we ran into Michael yesterday at the SunBucks on twelfth Ave. Even *he* kept saying I look familiar, he just can't put his finger on it. Like, *dummy*, we ran with the same clicks in high school – hint, hint."

Justin turns her seat all the way to face me. I know she wants some tea, but right now, my only focus is to devour her work of art. The way she added these fresh tomatoes and shredded goat cheese atop of the toast, *uhm mm*. Other than sunsets, the best rush I've experienced is always at the table with my roommate, my best friend. It's like an orgasm I not only could feel, but one that I could taste.

Justin's question floats around in my head for a few more seconds as I harass the omelet with my utensils, taking a swallow of orange juice just to make room in my throat for more. "Slow down," she laughs, "don't strangle yourself trying to get a taste of heaven."

"That's it, that's what you should name your restaurant – 'A Slice of Heaven' "

Justin doesn't care much about owning a restaurant, it's me who keeps pressing the issue. All Justin really wants is to be the whole package to the right man, whomever that turns out to be.

"I'm just saying, as good of a cook you are Justin, you really should. You could serve food from different cultures, and it will bring in lots of customers and revenue - *wink, wink*."

When I look over, I see Justin staring off into the corner, nodding his head. "You know," He says after a few seconds, "I always wanted to try an Asian guy. I heard they're passionate lovers. A restaurant could be my opportunity to draw in and taste many different flavors of men."

"Instead of the 'around-the-way' brothas you're used to catching," I add, "The kind of brothas who would go the extra mile to live the life of a straight man, but who deep inside are just as gay as you."

"Haha, yeah girl. but you sure know how to change a subject." she says with the snap of his fingers.

"I know how to change a lot of thangs."

Justin laughs out loud, "I wish you use those lame ass tactics when you're about to get the hell all up in MY business."

"You set it off by trying to get all up in mine, I just returned the favor."

"Chile, anyways."

"Yeah, *anyways*. But to answer your original question – yeah, he knows."

"Oooh girl, you didn't tell me all *that*! Wonder what he's going to tell his wife."

"As quiet at its kept – he's already got half of his wardrobe in *my* closet." I'll leave it at that. As I start over to the sink to wash out my dish, Justin feels to need to remind me of the time I woke up alone in a hotel room, after spending the night with Omar, "… so don't get too comfortable," she says, "a dog, is a *dog*."

"He left a note, his wife was rushed to the ER that night. He had to split."

"Well at least he left a note," Justin chuckles. This time her sarcasm gets under my skin. " Justin, have you forgotten? Everything is going as planned, don't start making me lose focus."

"Oooh," Justin sings with her palms upon her cheeks and her mouth wide open, "… where's my head? *April* is the Queen of bluff, the master of misfortune - How could I have ever forgotten about that?"

"Just know that I have it under control," I rage. In case you haven't figured it out yet, I'm trying to teach you how to play a player – and by the end of this game your mind will be blown. See, Omar is a research scientist for NASA. He's *paid* and I'm trying to GET paid. I'm so smooth with it that I'm not going to wrap him around my pinky finger, he's going to wrap *himself* around my finger while bending over to kiss my ass."

∞∞∞

As April finishes the dishes, she obsesses over her reflection in the stainless-steel spoon. Her eyebrow slightly arches and a warm sensation travels through her soul, " suicide note incoming." she chuckles wildly.

"you're so evil." Justin announces, "Now THERE'S the April I know." April glances over her right shoulder, then she glances over her left, "Where?"

She exits the kitchen without saying another word. Her thirst for his blood makes her insides tingle, and that feeling is aided by her drive to kill, steal - and destroy. By the end of it all, April would bring Omar down to a level that not even the devil himself could get under.

Chapter 18

Omar

People wake up with different feelings all the time. A person could be head over hills in love with you today, then fall back over that same hill and be out of love by tomorrow. Does that make them a bad person? No - it only makes them human. This is a concept I find it hard to wrap my head around, let alone trying to explain it to someone else. Someone who depends on me for love. The truth is, I *am* falling out of love with my wife, and I don't know what to do about it. Most of the time, I find myself pitying her under the pretense that I still care.

I often ask myself how a love that started out so strong, so powerful, could just fizzle out in the blink of an eye. How could the passion die so suddenly. I never wanted to change, I never wanted things to go this way. My heart breaks every time I try to pick up the nerve to say those words, '*I don't love you anymore.*'

I've practiced it in my head and my heart for months now but every time I part my lips, that same lie escapes. The expression on Olivia's face right now tells me I'm about to have to lie again.

"Omar, we need to talk," she says, greeting me with moist eyelashes the moment I step into our bedroom. She looks into my eyes, "Do you still love me?"

"Yes Olivia."

"Then why don't you say it anymore?"

"I luh you."

"That's it, I love you – just like that?" a tear slides down her cheek, "you use to smile when you told me that. You used to say my name, grab me in your arms and hold me close to your heart."

"Listen, Olivia – I love you baby. It's just that, things haven't been the same since Allen died, and I'm still having those nightmares every other night."

"The nightmares, they're back?"

"Yes. just last night I dreamed that he was chasing me with his head in his hands. Baby, I ran, and I ran – until I ended up in my grave. I Just fell right in. as soon as I hit the dirt, I woke up." As sad as it may sound, my nightmares have become my excuse to break loose – they're my escape from my wife. All I have to do is tell her I've had a nightmare, and she will automatically understand my disconnect from her. "Is that why you jumped up and ran into the restroom last night?" She asks as she wipes her eyes with the sleeve of her night gown.

"Yes," I lie again. The truth is that April had called. She was stranded in West Covina and needed me to wire her two-hundred and fifty dollars so she could have her car towed to the shop.

"oh baby," Olivia thrusts herself into my chest, and wraps her hands around my waist, "I've been so selfish, I'm sorry."

"it's not your fault," I slowly squeeze her back, "Look, I'm about to meet Michael so we can go over the details of our high school reunion. You gonna be ok until I get back?"

"Yes."

"Alright?" I kiss her forehead, "see you around ten."

Olivia steps back and glances at the new time-teller on our bedroom room wall, "ten O'clock *tonight*?"

"Yes, we're meeting up with some old classmates and going out for drinks after."

"Baby, today is Thanksgiving, I was hoping we could-"

"Put my food in the oven for me, I'll eat when I get back."

"Omar-"

"Listen, I'm not exactly in the holiday spirit. It's only been three months since Allen was killed. Really Olivia, I'm just not feeling it."

"Oh," Olivia hangs her head, and her voice softens, "okay." In the course of our relationship, I have opened up to my wife in the most intimate ways, ways I'd never opened up before. I have shared with her, my every fear, my every secret and my every waking nightmare. But the one thing I can't share with my wife is the fact that I'm having an affair. I don't know how to snatch her heart from her chest and squeeze the life out of it like that.

The biggest part of me hates myself for losing the battle that I'd fought against these feelings. Honestly, I want to be in love with her. I *want* to want her, but those feelings are just not there anymore.

As horrible as it may sound, I could barely stand it when she kisses me. It doesn't help that she's become so insecure with herself, that her body has visibly changed in form and well, it's a turn off. Her change so obvious, that even Michael notices it.

∞∞∞

"... seems to be her new swag; slumped over and vulnerable," Mike puts his car in drive, "and what's up with the red hair?"

"Red hair?"

"Yea bruh, red hair. It's been like that for like, two weeks now," he pulls into traffic while giving me the side-eye, "You haven't noticed?"

"Nah."

"She's been caking that makeup on too, and when have you

ever known her to wear makeup? It's almost like, she's trying to catch *someone's* attention." He nudges me and shakes his head, "You gotta do better man. This girl April, May, June – whatever the bitch's name is, she is taking you out of your element. Bro," He raises his voice, "THIS GIRL IS GOING TO DRAG YOU TO HELL."

"You don't even know her."

"And I don't want to, She's too perfect: perfect hair. perfect nails. perfect skin, perfect body – females like that, they have something to hide. They decorate themselves like royalty but those are the ones you have to watch. They don't give a rat's ass about other people." In attempt to downplay his observations, I clear my throat, "Um, Yeah."

"Uh, *yeah*."

Confession: I know Michael is right. Two weeks ago, I had come home to a candlelit dinner for two. Soft music played in the background and a relaxing foot massage was awaiting my arrival. The scene nearly took my breath away, made me feel bad about leaving work early to have dinner with April. I'd just dropped her off at home after a night of wining and dining.

On the way her house we'd cruised the highway, and I tried to open up to her, "bae, lately I've been thinking about Allen, my friend who I told you was murdered. I had a nightmare about him last night; He walked right up to me, put a gun to my head and told me to make a wish. Baby, I ---"

"Ugh," April huffed, "do we have to talk about that man, *again*?

"I, I just – It's getting the best of me."

"Yeah, it's getting the best of me too. It's so depressing. So, let's change the subject."

I shrugged my shoulders, "Alright baby, I'm sorry." Talking about the dead is one of April's boundaries. Before I could form my next thought, April took my dick out of my pants and started swallowing. It felt so good, I had to pull over at a turn out, and as soon as I exploded in her mouth we were back on the road. For some strange reason, she loves it when I say I'm sorry. I never understood it, but I've learned to just, enjoy the aftermath.

When I made it home that night, Olivia had the same sweet tooth, but my soldier couldn't stand up to her. I had already gotten everything I needed to make my night perfect and complete. The disappointed look on her face made my heart throb. I felt so sorry for her.

I softened the blow by telling her about the nightmare I had the night prior, where Allen was literally dragging me to hell. She responded by rubbing my back and suggesting I go see a grievance counselor. But of course, I refused that. Once she relaxed and ran me a bubble bath, I made a mental note to be more discrete about how I move around.

That night, I promised myself that I'd make sure not to raise an eyebrow, or to evoke another tear. I'm not sure how things in my life spun out of control so fast, but one thing I know is that my love for April has shifted things around in my head. Now back to my conversation with Michael. I shove my fist into his shoulder, "You're right, I gotta do better." Michael rubs his goatee, "*Do* better, *be* better bro."

∞∞∞

The tang of seared steak and fried green tomatoes punch me in the nose when I stumble into the house. Had I not just been fed like a King over at April's, I would jump right into my seat and pig out. But right now I can't stand the stench, I'm already, 'good food' wasted.

In my mouth, the aftertaste of turkey dressing with extra sauteed celery, cranberry sauce, baked mac and cheese, and collard greens dance along my tastebuds. The moment I step into the living room, Olivia's silhouette appears. "Hey baby," she says, rushing over to grab my arm and leading me into the dining room, "I know it's Thanksgiving, but I made your *favorite* dish."

She pulls out a chair and I sit down in it, scooting myself to table. Then I grab a fork. As soon as Olivia put the food in front of me, I start pigging out like I hadn't eaten in days. Ten minutes later, I'm stuffed like the Thanksgiving turkey April had slid in front of me only hours ago. So I wobble into the bedroom and lay back on the bed as I loosen my belt buckle and let out a huge sigh.

Olivia walks in my footsteps, and once she reaches the bed I roll my head in her direction, "whew baby, that was delish – I'm stuffed."

"Glad you liked it."

"I loved it. Come here, gimme kiss."

She slides into bed next to me, leans over and places her lips upon mine, leaving them there for a few drawn-out seconds before she finishes with her usual, '*mwah.*' Quietly I lay here, thinking about April. Among my thoughts is the realization that my morals are somewhere in a far-out place, way out of my reach.

Soon after that, another thought enters my mind, '*I'm going to be a daddy.*' I know it's messed up, but I always wanted a son. Olivia's last miscarriage threw me for a loop, I thought that we were in the clear after the one before that, but apparently her body still wasn't ready. With April though, I have another chance.

"Did I hit the spot or nah? I haven't seen you smile that hard in weeks."

"You know a good steak always does something to me. Oh, *and* I get a foot massage?"

"You're worth it daddy."

Daddy. Hearing that makes me feel like a superhero, and I can't wait to hear my baby's first words. *'daddy'* – I know that's what it's going to be.

"You're so tense. Try to breathe in deep and relax."

I do as my wife tells me, then I moan out in pleasure as she works out the kinks in my foot. grasping my heels with her palms, she circles her fingertips upon my ankles using the right amount of pressure as she inches toward my soles. Then she targets my toes, gently tugging on each one, and finally putting me to bed with the usual *snap, crackle, pop.*

Chapter 19

Omar

The sun hits my face with the force of a raging fire and when I peel my eyes open, I see Olivia dancing around the room, pulling back all the curtains. Something she hasn't done since forever. "Damn bae," I snatch the pillow from behind my head and use it to cover my face, "You couldn't give me five more minutes?"

"I could have, but you told me to wake you up early. So, what's a loyal wife to do?"

Sh, damn*!* I told April I would give her roommate a ride to work. I jump out of bed and prepare myself for the task ahead. Let me tell you about this guy, *Justin.* He's an asshole – and he's proud of it. The little twat is way too loud and flamboyant. I think of him as the worse person in the world, other than Satan himself.

He almost won me over at dinner last night, but just as I thought we could be friends he had the balls to ask me, *'So, is wifey gonna be godmother, or stepmother?'* that pissed me off so bad I almost reached over the table and ripped his eye lashes off his face.

But instead of doing that, I responded, "When are you going start minding your business?"

"Girl," he switched over to April then leaned toward her face, "you better get'em before I do." All of that because I had requested that April and I spent the last couple of minutes of our time there alone. I mean, I appreciate that he had cooked, but all I wanted was privacy so that I kiss up on my love. Really, that's the only reason I agreed to take him to work today – it's my way of saying thank you for the meal.

Justin tries to be more woman than any real woman could ever be, and that's the part that bothers me the most. He thinks he's the epitome of femininity, always switching, snapping his fingers, and rolling his long ass neck to make a point. Every other sentence he smacks his lips like he still has the aftertaste of cum on his dick suckers. On top of all that he has the nerve to be disrespectful.

Case-and-point: Last Thursday, April had called me asking for help to pay her part of the rent. I was ecstatic to run to her aid. I had been trying to find an excuse to see her again so when she called me, I jumped on the opportunity to be in her presence. I really wanted to feel her soft lips against mine.

I pulled into the driveway of the duplex and as soon as I exited my vehicle and started walking up, the door split open. There stood Justin with his arms folded across his chest. My anxious walk turned into a slow, reluctant creep. When I reached the porch, I spoke, "hey, where's April?"

"No hello?" he asked with his normal attitude as he placed his hands upon his hips. He stood there, guarding the front door like he was daring me to try to come inside. I glanced at his new hairdo; he had a fresh fade with a bow shaded in on the side.The sight of it made me chuckle, "Hello, Justin," I looked down at his red suede boots, "where's April?"

"Umph..." he huffed before he went in, closing the door behind him. I stood there with my hands in his pockets until April finally emerged from the house, a whole ten minutes later. When I saw her, I threw my hands up, "What took so long, you know I have a project to start."

"Sorry bae, I had to set Justin straight."

"Good luck on *that*." I laughed out loud.

"Not too much on my best friend." April says in a stern tone,

"Besides, she's going through some things right now."

"Oh, ok." I tried to catch a glimpse of her unique eye color before she committed her usual look-away. Her face was still glowing from the spa treatment I had paid for her and Justin to enjoy the day before.

It was April's treat to Justin, to reward him for finally making it on that one show called, 'Top Chef.' April told Justin that his spa treatment was complementary of me, but the little cum-guzzling bastard never even said thank you. And now here I am, being too nice to him again by agreeing to drive his ass to work. I run all this through my head as I shower and dress, then I peek in the room at my wife, "iight, Imma head out."

"Oooh, you're using Ebonics again, What gives?"

"I'm on my way out." I correct myself without responding to her inquiry. Before Olivia could pucker her lips, I twist out of sight, closing the door behind me. I then hop in my ride and dial April's number.

"Have him to be outside, I'm on my way."

"Ok daddy, can I have some money?"

"How much do you need?"

"Three-hundred dollars. I want to have my alternator fixed and hopefully get my nails done for our date tonight. *After* you give me a tour of NASA'S dormitory like you promised." And now I am here, handing April three crispy dollar bills just as Justin squeezes into my car and turns my radio on like he owns the bitch. This whole drive he keeps asking me to stop here, and stop there. Pulling out of a fancy flea market I finally ask, "What time do you clock in?" Justin checks his watch, "in one hour."

'I could've slept in', I think to myself as I hit the gas and take off at the green light.

∞ ∞ ∞

April gently tucks on my earlobes and presses her lips against mine, causing my penis to twitch. She stands close to me long enough so that no one else gets a glimpse of what's rightfully, *hers*. When my erection finally dies, she steps to the side, "So this is the lab, wow."

"yes, and this here rocket," I wave my hand toward the space shuttle, "I designed this one myself."

"Damn," she sings in amazement, "this is cool."

"Wait baby, hold on a second," I grab my stomach and ease to my knees, "*shit*." Watching April's purse lower then tap onto to the marble floor, my eyes become covered in a film of tears as she dips into view, "What's the matter?"

"I…. I'm not, I feel… I, *shit*."

Trying to force out a sentence to explain my agony proved to be an epic fail. I grab onto April's pant leg and groan, trying not to be so loud as to alarm my partners, who are congregating in a conference room nearby. In the next breath, a stream of digested lunch spray from my mouth and land on the floor before me, barely missing the brown Christian Louboutin boots I'd bought April for her birthday.

"Oh my God," she whispers, "Omar, are you ok?'

I try to ask her for a minute to pull myself together, but my mouth refills with vomit faster than I could take *another* breath. Then all of a sudden, the world around me starts spinning and I feel my hands tremble. This moment is way too much, and it feels like I could die.

"What did you do to me?"

"I got you pregnant," she chuckles, "it's just a little morning sickness. Come on babe, I got you." After a few moments of dry-heaving, I'm able to stumble to my feet. April cleans up the mess before anyone noticed. Needless to say, we cancel our date. I don't recall my drive home, but next thing I know, my wife is helping me into the tub.

∞∞∞

My lips meet Olivia's cheek with a careful tap. She doesn't budge, not even when I whisper in her ear, "You up?" *Perfect.* Now I can I call April. I need to do damage control – make sure I didn't gross her out to the point of not wanting to see me again. The second she says hello I hear Justin in the background.

"Girl didn't he just part from you like, two hours ago? *Damn!* I can't have no man calling me all day every day like he do. straight up bug-a-boo..." The sound of his throat opening and closing to release those words piss me off. So I slide my finger across the screen and end the damn call. April never puts him in his place, no matter how much I do to help them both out. She never says a word to him about his rude ass demeanor. Twenty minutes later I finally decide to answer my phone, "yeah,"

"*You* still up?"

"Obviously, I answered my phone, right?"

"What's up with that bitch in your tone?"

"What's up with that bitch in your background."

"Not too much on my best friend."

"Whatever April, I'll holla at you later."

Click

I don't know if it's the wheeziness I'm feeling, or the Pepto bismol that my wife forced down my throat, but I'm feeling some type of way and right now - I'm sick of April, literally. I think it's time I give her some space. I need to focus on frying bigger fish anyway.

Like, how I'm going to break the news to my wife. I just can't bring myself to tell her such a thing but somehow, I'm going to have to make that move. Olivia doesn't make this an easy task, being the perfect wife the way that she does.

"Omar," she calls out as she pulls the curtains open, allowing the sunlight to warm my skin, "baby, it's time to wake up. Are you feeling any better?

"Yeah," I groan, "a little"

"What happened to you last night?"

"Had too much to drink."

"What were you drinking, the devil's piss?"

"Something like that."

We laugh in unison and as soon as I sit up, Olivia sits the tray of food across my lap. Staring down at a ribeye steak topped with diced tomatoes, cilantro and a side of eggs sunny side up - my mouth instantly waters. "Why are you showing out?" I ask with a slight chuckle.

"Because baby, you have been working so hard, and you deserve it. You're so good to me." I don't understand why she insists on living this façade. Maybe she's trying to speak the lover she once had back into existence. I hang my head and sigh, "you didn't have to do this."

"I know but I did, so get over it."

"Thanks baby."

"You're welcome." Olivia turns to walk away but spins around with a second thought, "hey, who's Justin?"

"Huh?" I almost choke on my food.

"Yeah, Justin. The guy who drove you home last night. What's his story, is he alright?"

"Iono, why you ask that?" Olivia gives me the side eye, "because, he walked up to me and handed me your key. He seemed nice and all, but he walked away snapping his fingers and cursing at the wind." I take in a deep breath and produce a quick response before she could ask any follow up questions, "Remember Daisy from Dorsey? That's her brother. He's harmless and all, he's just a little gay."

"A *little* gay?" Olivia laughs, "well, tell him and whoever drove the car that trailed him here, that they need to get that raggedy ass engine fixed." The second Olivia pulls off in her car, I grab my phone and dial the right number.

"April?"

"Yeah?"

"Don't ever do that again. Like what were you thinking?"

"I was thinking you need to get home safe, you passed out in that parking lot!"

"Yeah well, that wasn't cool."

"Ok baby," her voice suddenly softens, "It won't happen again." Thirty minutes later I'm pulling up to April's house to drop off some money.

Before I exit my vehicle, I tap my neck with a few spots of Dior Sauvage cologne – that always makes her melt all over me, and I'm hoping for a quickie before I meet up with Michael for basketball. I know I can beat his score if I score with April first. Hesitantly I knock on the door, and that annoying as voice comes blasting from the opposite side.

"Who is it?" Before I could respond the door swings open, "I said who is it?!... See girl, that's what I hate about these *straight* men - they can't answer simple questions. Who is it?! who is it?! how hard is that to answer?!"

I take it this little bitch needs a pole up his ass. He turns his back to me, "April - girl your lil friend is at the door. You need to teach him some respect for when he comes to people's house!" He continues to bitch as he walks away. My tolerance for his gibberish allows me to overlook his attitude, but I don't know how much more I can take of this type of pussy.

In replacement of Justin's presence, a silhouette appears in the doorway, wearing high-rise cut-off jeans and a strapless Gucci shirt with the matching lace fashion gloves, which April had picked out during the shopping spree I surprised her with on our anniversary. I spent a total of five-thousand dollars just to show her how much she means to me. I mean, she'd told me that she deserves the finer things, and I believe her. I wink at her swag, "You look tasty."

"Thanks baby" she walks down the steps and greets me with a hug, "Did you get the bracelet I asked for?" I reach into my coat pocket, remove the twenty-four-carat diamond tennis bracelet from its box and snap in onto her wrist, "Have I *ever* let you down?"

"Daddy never disappoints." she winks then admires her sparkling arm. I let her stay lost in the bling for a few extra seconds, then I wave my hand toward my car, "The Polo Lounge awaits us."

April bounces on her toes, "Daddy," She wines, "we have to hit the Lakewood mall first, I saw a pair of Dooney and Bourkes that would go good with this outfit." she swivels her body and glances toward her hips, "They only cost three-hundred dollars."

"*Only* three hundred?" I chuckle, "you said that Gucci set would only cost Three hundred and it ended up costing five. You sure you need new boots?"

"What do you mean '*am I sure*,' so you're questioning my needs now?" She asks in a voice so soft and sweet that I cannot deny her. "Every time we make love you say I deserve the best of the best. Wait, are you just *fucking* me?"

I think about her question for a short second before I

respond, "I'm sorry baby. No - you do. You deserve the best. I'm just saying, I've spent over ten- thousand dollars on clothes in the last month. I could have put a downpayment on a new car for that price."

"Oh baby, oh baby!" She jumps on me and wraps her legs around my waist, "You're going to buy me a new car?!" I ease away from the door and walk towards my car, then I place April in the passenger seat. Avoiding her question, I tell her to buckle up, then I squeeze into the driver's side. The sound of her ranting and raving about the type of car she wants fades in and out of my auditory canals.

A new car isn't in my budget, but making April happy is *always* on my agenda. Seeing her happy is the best thing in the world to me. In some strange way I *need* her to need me – it's a sure way to keep her coming back. It's been almost a year since she's been in my life, and she's managed to leave a lasting impression upon my heart. So how can I turn her down? After seeing the joy on her face and hearing the rise in her voice as she talks about her new car, saying no to her would be so wrong in my eyes.

I glance at myself in the rear-view mirror, "yes baby, you're right - you would look good driving a lexus," April leans over and kisses my cheek, sending chills down my spine. The softness of her lips makes me slave to her every demand. So much so, that later that evening when we make it back to her house and she demands I stay the night, I comply.

Chapter 20

Olivia

The words, 'love should have bought your ass home last night,' hit different when you're married. If I could express that to my husband right now, I would. But here it is, nine o'clock in the morning and my calls are still going straight to his voicemail. I can literally feel my blood boiling, melting through my veins. I hate to put other people in the middle of my drama, but what other choice do I have? *Huh?* Only thing I could do at this point is call Michael. He picks up on the second ring, "Hello?"

"Hey Mike, is Omar with you?"

Michael pauses, as though he's deciding whether to lie for Omar again, or tell me the truth. I guess he learned from that time he told me Omar was being questioned by cops, that I would only ask to speak to my husband while racing my Equinox to the scene. Three whole seconds later he finally responds, "Uh, no – he's not here sis."

"Oh, we're doing *this* again I see."

"I wish I could tell you more. He didn't even show up to our game last night, or this morning."

"Oh really? You know what Mike, don't even worry about it."

Click

After all the counseling and praying just to keep this marriage on track – Omar is at his dog shit, *again.* I cannot believe this. Like seriously, where did the love go? I've just about had it up to the top of my head with feeling like an option in this man's life. Hoping to finally get through, I call his phone again, "hello?" he finally answers. The mellowed sound of his voice sends me into a rage and a flow of warmth streams down my legs, "Where are you?!"

"I'm at a friend's,"

"At a *friends*?!" I yell with tears dripping onto my night gown, "What friend?!"

"Remember James? Chloe's brother?"

"Yeah, what about'em?!"

"I ran into him after work, and we linked up. Sorry I didn't call you baby. We went bowling and I had too much to drink. I ended up falling asleep in my car. I'm on my way home now."

Call me crazy, but I know I just heard laughing in his background. I don't want to scare him away and make him reluctant to come home, so I'll play it cool. As soon as he gets here though, I have some choice words for his ass. A full three hours later here he comes blasting through the door with a bouquet of tulips in hand, "Baby," He says as soon as he reaches me, "I'm sorry."

"Your'e sorry, *again?*"

"Really baby, listen."

"What'chu gonna say this time?"

Omar looks up at the ceiling, "I juh, I'm just dealing with some heavy metal. I fell asleep at James's house for five minutes and that quick – Allen was trying to stop me from breathing. Baby he literally threw his fist down my throat and snatched my heart out through my mouth."

The gasp of breath that swirls into my mouth is unwelcoming. I blow it back out slowly as I look into my husband's eyes and allow him to finish his statement, "Had me shook up so bad, I tried to drive home. But once I made it to my car baby, I just fell asleep. I ain't gone lie, I was drunk. Listen, sometimes I lose my way – but I always make it back to you, don't

I?"

"You always make it back half the man you were when you left."

"Ouch." Omar grips at his heart, "that hurt."

"You can sleep your ass on the couch tonight."

"Got it." Omar agrees to that so easily it almost seems like that's where he'd rather be – in the living room on the couch, far away from me. Before he turns and heads for the bathroom, he says to me, "I've never seen you so upset."

"Yeah, I bet. It's almost like you've never seen me at all. I took this vacation from work for nothing, and you still haven't taken me on our honeymoon like you promised! it's going on a whole 'nother year!"

OUCH. Those words leaped from my voicebox with such force, my throat feels like it ripped open from the inside. I grip my neck with one hand and cover my mouth with the other. A few good coughs later, I'm sinking towards the floor. The space surrounding me starts to spin and vibrate. It takes my breath away. Omar springs from behind the bathroom door, runs through the hallway and rushes to my side, "baby, you ok?" he swipes my bangs from my face, "What happened."

"Nothing uhm fine."

"You don't look so good."

"*Now* you tell me."

"No, seriously Olivia," he takes my hand and guides me through the living room to the couch, "What's this?" he lifts my hair and motions toward my neck, "this looks like another allergic reaction."

In the blink of an eye, my distant husband is sealed within my space. As bad as I want to push him away, I've been craving his attention for so long that right now, I'll take any of him that I could get. I cover the spot with my hand and tell him,

"I know, it's been there for the last week, and it burns like hell. It's something going around at work, but supposedly - it isn't contagious."

"Don't worry," my husband assures me," I'll talk to Jess. He's got something for everything. That's a mad Scientist for ya." We laugh together, and it feels like he just made love to me right here. The way he touched me and the way he just kissed my forehead. There's something in his eyes that makes me feel like somehow, somewhere – the love is still there.

Chapter 21

Omar

"You're getting some *good* pussy tonight." April grabs the paperwork and rushes to the driver side door, "I shall call her, 'Pearl Jam.' Now, let's *jam*." She drops into the driver's seat and pushes the start button. The car purrs like a cat in heat, and April imitates the same. While dipping into the passenger's seat, I click on my seatbelt, "You happy now?" I ask, giving her the side eye.

"I'll be happier when daddy's home. The baby needs you, and I need you. You promised that by Christmas you would--"

"I know, I know. I just need more time."

"Damn baby how much more time you need?"

"More."

Looking straight ahead, I perform a mental calculation of the amount of money I've spent on this woman to make her happy: Two hundred fifty-five thousand dollars and counting - in less than a year. I'm not tripping though, because every dime spent is worth a lifetime with the woman of my dreams. And all of that is fine, until I remember I promised Michael I'd pick him up at the train station.

I curse aloud.

"What's wrong baby?" April looks over and places her hand on my knee. Staring past the glare of the window my eyes find some guy in a royal blue cardigan, following closely behind a woman racing toward a yellow Mercedes. *TYPICAL. Bet I can predict his future: He's getting some good pussy tonight.*

I finally tell April, "We need to go pick up Mike from the Union Station," I check my watch, "He's already there. Make a right up here at the next light."

"*We*?" April says with her face twisted and her eyes rolling in their sockets, "Why can't you pick him up in *your* car?"

"Because he's been there waiting for over an hour now. Let's go," I demand. April twists in her seat and smacks her lips, but she makes the turn at the light. About forty minutes later, we're pulling up to the pickup spot at the union station. I text Michael

pulling up in a two-tone pearl colored Lexus.

From the distance I see Michael rushing over, but when he spots April in the driver's seat, his stride slows from a light jog to a two-step walk. Once he makes it to the back passenger seat, he opens the door and drops in, "Thought you'd never come."

"You can't speak?" April says before Mike could even greet her. I see them lock eyes through the rearview mirror before Mike says, "Hey."

"Hey *April*." She tries to correct him. Michael repeats himself, "Hey."

April's head sits firmly upon her neck, bouncing between her shoulders with her thumb curved over her back, "See, this is why I don't like this guy."

Michael sways his head, "aww man, here we go with *this* again." As quickly as he had snapped his seatbelt on, he pushes the button and frees himself, "Look O, You can just let me off here. I can catch the bus. I'm not 'bout to do this today." I do my best to calm him, "Relax man, it's cool. Just be easy."

"Easy my ass bruh, I can't do it."

"I know you can't it - you can't keep a woman, you can't have kids. So what *can* you do?" April laughs aloud. Trying hard to keep this situation from escalating, I turn to April, "Yo, that was too much." A red light stops us from moving forward and April takes that opportunity to grab her phone.

Her fingers go to work at three taps per second. "too much? You think *that* was too much? Watch this." By this time, we're just four blocks from where she lives, so I already know what train of thought she's riding. It takes all of two minutes to pull into her driveway and the second she presses down on her horn my arc enemy pops out of the house. "What happened?" Justin rushes over, his hands waving through the air like he's fanning flies away.

"This basehead-looking trashbag *must* be smoking on cock," Mike barks, "I'll send those crooked ass teeth sliding down his throat." If you knew Mike like I know Mike, you'd know not to throw yourself in his way. Humble as he is, I've seen him beat niggas to a bloody pulp in just a few thrusts of his fist.

But I guess April thinks I'm going to save Justin from the ass-beating he was supposed to get the last time he stepped to Mike. This time, I'm not stopping *nothing*. Justin takes two more steps toward the car, prompting Michael to pop out of the back seat, "what's up?"

"what's up?" Justin removes the studs from his ears one by one, "what's happnin?'

Mid-way to his opponent, Michael plants his right foot forward and shifts his weight to his left foot. His left fist is blocking his chin, his right fist is ready to strike. He flinches at Justin, "You trying to move something or naw?"

Now I'm not saying that Justin doesn't have hands – I saw him knock out a big dude two weeks ago for calling him a fag. But he's not ready for Michael's swift beat. Still, he squares up, "what you trying to do?"

"Yo come on ya'll chill." I jump in front of Mike and try to stop the fight before it could get started. But April does not make that an easy task. She jumps out the car, "Nah babe, you always trying to save him. He been asking for this ass whooping."

"Ass whooping?" Michael asks with a chuckle. "dude if I smack you, you're going to sleep. " With my back turned to Justin and standing face to face with my best friend, I tell him straight up, "Yo, he ain't even worth it." Justin's breath warms the back of my neck, "Its *she* to you."

I almost turn around and sent his teeth trailing down his throat, but that would only make things worse. April would swear we're double-teaming him, and she'll jump right in the fight. I don't need that – she's carrying my baby and this time, nothing's going to stop me from being a dad. Right now, I'm looking right into Michael mouth, watching his words pour out, "you want to be a woman so bad, but you will never be that."

"And you wanna be relevant so bad, but you will never be *that*."

"You're talking too much," Michael squats into his boxing stance, "Move something, *bitch*."

The way Justin's body tenses up, it's clear Mike struck a nerve. Two words Justin hates being called: Bitch, and fag. The thug comes out of him so quick, it scares the ghost out of *me*. Suddenly I feel myself stumble to the side as Justin pushes me out of the way and charges towards Michael. The second he's in arm's reach, Mike's knuckles meet his chin with speed

Bink, bink

Boop, bop

Whoop

whop

tack

Justin spins into the worldwind of blows, then he swipes his thumb across his nose as he walks backward toward the house. When I turn toward his direction, he's looking dead into my eyes, "nigguh hit like a bitch,"

He looks at the red color dripping from his thumb, "It's cool though. I can't wait 'till you find out what's really up. The truth is gonna beat *your* ass better than I can beat up that bitch standing next to you." He turns, then walks up the steps and into the house without another word.

"What's he talking about?" I ask April

"Nah, bump all dat. He just put hands on my bestie?" I look at her with my face twisted as I stare at her moving lips, "He was bumping his gums for nothing though. Making all that noise for what?!" Justin's muffled voice comes blasting from inside of the house, "It's *she* to you, fuck boy."

"Your'e breathing all that smoke from behind the wall though!" Mike interjects, "Come out here and get'chu some mo." Mike walks towards the steps with his fists still balled into knots but April jumps in front of him, "You're not welcome in my house," she raises her hand, causing me to grab her arm and guide her toward the car, "Come on bae, chill,"

With her arm squirming free, she snatches her hand away from me then grips at her wrist, "get your lil friend then, cause he doing too much!" She throws the car keys into my hand, "Go on, and drop this little pussy off somewhere. get it outta my face."

She leaps up the steps and disappears behind the door in the same moment I dip into the driver's seat, "Come on Bro, let's go!"

Mike snatches his sweater over his head as he walks toward the car, "I knew that sissy ain't want no smoke. The hoe didn't bust a move – all talk, no walk. Remember, he said next time he saw me it was 'hands on sight," Mike sticks his head from the car window and amplifies his voice, "BUT YOU IN THERE JUST FLAPPING YOUR WRINKLED ASS PUSSY LIPS."

The engine purrs when I push the button on the steering wheel. "April ain't gonna let me live this down, she acts like she loves *him* more than she loves the baby in her stomach." As I pull off, Michael turns and looks at me with his face twisted, "Nigga, what *baby*?"

Chapter 22

Olivia

Exactly four weeks after Omar ran into a high school friend and forgot where home was, I sit here alone, again. I guess he thought dropping dick would pacify my broken heart, and it did for just that fifteen minutes he was inside me last night.

Lately he's like a ghost in our home. I can hear him, smell him – even feel him here. But I hardly ever see him. The breakdown of our marriage is making me weak and to make matters worse, I might be pregnant, *again.*

I can't even enjoy a cup of orange juice without throwing it up, and even the smell of my own husband makes me sick to my stomach. A few minutes ago, the lingering scent of Dior Sauvage cologne punched me in my nose. I followed the smell to the garage but by the time I open the door and stepped out there, he was already gone.

I peeked from the window just in time to see him turn the corner, and he was in the wind just like that. I rush to the bathroom, and the apple sauce I'd eaten a few minutes earlier expelled from my mouth and into the toilet. Omar doesn't even seem to care that he's hurting me this bad.

I hesitate calling him, but it seems my fingers have just taken on a life of their own. As I start my grounding countdown they aim for the numbers on my screen. Then the ringing begins.... *10*

"Hello?" Omar answers swiftly, "can I call you right back, I'm driving."

....9,8

"Honey, do you know what today is?"

"Uh, no – inform me."

7,6.... 5

"February 14th! We're supposed to be leaving out for our honeymoon!"

"Ah, *sh*. Look, I'll get back to you on that as soon as I can."

"As soon as you can..."

...4

sniffles

"...do you realize it's been going on two years since we got married?"

.....3 ....

"You've put our honeymoon off three times already! Omar," *.... 2*

"Tell me what's going on..."

..... 1

"Are you having an affair?!"

"Do we have to do this right now?"

"Yes!"

After about five seconds of silence he finally responds, "No, Olivia. I am not having an affair, Ok. Things are just – look, it's complicated. But I can't talk about it right now. I'm late for a convention in Mission Hills. I will have to call you back."

I fix my lips to stop him from hanging up but before I could utter another sound, an incoming call interrupts my thoughts. At the top of the screen, my Doctor's name stands out in neo-green. I swipe right, "Hello?"

"Hello Mrs. Parks. This is Doctor Stokes."

"Yes, I know. Hello Doctor."

"How are you feeling?"

"Very sick. A lot of morning sickness. But I'm ok."

"I see..."

I could hear pages turning from the other end of the phone, then he clears his throat and continues, "We took comprehensive lab tests, and the results are in. When are you available for a follow-up appointment so that we can review your results?"

"I can come in on Friday if you have an opening."

"Let me check," a few more pages flap through the air, "Can you come in at ten o'clock a.m, this is pretty urgent."

"uh, I sure can Doctor."

"Ok, I will have my receptionist to schedule you. You should get a confirmation email in about twenty minutes."

"Ok, see you Friday." I hang up the phone then walk back into my bedroom and sit on the bed. Just then my attention is called to the closet door. I notice it ajar, and when I walk over to push it close, some unknown force makes me pull the door open instead.

The emptiness I find inside nearly makes my heart explode. All the clothes and shoes on Omar's side are gone. Everything from his suits to his belts and even neck ties. In a sudden panic, I grab my phone and call him up. The second he answers I start demanding answers, "Omar, what's going on?!"

"What do you mean what's going on?"

"Why is your side of the closet empty?"

"Oh," He says after three seconds, "I'm giving my wardrobe a makeover. I'm taking everything to the cleaners after the convention." Looking at the missing items on the top shelf, I know something isn't right. My high hopes for our love makes me believe that I'm just over reacting. But then Tuesday rolls around.

Wednesday blows by.

Thursday comes to town

… and now here we are on Friday - still no Omar. My hands shake as I grip the wheel and drive to my Doctor's appointment. All I could think of is what I'm going to tell my family and friends.

With more than thirty minutes to spare, I stop by Michael's to see if he's heard anything from his friend, but his empty driveway lets me know he's not home, so I speed down Rodeo Drive and continue my route. The cool air brisking through my window caresses my skin, offering a sense of calm.

Fifteen minutes later, I'm in the waiting room sitting in this hard ass chair with my entire body aching beyond belief. This whole fiasco is taking a toll on me for sure. Just as I start dialing Michael's number, the door opens and a tall slim figure appears, "Olivia Parks," She calls out and motions for me to follow her. I stand up and trace her steps to the examination room.

"The Doctor will be with you in a second," she says with her eyes sinking towards the twist of her lips. She then pulled the door, closing herself out of view. Now I sit here going over my life in my head, trying to sort out my thoughts. Mid-reach to my singing phone the door swings open again and in walks Doctor Stokes, "Mrs. Parks," He says with his chin touching his chest, "I'm afraid I have some bad news."

Bad news? I just don't understand how things can get any worse than they have been, especially in this past week. Doctor Stokes removes his glasses, "Your pregnancy test was negative." I take in a deep breath and explain to the Doctor, "Given the way things have been going for me, that's *good* news."

"… that's not all."

"What else is there, Doc?"

"You were concerned about the recurring rashes and fevers, so we ran comprehensive blood work."

"And?"

"Mrs. Parks, you tested positive for HIV." On my way to the floor, a ball of air travels through my lungs, shoots to my throat and gets stuck there. I can't scream. I can't push a puff of air from my mouth. Seems like it takes forever for my knees to finally hit the ground. The Doctor watches me struggle with myself for a few moments, then he continues, "I'm sorry to inform you that your T-cell and CD4 counts are low, extremely low."

"Wha – what does that means?" My tone is so harsh, I can't even recognize my own voice. Doctor Stokes looks down at the paperwork in his hand, and his eyes stay there for the rest of his speech, "Well," he says, "You tested negative for your screenings in the year twenty-twenty, and twenty-twenty-one. We don't have any follow-ups here since then. But looking over your records I see that you were in the emergency room last year?

"Yes," I cough out the words, "I had a miscarriage."

"Ah, I see," The Doctor places the clip board near the sink and turns toward me, "what this means, judging by your cell count, is that the virus is fairly new. You've had HIV for at least six months, and for reasons we can't quite explain, the disease is rapidly progressing into AIDS." Those words turn my world black, and I before I could take another breath, my face hits the cold marble tile beneath me.

Chapter 23

April

My best friend Justin, she's got bars for days. That's something I failed to mention about her, and I always forget that because her skills don't really show unless she's in the mood. Like a few minutes ago after running into the duo he can't stand. Their faces set her off and she fired'em up with passion. In her defense, the bitch that fell victim to her rhymes should have been minding her business.

Instead, she looked dead in my face as she walked up to Omar, "Where's Olivia?" She questioned. When Omar tried to walk away pulling me along by my hand, this hoe followed, and her unwanted presence pissed Justin off. She and Omar are finally making amends and Omar wanted to commemorate their bond by treating Justin to the cheesecake factory. When Justin realized our steps had slowed, she turned around and snapped, "Damn, can ya'll hurry up, I'm trying to push this cake down my throat already."

"I see that's not all you're trying to push down ya throat." The tramp said with a loud chuckle. Justin turned around, realizing the tag-alongs were still in tow, "Honey look," she said, "I ain't the one, *or* the two. You might wanna slow yo roll lil boo."

"I ain't gotta slow nothing"

"Shay!" her friend calls out to her, "come'on gyal, we nuh do dis now. Yuh kno mi wuk here." See I know both these bitches from way back when, one better than the other. Shay has always been the in-your-face type of female and Tracey – well she's just an all-out nightmare on wheels.

They both look at me with twisted faces – but neither of them seem to recognize me. One thing I've always hated about this bitch Shay, is that she's relentless in her annoying ass ways. Instead of just walking away, she repeats herself, this time swinging her body ahead of Omar and stopping directly in his face, "Where's Olivia?" She asked with her finger pointed at his nose.

"Bitch!" Justin had Blurted out, "Where's your bizness? Where is your fitness? You walking 'round like a fat ass clown," she looked at Tracey, waved her hand in the air then looked back and Shay, "Bitch you need to check yo friend list."

Omar and I couldn't help but to burst out laughing, looking at shay dressed in a pair of overhauls, a bright red plaid shirt that she was bursting out of, and face full of exaggerated make up. Her head is adorned with a wavy blue wig and then she has the nerve to be wearing the clown suit like, *'I slay'*.

"Bitch," Shay says after she looks over herself, "I'll knock your face off." Justin laughs hard, "hoe these ain't the problems you want. Bad-body-built ass bastard. Bitch look," she points and laughs, "Looks like yo whole body is twisted on backwards."

By then a crowd had gathered, and they were looking for some action. But Tracey thrusts herself in front of Shay, and now she's walking toward her. As Shay backs out of sight, she screams aloud, "I'll see yo tramp ass again."

"Go now an go quietly before yuh start a show." Tracey demands. They're almost out of the door when Justin gets her last words in, which thrills the crowd. With her arms wailing and her fingers rhythmically pointing one at a time, Justin yells, "Yeah ho, go quietly back home to yo momma," she turns around and throws her little booty in a circle, "bitches mad 'cause they getting all those *periods* but no *commas*. Tweakin' ass bitch, clout-seekin' ass bitch. Every month got'cho twat leakin' ass *biotch*!

Laughter waves through the small area and as soon as

the door closes behind Tracey, we follow our waitress to our table and peel open the menus. Now we sit in silence, and I'm wondering who's going to break the ice. It's no surprise to me that Justin parts her lips first, "Damn, she screwed up the whole vibe," Her eyes scroll down the list of entrees as her neck swerves, "I wanted to mush'er in her weird ass face."

"Yeah, I know. It's like they pop up out of nowhere. Babe," I look at Omar, "You think they're following us?"

"Most definitely they are," he responds while staring down at the choices of food like his eyes are too heavy to pull up, "Olivia has been calling and calling. I did block her number, now all of a sudden, *this.*"

"Well," Justin says, "I'm putting a tint on my bedroom window next week. I feel like dem hoes be watching me, peeking through space." I guess Omar found the strength in his eyes, because he finally looks up at me, "huhm," his eyes falls back to the menu, "next week huh?"

"Yeah, next week. Or the week after that. I don't know but soon." Justin looks up at the approaching waitress, "I'll have the almond-crusted salmon salad and the Godiva chocolate brownie sundae. I'll take those at the same time, *together.*"

Omar orders his usual orange chicken and white rice, and I get the sweet corn tamale cakes with a side of hot spinach cheese and dip, and of course my favorite - strawberry cream cheese cake. We spend about thirty minutes silently enjoying our meals, then Omar calls for the bill. Before we lift from our seats, he places a crisp hundred-dollar bill upon the table, then he starts walking out of the building with me on his heels, and Justin on mine.

∞∞∞

We pull up to the house, and as soon as Justin steps from the back seat of the car and closes the door, I hear the locks drop. Justin turns around and throws her hands up, watching the car back out. Holding eye contact with her, I shrug my shoulders as Omar drives off.

"What's going on?" I ask. My question stays void of an answer for the entire drive. After speeding past about five miles of colorful boutiques, designers stores and palm trees, Omar turns right on Wilshire BLVD, makes a left on South Camden Drive, a right onto West Pico BLVD, then he makes another left onto Gateway BLVD. My guess is that we're headed to Venice Beach. Looking left, then right, I finally ask, "Is this a set up?" Omar remains quiet. All I could hear is the sound of air entering through his mouth and leaving through his nostrils.

Okay - now, I'm uncomfortable. I know that Michael and Omar meet three times a week to play basketball in the morning, and today is Thursday – the day they usually ball at night. I look over my shoulder just as Omar makes the right onto Rose Ave and slides into an empty parking space. Staring blankly ahead, he says to me, "This might be the end of our road."

"What, why baby?" I turn to face him, "Listen, I know---"

"April, stop. Just stop it right now."

"Omar..."

"Please," he slightly rocks, crunching his fingers into fists, "Stop!" Omar faces me, his forehead wrinkled to the point his eyebrows are nearly touching, "You told me that when I move *in*, Justin was moving *out*," He slaps the back of his fingers into his palm, "It's been two months, and he's still there!"

"I know baby, but look... the place she was going to rent, well – they gave it to somebody else, and..."

"Whose problem is that? Our son will be here soon, and I don't want him growing up around no fa-!"

"Come on Omar," I rub my stomach with one hand, and place

my other hand on my fiancée's shoulder, "I can't just put her out on the streets."

"*HIM!*"

"I'm sorry baby, *him*. I, I can't just put him out on the streets. He's my best friend." Omar thinks for a second, staring forward and never blinking. Two seconds later he restarts the engine, "I tell you what," he looks over his shoulder and simultaneously puts the car in reverse, "*I'll* put him out for you."

"No baby, wait…"

"There is no more, '*wait*' here April," He puts the car back in drive, slides forward a few inches, and now the car, once again, is in park, "it's either him, or it's me!"

He must be forgetting that I don't take kindly to demands, especially from *him*. Nobody tells me what to do, I run my own program and call my own shots. After I take in a deep breath, I slowly push it back out, "Ok."

Staring at the colony of seagulls as they glide through the wind then meet in the sand ahead of us, my lips finally twitch, "You can go."

"Me?!"

"Yeah, *YOU*."

"I know *you* lying." Omar chuckles and throws his neck back onto the headrest, "Your'e cappin' right now."

"You act like you don't have the money to get us another place."

"*Us?*" Omar laughs, "*Another* place?"

"Yeah, you got the money. If you want us to be together so bad, then instead of you moving in with me, how 'bout you get us our own place. You know Justin is still struggling to pay off his student loans. You said you would help him pay that off so he would qualify for his own apartment, but you ain't even came through like you said you would."

"I paid over half of it off already."

"Well, what about the remaining balance? Creditors don't respect half-payments, Omar. You want him out so bad, help him get out. Either that, or you get us a home of our own and he can keep that place while he pays off his debt. Then me, you and the baby can live happily ever after."

I grab Omar's hand to put it on my stomach, but he pulls back and grips the steering wheel. That was *his* bad. *His* lost chance. From my peripheral view, I see him shake his head, "this is getting ridiculous, I should have stayed with my wife."

"Then why *don't* you go back to her, and take this baby with you?" I push out a tear and a sniffle, "You never really wanted to be with me anyway."

"Here you go with this blame-shifting again," Omar huffs, "You know what, I just *might* do that." We go back and forth for another half-hour, then Omar starts the car, backs out and heads to my place. With his chest, he says to me, "I'm taking pearl jam with me."

"No you're not!"

"Yes, I am! My wife would love to drive in that."

"Only problem is, the car is in *MY* name. so, your wife is going to have to keep driving that tin-can Equinox."

I clap my hands, throw my head back and laugh. Omar must have been thinking about this for a while. He laughs in return and says, "You know damn well you can't pay that car note off with your call-center ass job. So," He rubs his waves, "like I said, *Pearl Jam* is coming with *me.* and you can hand me back that black card too!"

"I ain't handing nothing over!"

"Look at you April, you can never even look me in the eyes - that's how I *know* you're full of it."

"Full of what?"

"Shit!"

Before I could breathe in a gulp of breath, my sweater comes off over my head and I toss it to my feet. Only thing I know right now is that *this* is it. It's time to finally break'em. He just reignited the flame to the bomb that started this war between he and I, so let's *go*.

What he doesn't know is that I never really needed his money, I just wanted to spend it up. Omar has been nothing more than a meal for me to devour, and it's about time for me to swallow. And one thing for sure – when I go off, I'm going out with a *bang!*

Chapter 24

Michael

The word *'Stupid'* has never stood out to me as much as it does right now, stretched out in bold letters across my brother's forehead. The light fizzing on the tip of this Montecristo only illuminates the proverbial sign. I sit back and take a puff, looking at Omar with my eyes squinted. Finally, I ask, "bro, when you do all *that?*"

"About two, three months ago," Omar huffs, "Just packed up all of my things and left." I can't believe what I'm hearing. My body must be reacting to this charge of dirty energy because I feel myself sink deeper into my chair, and my right foot slides forward, "You left, and went to *that* bitch?"

"Uh, yeah"

"Ok so now what? You want me to soften the blow by telling you everything is going to be ok? I told you the moment I laid eyes on that trick that the hoe was trouble. Now you've gotten yourself stuck in an *entanglement,* and you want my help to pull you out of it?"

"I need you man."

"No, you need psychotherapy," I reach over and twist my cigar into the bottom of the ashtray near the fountain of swimming fish, "*you* made the bed, *you* lay in it – stupid ass nigga."

"I know man, look. All I want is to talk to her. But, but – she's disappeared. I went to the house and waited on her for three days, and she never came back home," Omar hangs his head and interlocks his fingers onto the back of his neck, "I know I've been out of sight, and out of touch but—"

"I haven't heard from you since that play at that bitches house. That witch 'uhn had you under her spell like *that* fool?"

"It ain't even like that."

"How the hell you can't find your wife then?"

"Man look," Omar stands up and glances around the patio, "I wouldn't have come here if I thought you, of all people, who react like this. What happened to being a brother?"

This fool didn't just say that to me. I guess he forgot about how heavy that wedding ring on his finger *was*. At this point I'm just as done with the conversation as he is, so I stand up and pour the last sip of D'usse down my throat, and I look him square in the eyes

"I tell you what," I pinch my leather fedora hat up from the table and place it back on my head, "Since you like to disappear and then re-ah-fucking-peer, why don't you be a genie. Go squeeze your ass into that urn with Allen." Looking at my brown Stacy Adams loafers I shake my head, then I look up at him from the corner of my eye, "Maybe *he* can tell you." No further words are needed; I slide my hands into my pockets and walk towards the back exit, and I look over my shoulder to see Omar heading towards the front.

∞ ∞ ∞

I need another shower. That conversation with Omar got me so heated, I need to cool off. It feels like he spit his grime all over me. I'm disgusted beyond belief. I start the shower and let the water warm up as I dial Olivia's number. No answer.

Three times, my calls go straight to voicemail. Before I step into the shower, I try one last time. Following Olivia's prompt, I speak into my phone, *"Hey sis, I'm sorry I haven't been in touch.*

Things have been hectic since I got back in town. I haven't talked much to 'O' either, but I want to come by there and chill with ya'll before I take my next flight. Call me back when you get this message."

The guilt I feel right now is bad, *real* bad. I'd been avoiding sis *and* Omar for months now because I didn't want to be smiling in her face knowing Omar was creeping around with that weird looking bitch. and then apparently, there's a *baby.* I never thought he'd leave her though - I mean, he did talk about it a time or two, but I always thought that once he got through the mourning Allen stages, that his love for her would regenerate. But I guess that didn't happen.

I spend almost an hour in the shower, then I lotion up and dress. For some reason, I still feel full of dirt. I can't shake the feeling of being covered in it. The next hour consists of me deep cleaning my house - I mean dusting, mopping and decluttering all my cabinets.

Still, I feel filthy. I *see* filth. Everywhere I look, there it is. Without even thinking twice I grab my car keys and dash out the door. On the way to my car, I almost run right into my favorite trio; Tonia, Unique and Star – the triplets from, *'around the way.'*

"Sorry ladies," I touch Star's shoulder as I ease past, "kinda in a rush."

"It's ok, you can run into me anytime." Unique says with a giggle. Tonia heads toward my side-gate, "We're just here for the avocados," she winks as she looks over her shoulder, "I'm making fresh guacamole tonight, and Mike – Thank you for being so generous."

"You're welcome," I swing open the driver's side door, "Grab as many as you need." I drop into the seat and look from the passenger side window to see the girls following in Tonia's footsteps, "No strip show today?" Unique shouts from the distance, "I'm pressed." She grabs a bill from her pocket and waves it, fanning a wayward bumble bee away. I shake my head as I start the engine and pull off, then I head down the block, turning left onto La Cienega Boulevard.

At thirty-five miles per hour, I hit enough corners until I find myself driving passing the line of palm trees on Carmelita Way. Then I make a quick left, quick right and boom - I'm at Omar's house. Olivia's car is in the drive way with its tires surrounded by leaves, dust and debris. Something ain't right.

I grab my phone and call Omar, "Yo, I'm here in front of your house and the place looks abandoned."

"That's what I was telling you."

"bruh, the grass is overgrown, and the yard is filled with leaves and garbage. looks like Olivia's car hasn't moved in ages. I'm walking up to the door now." After a series of knocks and yells but no answer, Omar says, "I told you she ain't been home. I don't know *where* she is." I could hear the panic in his voice become condensed onto the back of his throat. Then his voice trembles, "Bro, we've got to find her."

"You're right man," I look both ways and head back to my car, "you're right. Meet me at –" Before I could finish my instruction, a car pulls up and a group of Olivia's friends pop out simultaneously. Veering their way I yell, "Aye ya'll, what's up?"

"Who's that?" Omar asks.

"it's Champagne, Shay and Mo."

"Mike," Shay runs up and wraps her arms around my neck so tight, it feels like with just a little more squeeze, she'd decapitate me, "Oh my gosh, it's been so long since I've seen you. How you been friend?"

"I'm good," I squeeze her back softly before I release her and ask, "Anyone heard from Olivia?" the girls look around at each other for a few seconds, their faces twisted and their mouths nearly hitting the floor.

"You haven't heard?" Champagne asks with her eyes wide open.

"Heard what?"

Omar's voice comes through the phone, "what's going on? Ya'll stay there, I'm on my way." The screen on my phone flashes, then goes black. I look back at the girls, "heard what?" I repeat with Omar's question now attached to my inquiry, "What's going on?'

"Michael," Shay's voice softens, "Olivia is in a mental institution."

"What, why?"

"She had a psychotic melt down. We're just grabbing her some more clothes."

"Shit."

"Omar left her." Mo announces.

"I just found that out. I swear, I didn't know. Omar just told me a few hours ago. I understand she'd take it hard, but –" Shay touches my hand, "Micheal, he left her, sick."

"Sick – sick." Mo reiterates. I look back and forth between Shay and Mo, awaiting elaboration. At first there was none, but then Champagne walks up from behind, places her hands on the back of my shoulders and whispers in my ear, "Michael, Olivia has HIV."

I sank to my knees just as Omar pulls up in that two-tone pearl-colored Lexus I hate. He rushes over to our huddle-puddle, "what's up, what's happening?" I could feel his eyes burn a hole through the top of my head, "Somebody tell me something!" He demands.

"Olivia has been trying to reach you," Shay's eyebrows arch, and her voice thickens, "She's been in the Psychiatric ward of Ronald Regan Medical center for months, thanks to *you*." Omar slaps his palms onto his forehead, "Shay, this is not the time for your dramatic shit, ok?!" he looks at me, "Mike, can you drive me there?"

"Yeah man, let's go," heading towards my driver's door I look over my shoulders to see the trio standing there, resembling the *'see no evil, hear no evil, speak no evil,'* monkeys as they watch me start my engine and drive off. For the first few seconds of the ride there is hardly any sound. *Should I tell him?* No, I can't bring myself to do that.

All I can think about right now is that bitch April, and the many times I warned Omar that she was nothing but trouble. The silence is broken by Omar's ringing phone. He answers it swiftly, *"What* April?!"

A muffled voice comes through from the other end. It seems the slut is giving Omar demands to which he replies, "I ain't giving yo ass nothing."

A few more seconds of silence, then he says, "What 'chu talking about?" he looks at me with his face frowned, "hold on Mike, pull over." I put on my right signal, then clear the lane and swerve into Ladera park. The second I pull over and turn off the engine, Omar pops out the car.

After I free myself from the seat belt I step out, walking over to the passenger's side where I witness Omar screaming into his phone, "Pull up then, bitch! Since you right here," He starts pacing back and forth, "that's your problem," he yells, "you never put that lil bitch in his place."

The sound of tires screeching to a halt calls my attention to the space behind me. I spin around to see the driver and passenger doors of a grey Mitsubishi swing open at the same time, and out walks this crooked ass bitch and her musty lil side-kick, "what's that?" April says as she heads our way, "You popping yo shit Omar?!"

With her neck zig-zagging and her fingers pointing, she screams, "you got me driving this raggedy piece of junk, just because I wouldn't put my best friend out on the street like a dog?!" She stops in her tracks and continues, "You ain't right. You don't even care about this baby." She rubs her belly and spins around, screaming amongst the trees above, "that's alright, cause child-support, so we gone be good!"

"Mike, I'm about to beat this bitch up."

"You can't hit no woman bro."

"I'm not talking about her, I'm talking about the bitch walking in her footsteps." Just then I notice Justin walking up behind April. He steps up and slides to her side, then opens his dick flappers, "it ain't nothing but space and opportunity out here – what's up?!"

"What's up?" Omar leaps forward, "I'm with all the smoke today." He makes it about twenty feet to Justin before April thrusts herself in front of him, "You ain't gonna touch my bestie, bitch." Omar spits on the ground, *"Bitch?...* I ain't neva been a bitch!"

"Little do you know," Justin laughs out loud, "you've *always* been a bitch." Omar reaches over April and points his finger in Justin's face, "You better get this lil fruit loop" he says to April, "Before I fuck'em up!"

Justin points back from the distance as he takes a step backward, "you *been* fucked up." Something about the way this is playing doesn't seem right. One thing I learned from Omar is how to read people – he's always been so good at it that he inadvertently taught me the ropes. But right now, he's too focused on his target to pay attention.

"Yo, I told ya'll to stop following me," he shifts his weight from his left leg to his right, "I'm two seconds away from getting sick on you bitches." He flinches, but I rush over and tug him away, "come on man, it ain't worth it. *They,* ain't worth it."

"Nah, you the one ain't worth it," April says, her voice plummeting from one octave to another, "talking about, *'two seconds away from getting sick.'* Bitch, according to my calculations – you *have* arrived. Now tap dance on *that.*" April flaps her feet against the concrete in rhythm and twirls into a three-sixty, throwing her lace-covered hands over her head wildly. Once she reconnects with Omar's eyes, she says to him, "copy that?"

This cold, conniving *bitch*! She had been planning this all along. "Roger that," Justin concurs. I cover my mouth with my palm, trapping the rest of the draining air I have left within my cheeks as to avoid losing further wind, "Omar," I tug at his elbow, "we need to talk."

"Nah son, I'm done talking yo. Now I want action. They wanna fuck with me after they spend up my money, help me lose my wife, and damn near my career. And then this bitch, wanna talk about some fucking child support."

In an instant, Omar's sanity becomes a boiling pot of hatred. I haven't seen him this pissed off in years.

"My wife is laid up in a mental ward, and I'm here wasting my time with yo trifling ass."

"Not too much on my best friend," Justin snaps his fingers, "hold tight lil boy."

"April And you still letting this loose-booty bitch disrespect me, after all I've done for you."

"Aww, '*After all I've done for you.*' You really sound like a bitch. You a stupid ass, nothin' ass nigga, I swear."

"How 'bout I really be a nothing ass nigga and let you raise that baby by yourself, You prepared to be a single mother, *bitch*?!" I literally saw those words flip from Omar's mouth. With that threat, April and Justin slap hands then burst out laughing.

"Do you believe in magic?" April asks rubbing her belly, "Now you see it," she snatches the silicon bump from underneath her shirt, "*now* you don't."

"Ha ha," Justin laughs, "*What* baby?"

"Oh, I forgot to tell yo dumb ass – I *can't* get pregnant," she looks at Justin, "Best friend, what today is?"

Justin cackles, "April first."

"Your bad." April says to Omar, her voice changing tone with every word she speaks. Sounds like she must have went through some type of metamorphosis overnight, or something.

"...So there - *trick*." Omar flinches towards her again but look, no matter how bad this situation is, she's still a woman and I don't want my brother going to jail for beating this bitch's ass.

I pull him back, "Come on, let's go." His strength fails him when he tries to squirm free, then a tear slides down his cheek, "I gave up everything for you. Everything – my wife, my *life*. Bitch," he spat on the ground again, "I gave you my whole soul yuh hurd me?"

I study April viciously, and pieces of this puzzle starts coming together one by one. The post Allen had made on FakeBook right before he died comes to mind, '*I can't wait for everyone to meet my new bitch.*' Is what he had said in his rant.

But hell, I can't tell if he was talking about Justin, or April because right now, they both seem to be gunning for Omar's throat, and it's clear that they both are bitches. Then, something Justin once said replays in my head, '*the truth is going to beat you up better than I can beat up that bitch standing next to you.*'

The blurry picture I see in my mind becomes clearer by the second. I look at Omar's sweating forehead, then I sway my head to look at Justin. But my eyes are forcing me to focus on April. I turn to look at her and in that same moment, she snatches off her glove and starts tugging at her sleeve.

My eyes blink uncontrollably as my brain tries to see the picture for what it is. The D'usse I had earlier must just now be kicking in, cause I'm *tripping*, tripping.

This can't be right.

My peripheral vision shows me a glimpse of Omar's out of control demeanor, and the sound of his heavy breathing makes it hard for me to make sense of what's unfolding right before my eyes.

I look at him, then back to April. That's when I notice her scratching her hand so hard, that a spot on her wrist turns from cocoa brown, to a dark, protruding purple. My heart starts racing toward my stomach, and my eyes burst wide open. I grip Omar's forearm and try to inform him, "Sc--!"

"Here," Justin tosses a few single dollar bills at him, "maybe you can use this to buy a clue."

"Nah, I'm straight." Omar says while taking in deep breaths and blowing them out in a whistle.

"You sure," Justin asks with a wicked laugh, "You sure you straight."

By now, Omar is pacing the sidewalk, gawking at April as she drops into the passenger seat of the car. Her shaking shoulders tells me that she's still digging into her skin, and as Justin spews hateful words towards Omar's ears, I try again in my attempt to inform my brother.

"Scuh---" I manage to choke out in between their verbal sparring, "Schaah!"

"I thought you wanted all the smoke," Omar says as Justin backs away and heads toward the driver side door.

"Nah, you already *burned out*. Tuh."

"I swear if I didn't have everything to lose, I'd choke the bitch outta you right now," Omar's words are fugitive to his locked jaw and his clenched teeth, "Fucking prick."

I'm still trying with all my might to push out what Omar needs to hear, but it feels like the words are stuck to the back of my throat. *"Schu!"* I cough, looking into the face of death and watching it scratch the truth to light.

"You ain't gone do nothing." Justin laughs

"Scuh!"

"Yo you mad disrespectful."

"and you're just mad cause I was all in yer bag, while you was always sad, like another lil bitch on ya rag!"

"Ayo no cap, you betta disappear 'fore you get folded up fuh real." April's distant laugh nearly shook the earth. The crows must have felt that, because they burst from a tree with their wings pushing them toward hovering clouds. Justin looks at his Rolex then drops into the driver seat, "oh, and thank you for everything, *trick*."

"*Scah-*"

"Yo, I swear," Omar swings his fists back and forth with his head toward the sky, "You broke bitches are weak."

"Scuh, Scah!" I'm pointing at April's twitching hand as she scratches, and scratches and *scratches*. My eyes, my reality and my focused mind must be deceiving me. Finally, the strength to shake Omar up comes to hand. I jump in front of him and push him a few good times, causing him to stumble backward and blocking his path to Justin's receding car. "Scar!" I finally manage to scream, pointing at April, "Scar!"

Omar charges toward me and thrusts his chest into mine, "man what the hell are you talking about?!"

Lace-front in the air, whipping back and forth - clutched in the tight grip of April's hand.

"Scar!" is all I could say over and over again, "Scar!" Omar looks over my shoulder and as Justin's vehicle disappears into traffic, It finally hits him.

He grips at his heart then collapses and vomits all over the pavement. As the seat of his pants change from turquoise to midnight blue, he reaches into his back pocket to grab his singing phone. *'April'* flashes on the screen of the caller ID.

In the midst of his labored breathing, Omar pushes the speaker icon and from the other end I hear Allen's voice, "April Fools nigga," He laughs wickedly in his masculine voice, then his tone hikes back into his feminine voice, "Jokes on you."

Chapter 25

April

'Imagine what a buck could do,' This was the prompt in a twister post from the California Lottery that snatched me up from my bed one day, and pushed me into the seven eleven down the street where I purchased my first lottery ticket in over three months. I had given up on winning, but that day some unknown force gave me the luck to do it.

So, for anyone wondering – let me give you a little hint. A buck could change you as a person, literally. May not be that easy for you, but for me – all I did was play the right numbers and *bling*, I was in the money!

In that same instance, I already knew what moves I was going to make. I'd been contemplating how to exact my revenge for so long, that as soon as that money hit my account I started moving faster towards a new life.

My luck didn't stop there though, because soon after that, my Uncle Stan was promoted to lead homicide investigator. When people say that death comes in threes, they leave out the fact that, so does luck. Seemingly overnight I gained riches, a get out of jail free card, and a different gender.

The game of operation had actually been under way months after Olivia and I split. It was a surprise to me that she didn't notice I was wearing a dildo the day she cheated on Omar, but that's just how she is – gullible and simple minded.

Had she used her hands like she used to, she would have reached down and noticed that something was missing. See, my surgeon was skilled - all he had to do was cut some strings, remove a few things and basically turn me inside out. I'd traveled all the way to Miami to have myself remixed from my breast implants, all the way down to my Brazilian butt lift.

Gender reconstructive surgery, look it up!

The finishing touches in establishing my new identity was a reconstructed forehead complete with eyebrow and eyelid lift, a few bouts of hormone therapy, a lowered hairline, and a rearranged jawbone.

Facial feminization surgery, it's a real thing!

The iris color replacement surgery and my implanted personality was just the icing on my cake. Winning that powerball was my stroke of luck, it sped up the process and helped me become the woman I am today. So unlike you, I no longer have to just imagine what a buck can do, because I'm actually living it out.

Now let me say this, if people knew me like they thought they did, they would've noticed the change in my walk and the change in my talk. But everybody was too busy helping Omar cover up his back-stabbing nature to realize that inside the man they called a brother, lived a woman who was fighting to get out. And she finally got her way. Say what you want about me, but everything I set out to do, I did – and that's what you call a *BOSS*.

People always say, '*If you can see it, you can achieve it.*' And those visions of Omar dying each time I blinked my eyes – well, let's just say I achieved it. He's not gone yet but by now, he should be well on his way. And I don't feel one bit of remorse - I feel vindicated, accomplished, and victorious. I climbed my way to cloud nine with a vengeful heart and now that I'm up here, nothing can snatch me down.

Nothing that is, except these nagging twats I need to finally get rid of. After all the ground I've covered in this plot of mine, here I am – back at square one.

The sign ahead of me commands me to just do it, and I'm

finally going to make it happen. The wheels have been in motion for a few good hours and as I sit behind this steering wheel, my life flashes before my eyes.

Scene by scene, I see Olivia sway into Omar's arms in the same moment he thrusts the proverbial knife into my back. The piercing agony sends me edging toward the ground. Just as my knee hit the concrete, I look at my blood covered hands and I hear people begging for their lives: that wedding instigator, the girl who wouldn't stop smiling at me even after I warned her that her number was coming up, Sobbing Sam, Quanny, that silly bitch who flashed her teeth at me an hour ago....

I can keep going, but you get the point; Don't smile at me unless you're ready to meet your maker. Scene after scene, my thoughts push me down memory lane. In the next flash, I jump into the Uber and hurry off to the airport as Uncle Stan covers my tracks. The smile that grows across my face is palpable and my heart is content. It sucks that these measures I had to take, but I said I would leave my imprint on the world, and I have.

The only person I'm worried about is Justin – I don't know how she's going to take all of this in. I know for sure that by now, she should have received the letter I mailed to her day before yesterday. I wouldn't know, because I left everything I owned – including my phone, in a pile just outside of the new home I'd bought for her before my goodbyes bled out and onto the paper.

So now, here I sit once more – begging for silence. Mrs. and Mr. Wright, they're at it again. With their kids cloning their behavior, they argue back and forth about another chance at life – one that I don't give two shits about living. Only thing I want to do right now, is watch Omar run from the building screaming to God, *'why.'* But I can't even think straight for the sound of Ying flapping her lips towards my ears, *'You've caused enough pain,'* she says, *'think about this for a second.'*

'What's there to think about?' Yang yells in my direction, *'If they catch you, you're finished! Either way it goes,'* he glances at Ying,

'He is baked!'

"it's *she* to you!" I look over my shoulder and yell. A group of friends walking past looks into my back seat, then they look around at each other with their faces frowned. *'She's baked!'* Yang reiterates my correction. These people must think I'm crazy, but by now it should be a known fact that I don't care about what people think.

Crazy part is – this time, Yang is right. I'm either going to jail, or I'm going to hell. I'd rather chose the latter. The sounds of this arguing couple and their kids travel in and out of my ear, *'Don't do it!'*

'It's now or never!'

'Wait Al!'

'Just do it!'

I grab my head with both hands, "I wish you motherfuckers would shut up!"

tick.... Tick... Tick.

After slamming my palm into my forehead three times, Daniel walks up and taps my window, "Sorry ma'am," he says with his face twisted as he looks into my eyes, "I thought you were someone else," He glances at the drying red blotches on my hand and his voice mellows, "Is everything ok?"

"Yes," I lie.

"Are you sure? We can get a Doctor out here if you need help." With my head titled away from him, my eyes stay plastered onto the billboard ahead, "I'm fine."

"Ok, well this right here is an outpatient mental health facility. Were you looking to come inside?"

"No."

"Ok. Well just so you know, that over there," He points to the adjoining building, "that's a medical clinic. You can go in there without an appointment and see someone if you feel that's what you need."

Silence.

What makes this asshole think I need him in my space, telling me what to do. "Well, take it easy," he walks away with his hands in his pocket, spewing his last few words as the door to the mental health facility opens, and a group of laughing people pour down the steps, "remember," he says as he walks over to the crowd, "help is just a few steps away."

If anyone needs help, it's you so-called *'happy'* people. Ya'll spend so much time faking it, that ya'll really think you're living a good life when in reality – all of ya'll are melted inside. If I'm lying, then what is this mental health clinic here for? Why is, *wait – what's going on?*

Suddenly the mental health center door swings open and out rush two Doctors. They head towards the medical clinic and as soon as the door opens, someone runs into them and falls to their knees. *Oh shit, it's Omar.*

"Why me?" he looks toward the sky and yells, "God, why me?" *mission accomplished.* The scene expands as Michael, Shay and Mo exit the door and rush over to Omar, followed by a crowd of other people – some stopping to watch from the ajar door.

Just as the Doctors reach the crowd, Michael looks up and starts swaying his head from left to right. Ducking toward the steering wheel, I start my engine and pull forward, then I make a right at the stop sign like Yang instructed. Left, right..... left - The entire time I'm lost in the Wright storm

'Do it.'

'NOoo!.'

'kill.'

'Steal.'

'destroy.'

Arrgh! straight through three red lights. It all ends here. Wailing sirens accompanied by flashing red and blue lights is my cue to pick up speed. It's all too clear to me at this point; it's now, or it's never.

My side-view mirror captures a picture of distant faces talking through held-hand microphones, "Pull over, now!" they demand to no avail. Fast-forwarding past a stop sign, palm trees flash by as the scene stretches toward the green light on Rodeo and Brighton Way. I ease my foot off the gas pedal and let my car creep to a stop, then I shift the gear to park and reach into my glove compartment.

"Hands up!" an Officers yells as they pop out of thier car with their guns leading the way. Surrounded by an ocean of headlights and widening eyes, I watch the color of the traffic light pop to yellow, then red.

'this is it, this is it' I grab the steel and I hold it in my lap for a few seconds. In my rear-view mirror, the halo above my head erects and stands at attention.

'what are you waiting for?! Do it!'

I push the door open and pop out, then I twist around and aim the gun at my temple. Ignoring the pleading Officers, my eyes veer toward the barrel, "any last words?" I say to the wrights. Ying speaks first - between sniffles she utters, *'yay tho I walk through the valley of the shadow of death...'*

"hands up!" and officer yells as Yang insists, 'do it!'

'I shall fear no evil.'

'Now Al!'

'for thou art with me"

"Ma'am, you don't want to do this," another Officer yells, "Drop your weapon!"

"This isn't what you want," his partner co-signs.

How the FUCK you know what I want, huh? Suddenly Yang

changes his tune, 'wait!' he cries out to me.

 Tick... I'm sick of this shit! *The rhytm that usually soothes me is now making me dance in agony*

 ....tick

ugh! I cringe. Joining in with Ying, my face starts moving, "Thou rod and thou shaft, they - " You know what, *enough. I'm over it, gone!*

∞ ∞ ∞

Allen's finger twitches and a sharp vibration sears through his skull, melting his brains. Weightless, gravity fails him. His flesh hits the ground, his soul dashes toward heaven then crashes back down into a river of fire. This was supposed to be an end to the end but to Allen's dismay, an eerie sense of discomfort comes in the form of a familiar, yet distant voice....

Welcome to hell

Epilogue

Three weeks later Michael and Olivia join to pick Omar up from the Ronald Regan Regional Psychiatric ward. He'd been there since he'd received his results, breaking down and talking to Allen as though he were right in front of him.

On a beautiful Sunday, his Psych Nurse walked in and noted him saying to his reflection in the mirror, "Ayo shorty – what you just say to me?! I mean yo eyes all bulging from your head, and you spitting all from your mouth. Yo, you need to chill!" He held conversations with himself daily, but his favorite words had been to Allen,

"I'll kill you *and* this bitch April!"

He repeated that every day until he'd started medication, and then his psychosis ceased. Olivia, being the woman she is, took hold of Omar's hand and led him back home where together, they would live this thing out the best way they could.

Supporting Omar into recovery, she quit her new job as a banker and resumed catering to his every need. But Michael? things were still heavy on his mind, and he remembered that he was due for a vacation. He stopped by Omar and Olivia's on his way out, to update them on the turn of events. "His DNA tied him to seven murders and counting," Mike shook his head then slammed his hand onto the table, "Domino! But yeah - Damn. Suicide though? I can't believe he did it."

"I'm *still* in shock," Olivia mumbles, looking across the table at Omar's bowed head and his moving lips, "and him," she whispers and nods in his direction, "he's just, not taking it well."

"Rightfully so."

After they'd played for hours on in, Mike sprinted down the steps and he headed to his car, "luckily, the face of death will never be seen around here again."

"Hopefully." Olivia cosigned as she waved. Omar struggled to the door using his walking cane and as he approached the porch, he stopped to glance at the picture of himself on the end table. He was standing with his partners, next to the prototype of the telescope drone he was contracted to build. The life he was forced to leave behind had been a good one, but now it's all over. "Have fun brother," he waved to Michael as he stood in the doorway.

Michael nodded his head, checked his rearview mirrors, then put his car in drive. He honked as he drove off and headed for Rodeo Drive. Four hours later he was driving into the sunset, shaking his head. He found himself ashamed when a thought struck his conscience, and he tucked the frightening possibility in the back his mind as he questioned aloud, "But can you really catch that shit from letting'em suck your dick?"

Moral of the Story: Strap it up!

Over 35,000 new cases of AIDS/HIV are recorded each year, and although this story is based off a recurring dream, let this novel serve as your official warning to always wear protection, and be mindful of how you're moving around in this world.

Thanks for reading!

Remember that a book review is one of the best gifts an Author could recieve. With that said, **please go to Amazon and leave your honest review (no spoilers please)**, and also - tell a friend about this book and the warning that comes with it. If you'd like to stay connected, follow me on TikTok

Username: queen_ _ i'm _ _ unique
https://www.tiktok.com/@queen__im__unique?
is_from_webapp=1&sender_device=pc

Podcast Website:
https://letsgopodcasting.com/

April's Fool FB Page: 'Back stories', 'behind the scenes' stories, and 'current events' stories. (Want to stand out? Leave your feedback/review on posts)
https://www.facebook.com/xApRiLsFoOLx

Other books by me:

- He Killed Me First (A cautionary tale of DV)
- Damn (A collection of short stories)
- Lemonaide: A Personal Development Workbook

More about me

- My books are available on Amazon/Barnes and Noble

- I currently host a podcast called, FLip ThE ScRipt
- I am a Libra
- My Dream Catchers book collection is based on dreams   I have while sleeping

Last words

SUICIDE IS **NEVER** THE ANSWER! YOUR PHYSICAL BODY IS JUST A VEHICLE FOR YOUR SOUL TO TRAVEL FROM ONE EXPERIENCE TO ANOTHER. IN ENDING YOUR OWN LIFE, YOU COULD BE SENDING YOUR SOUL TO A VEHICLE TO EXPERIENCE FAR WORSE, JUST LIKE WHAT YOU JUST SAW HAPPEN TO ALLEN.

If you or someone you love is suicidal or experience suicidal thoughts, please reach out to someone. There is help. JUST HOLD ON, THINGS WILL GET BETTER IN TIME.

Suicide prevention website:
https://didihirsch.org/services/suicide-prevention/

National suicide prevention hotline: Dial 988
National Hopeline Network, Suicide & Crisis Hotline 1-800-442-HOPE(4673)

Remember, today is the first day of the rest of your life. You can make it count; all you have to do is wake up, stand up – and move forward

Afterword

What better way to stand out to an Author as a supporter, than leaving a review?

Amazon has strict requirements for leaving reviews but as a self-published Author, I greatly value your feedback and opinions. If you are not able to leave a review on Amazon, I have created a post on my personal Facebook page just for you!

** EBOOK READERS **

Simply click the link below, and you will be directed to a page where you can talk your sh-- about the characters, plot and the whole story. Your opinion is greatly valued!

Make sure to:

1) Name the character that stood out to you the most
2) Be as specific as possible without giving spoilers
3) Mention how many stars from 1 to 5 you give

Review here

** BONUS READ ON THE NEXT PAGE**

Here's another cautionary tale; it's the story of Pa'Trice and her mother's husband, Ronnie. Refer to chapter 7 where Olivia and her friends played a game of questions and secrets were exposed. This is a Wattpad story, so you may or may not have to create a (Free) account.

Here's another way you can leave your review if you are not able to review me on amazon. Just sign up, and leave a few words in the comments. Let's get this conversation going ya'll, I want to see you come through!

Click the link below to read the bonus story

DO NOT READ Warning: explicit language, read at your own risk

UPCOMING BOOKS

- I like Making Babies Cry (A cautionary tale)
- The Diamond King (A love story)
- Rainbows
- Daddy Long Legs (Sequel to He Killed Me First)

www.ingramcontent.com/pod-product-compliance
Lightning Source LLC
Chambersburg PA
CBHW071147260626
47162CB00003B/954